CUPID PILLION

Barbara Cartland

Barbara Cartland Ebooks Ltd

This edition © 2023

Copyright Cartland Promotions 1952

ISBNs
9781788677431   EPUB
9781788677530   PAPERBACK

Book design by M-Y Books
m-ybooks.co.uk

THE BARBARA CARTLAND ETERNAL COLLECTION

The Barbara Cartland Eternal Collection is the unique opportunity to collect all five hundred of the timeless beautiful romantic novels written by the world's most celebrated and enduring romantic author.

Named the Eternal Collection because Barbara's inspiring stories of pure love, just the same as love itself, the books will be published on the internet at the rate of four titles per month until all five hundred are available.

The Eternal Collection, classic pure romance available worldwide for all time .

THE LATE DAME BARBARA CARTLAND

Barbara Cartland, who sadly died in May 2000 at the grand age of ninety eight, remains one of the world's most famous romantic novelists. With worldwide sales of over one billion, her outstanding 723 books have been translated into thirty six different languages, to be enjoyed by readers of romance globally.

Writing her first book 'Jigsaw' at the age of 21, Barbara became an immediate bestseller. Building upon this initial success, she wrote continuously throughout her life, producing bestsellers for an astonishing 76 years. In addition to Barbara Cartland's legion of fans in the UK and across Europe, her books have always been immensely popular in the USA. In 1976 she achieved the unprecedented feat of having books at numbers 1 & 2 in the prestigious B. Dalton Bookseller bestsellers list.

Although she is often referred to as the 'Queen of Romance', Barbara Cartland also wrote several historical biographies, six autobiographies and numerous theatrical plays as well as books on life, love, health and cookery. Becoming one of Britain's most popular media personalities and dressed in her trademark pink, Barbara spoke on radio and television about social and political issues, as well as making many public appearances.

In 1991 she became a Dame of the Order of the British Empire for her contribution to literature and her work for humanitarian and charitable causes.

Known for her glamour, style, and vitality Barbara Cartland became a legend in her own lifetime. Best remembered for her wonderful romantic novels and loved by millions of readers worldwide, her books remain treasured for their heroic heroes, plucky heroines and traditional values. But above all, it was Barbara Cartland's overriding belief in the positive power of love to help, heal and improve the quality of life for everyone that made her truly unique.

1
1658

It was dark in the coach and the flickering taper in the lantern seemed to accentuate rather than relieve the gloom, as the wheels rolled and bumped over the rutted, stony road.

The moon, however, was rising up in the sky, and after a while Panthea thought that she could see only too clearly the face of the man sitting beside her. He had taken off his broad-brimmed hat and was leaning back against the well cushioned seat as if at his ease, but she was well aware that his eyes were turned constantly in her direction.

She made herself as small as she could, so that she appeared to crouch in the corner of the seat making believe, with a hopeless hopefulness, that she was so tiny and insignificant that she might even be overlooked. She even prayed that the darkness might deepen and hide her completely.

He was watching her! She could see the sharp outline of his hooked nose turned away from her, and yet she knew that his eyes searched for hers. There was no need for the moonlight or the guttering candle to reveal to her the lines of his face. She knew the features too well – the tight, cruel, yet sensuous mouth, the square jaw which had a look of brutality, the bushy, longhaired eyebrows, which mounted guard over suspicious, glittering eyes that seemed to miss nothing. Yes, she knew his face as she knew her own – the face that had haunted her dreams and every hour of her waking life for the last two months.

She had been aware, Panthea thought, from the very first that she could not escape him. She had seen the look in his eyes when he entered the hall at Staverley and shrank from it in horror and disgust, but from that first moment it was too late.

She had known, though she hardly dared put it into words even to herself, that his next visit had been but an excuse to see her – then he had come again and again - always with the same excuse, always upsetting her father and frightening the servants into hysterics, so that she alone must remain calm in order to combat and defy him. And she had guessed that he enjoyed torturing them. She had seen it in the faint smile at the corner of his lips, in the depths of his eyes, which watched her as a cat will watch a mouse before it pounces. And then, at last he had spoken what was on his mind.

Almost involuntarily as her thoughts tortured her, Panthea made a convulsive gesture and instantly the man at her side leant forward. He was, for the instant, silhouetted against the window, and she saw his rounded head, the greying hair lank and straight.

"You are cold?"

His voice was very deep.

"N-no, I am warm, thank you, sir," Panthea replied a little breathlessly.

"We have quite a long journey before us. Are you sure you would not be wiser to put a shawl around your shoulders?"

He reached out as he spoke, towards the coats and shawls that had been placed on the smaller seat opposite the one on which they sat. Panthea's eyes were on his hands. There were hairs on the thick fingers, and she cried out again with a sudden urgency.

"N-no. I thank you, but I want nothing!"

He leant back again, but his face was still turned towards her.

"You may relax," he said. "There is no need for any further agitation."

"You can hardly expect me to think that," Panthea said with a sudden show of spirit. "In the morning my father will read the note I have left for him. He will be distressed, desperately distressed."

"He will be glad to know that his son is safe."

"Yes, he will be glad of that," Panthea replied, "if indeed Richard is safe! You are sure - absolutely certain - that you can save him?"

"I have given you my word."

"But as he has already been captured," Panthea said, "will you be strong enough, or important enough, to release him?"

"I assure you, the power of Christian Drysdale is quite considerable," was the answer given somewhat drily. "My friendship with the Protector is well known. My ability has never been questioned. I think it will not be hard for me to obtain the reprieve of a young Royalist more fool than traitor."

Panthea's chin went up.

"Must one be a fool to be loyal to one's rightful King?" she asked.

Christian Drysdale snorted.

"Such words are treasonable," he said. "I must ask you, now that you are my wife, to keep guard on your tongue."

"Were I twenty times your wife," Panthea replied, "I should not forget that our rightful King is Charles Stuart and that a usurper sits on the throne of his murdered father.'

She spoke passionately, all fear forgotten, her breath coming quickly between her parted lips. The coach turned a corner and a shaft of moonlight fell full on her face, revealing the exquisite loveliness of her large eyes, separated by the delicate artistry of her tiny, tip-tilted nose, and the way in which the soft waves of her fair hair framed the white oval of her forehead.

It was a lovely face, the face of a child, but the man who looked at it was not touched by its youthful innocence. Instead, his eyes narrowed a little as he reached out his hand towards Panthea's fluttering fingers.

"We will dispense with such nonsense for tonight," he said, "and recollect only that you are married to me."

His voice had an ugly, hungry note in it, and instantly Panthea forgot what she had been saying and remembered only where she was and at whose side she sat. She shrank into the corner of the coach again, hiding herself in the dark shadows as unobtrusively as she had done before, but now it was too late even to pretend herself invisible.

"Come nearer to me," Christian Drysdale commanded.

Her shoulders were already taut against the corner of the seat, but she pressed them even harder in the desire to obliterate herself. There was a silence between them which seemed to her to be broken by the noisy thumping of her heart.

"Do you hear what I say?" Christian Drysdale repeated. "Have you forgotten your marriage vows so quickly? You promised to obey."

"I-I am near you," Panthea faltered.

He laughed a little at that, and she knew that he was enjoying this moment of torturing her, knowing that eventually he must get his way.

"Come nearer," he repeated.

Panthea drew a deep breath, as if to give herself courage, before she answered.

"I am near enough. I have married you because you have sworn you will save my brother. I have come away with you now at dead of night, without telling my father, because I know he will be ashamed and disgusted at the thought that one of our family should marry a Roundhead. I have done all this, but you cannot – no, you cannot – make me feel anything but hatred for you."

Her last words were spoken hardly above a whisper, the terror and fear Panthea felt for the man whom she had married seeming almost to stifle her – and now, having spoken, she dared not look towards him, but could only stare blindly ahead.

It was then, as she waited, afraid even of her own bravery, that she heard him laugh, the amused laughter of a man who is completely sure of himself and of obtaining what he desires.

"So you hate me!" he said. "Well, it will amuse me to teach you what love means."

He put out his hands as he spoke, and at the touch of his fingers Panthea gave a sudden cry, half of despair and half of terror. Then, from beneath the sable and velvet handwarmer on her lap, there came a low growl and a snarl, and suddenly Christian's hand was hastily withdrawn. He muttered an oath beneath his breath.

"Zounds, but what have you in your lap?" he enquired.

"It is only Bobo . . . my dog," Panthea faltered.

"The cur has bitten me," Christian Drysdale exclaimed. "I did not know you had brought him with you."

"He goes everywhere with me," Panthea replied.

"He will not come to my house," Christian Drysdale announced. "I have no liking for animals, and especially not for one that has set his teeth in me."

"I am sorry if Bobo has hurt you," Panthea said. "He was protecting me because I cried out."

"Put the little beast on the floor," Christian Drysdale commanded.

"He is comfortable enough where he is," Panthea answered, her hands caressing the dog, who was still growling low in his throat.

"You heard what I commanded you," Christian said.

"Why should I obey?" Panthea asked. "The dog is mine. I love him and he may sit in my lap as he is always allowed to do."

Once again she spoke defiantly, yet holding in check her hatred of this man who seemed with every word he uttered to grow more intolerable, more horrible. It was as if her tone and her manner stung him for the first time.

"You shall do as I tell you!" he shouted. "Put the dog on the floor."

The coach was going uphill, the horses drawing their heavy load steadily and without haste. Panthea sat upright and very still, making no movement to obey her husband. As he waited, she could feel the tension growing between them, and she lifted the little dog in her hands and put her cheek against his head. It seemed as if the caress snapped the last self-control of the man beside her. With a sound that was half an oath and half an expression of unbridled anger, he reached out his hand and snatched the dog from her.

There was a snarl and he winced for a moment as the animal's sharp teeth buried themselves once again in his finger, and then there was the dull thud of a heavy stick, a cry of horror and agony from Panthea, and the sound of a small, unconscious body being thrown on to the floor of the coach.

"You have killed him! *You have killed him!*"

Panthea would have flung herself on to the floor had not Christian's arms held her back. For a moment, she was quite unaware of anything save the horror and misery of knowing that her pet had been injured.

"You have killed him, you beast!" she cried again, and then was suddenly aware that Christian's face was very near to hers, that his arm was round her in an almost vice-like grip, and that his other hand – the drops of blood from the dog's teeth scarlet in the moonlight – was moving upwards so as to hold her chin and lift her face towards his.

"You have killed him," she moaned, and even as she said the words the meaning of them slipped from her thoughts, for another and more terrifying fear came to her.

"You silly child! I will give you something to think about," Christian's voice said, thick and silky now, and then his lips were pressed hotly and firmly on Panthea's mouth.

She tried to struggle, tried to fight against him, but she was utterly powerless. She felt as if a darkness more terrible and more frightening than anything she had ever imagined in her whole life encompassed her, taking away her breath, possessing her, forcing her down into a pit of despondency, deeper than the depths of hell itself.

She could feel his lips, the very nearness of him, sapping her strength, obliterating even her identity so that she was lost, forsaken and forgotten in a hideous darkness in which she could neither move nor cry out.

She felt she must faint and die from very horror, and yet she did not lose consciousness. Then suddenly, when the agony of mind and body was too much to be borne, there was a sudden jolt. Christian's arms slackened around her for one moment and she was able to free her mouth from his, gasping for breath. But before she was aware of what was happening, or what indeed had caused her release, the door of the coach was flung open and a voice, sharp and imperative, rang out into the night .

"Stand and deliver!"

She heard Christian mutter some strange words that she had never heard in her life before, but which she knew to be oaths, and then the same clear, commanding voice spoke. "You will oblige me by descending while my man searches the coach."

Christian began to swear again, but this time a pistol barrel came through the doorway and his voice died away into silence.

"This is an outrage," he spluttered at length, "for which I will see you hanged."

"Come out and quickly," was the reply, and taking up his broad-brimmed hat, Christian Drysdale stepped from the coach into the moonlight.

It was a warm night for February, for the air was still and there was no wind, but there were traces of a recent snowfall on the leafless branches of the trees, and the ground was white save in the darkness of the thick wood that flanked the narrow roadway.

There was a small clearing where they were, and one quick glance was enough for Christian Drysdale to see the predicament into which he had fallen. Both the coachmen had their hands above their heads. The horses were standing still, unable to proceed as across the road in front of them, his face concealed with a black mask, was a highwayman riding a thoroughbred mare. At the door of the coach was yet another gentleman of the road, dismounted with two pistols in his hands, while behind him, untethered yet waiting obedient as if for a command, was a magnificent stallion.

The highwayman facing him, Christian Drysdale saw, was much more elaborately dressed than the man on the horse. His coat of black velvet was beautifully embroidered, his riding boots were of the finest leather, while at his neck a ruff of priceless Venetian lace was pinned with a flashing diamond. For a moment, Christian Drysdale appeared to gasp for breath and then, in a voice that seemed to come snarling uncontrollably from between his teeth, he proclaimed, "White Throat! So it is you again!"

"Your servant, Mr. Drysdale," the highwayman said with a mocking bow. "I promised you last time we met that it would not be long before we encountered each other once more."

"You have been following me?" Christian Drysdale asked.

"Shall we say keeping a check on your movements," the highwayman replied. "As I told you at our last meeting, I have no affection for tax-gatherers, especially when they use their position to persecute the innocent and those who have no one to protect them."

"You insolent knave! I will make you pay for this," Christian Drysdale said.

"You made the same sort of threats to me the last time we met, if I remember rightly," the highwayman smiled. "On that occasion I made a grave oversight. I did not realise that you carried about with you a large part of the taxes you have extorted. This time I shall not be so stupid."

Christian Drysdale made a sudden movement, but the highwayman stepped forward a pace.

"My pistol is loaded, sir," he said warningly. Then turning to the two coachmen on the box of the coach, he shouted, "You fellows come down and tie up your master."

"He be no master o' ours, sir," one of the men said quaveringly, in the soft, broad accent of the county. "He hired we ter tak him to the church wi' his bride and then ter drive 'em oft on their honeymoon."

"A wedding!" the highwayman cried. "What devilry are you up to now, Mr. Drysdale? I'll bet a hundred guineas that 'tis something unsavoury if you've been planning it. Tie him up!" he commanded as the men scrambled down from the coach. "See to it, Jack," he added to his masked companion, who rode forward and drove Christian Drysdale before his horse until he came up against the trunk of a tall oak tree.

~9~

The second highwayman flung the coachmen a rope and, pistol in hand, instructed them how to rope the cursing tax-collector to the tree.

The man Christian Drysdale had called White Throat watched the little scene for a moment, with a smile on his lips, and then turned towards the coach. He looked inside and found Panthea crouched on the floor, the lifeless body of her small dog cradled in her arms. She was quite oblivious of everything that was going on outside. The tears were streaming down her face, as she felt with delicate fingers the battered skull on which the heavily leaded cane had descended all too heavily.

For a moment, the highwayman looked at her in astonishment, and then sweeping his hat from his head he spoke quietly.

"Can I help you, madame?"

She looked up at him and his masked face seemed not to frighten her. Instead, confidently and with the assurance that she might have shown towards an old friend, she held out the body of her dog towards him.

"Is he quite dead?" she asked, her voice coming brokenly between her lips.

The highwayman took the dog from her and stepped back into the moonlight. He looked at the battered head and then with expert fingers felt for the heart.

"Who dared to do this?" he asked and knew the answer even as he asked the question.

He glanced across the clearing to where Christian, bound to the tree, was telling the frightened coachmen what punishment awaited them when he was free again. Panthea saw his glance.

"My dog bit him," she explained.

She stepped out of the coach as she spoke, and in the moonlight the highwayman saw she was only a child. Her cheeks were wet with her tears and they glittered on her long dark eyelashes. The moonlight revealed, too, the immaturity of her figure, the short sleeves showing the thin, undeveloped arms and the hands, small and dimpled, which were not yet the hands of a woman. She was very tiny and, as she bent over the little dog he held in his hands, her fair hair fell forward and brushed against the sleeve of the highwayman's velvet coat.

"I am afraid your dog is dead," he said very gently.

She gave a little sob, which was choked in her throat, then she reached out and took the lifeless body in her arms.

"Could we . . . could we bury him?" she asked.

The highwayman seemed quite unsurprised at the request.

"Yes, of course," he said.

He walked round the back of the coach, took a spade from underneath the back axle, where it was kept at this time of year for digging the wheels out of snowdrifts or heavy mud. Then he led the way across the road, and walking through the wood came to a small stream. The moonlight shimmered through the bare branches of the trees. Beneath a silver birch, the highwayman began to dig a deep hole. It took him but a few minutes for the ground was soft, and then, still without a word, he took the dog from Panthea's arms, laid it in the grave he had made, and covered it quickly with the loosened earth.

When he had finished, Panthea knelt beside the little mound. She looked very small and pathetic. Her wide skirts of satin and velvet, billowing out around her, accentuated the fragility of her sweetly rounded neck and the grace of her bowed head. The highwayman waited until she rose and as she wiped the tears from her eyes, fiercely and impatiently as a child might have done, he asked, "Why have you married this man?"

"I had to! There was nothing else I could do," she answered. Then she looked down at the little grave and added fiercely, "I hated him before, but now that he has killed Bobo I will hate him until I die."

There was something pathetic and helpless in her anger. The highwayman repeated his first question.

"Why did you marry him?"

Panthea raised her eyes to his, and he saw a look of desperation on her face.

"My brother is under arrest. Mr. Drysdale promised to save his life, but he would do this only if I married him."

"Are you quite sure he will save your brother, now that you have done what he wished?" the highwayman asked.

Panthea made a little gesture with her hands.

"He has promised," she said.

The highwayman stood looking down at her, and when he did not speak, for perhaps the first time, she looked at him appraisingly. There was little she could see of his face save the firm chin and a mouth that seemed to her kindly and without cruelty. His hands were thin and aristocratic, and on one of his fingers he wore a signet ring with a green stone in it.

There was something elegant about him, something too that told Panthea all too clearly that she spoke with a gentleman of her own class. Then, as she stood looking at him, she heard in the distance Christian's voice raised in anger. He was still cursing and swearing, and a shudder went through her that seemed to shake her whole body. Involuntarily, she went nearer to the highwayman as if in need of his protection.

"Have you no relations?" he asked almost angrily. "Why did they not stop you from doing this thing?"

"I did not dare tell my father," Panthea replied. "He has been ill for a long time. If I had told him that my brother was imprisoned, it would, I think, have killed him. He will know now that he has been in danger, but that he is safe."

~12~

"So, you ran away to get married?" the highwayman asked.

"I waited until everyone was asleep," Panthea said, "then I crept downstairs and cut through the garden entrance. He was waiting for me outside the lodge gates."

"He was waiting!" the highwayman repeated. "Mr. Christian Drysdale, the tax-collector, the man who squeezes the very lifeblood out of widows and children, who has extorted money from Royalists in expiation of the crime of being faithful – and when they have no more to give, he has denounced them."

Panthea gave a little cry.

"You mean he has pretended to help and then betrayed them?"

"Not only in one case, but in dozens," the highwayman said grimly.

Panthea's eyes, wide with terror, made him catch his breath.

"But suppose," she said, "suppose that he will not save my brother after all?"

The highwayman's lips tightened.

"Perhaps in your case he will behave honourably," he said, but his tone was unconvincing and she knew only too well that he was trying to comfort her.

Panthea put her hands up to her face.

"I knew in my heart that one could not trust him," she said.

The highwayman sighed.

"You are too young for all this. How old are you?"

"I was sixteen last birthday," Panthea replied, "but I am not concerned with myself, it is my brother of whom I am thinking."

"Will you tell me your brother's name?" the highwayman asked, and added quickly, "Believe me, I am not asking out of vulgar curiosity. My man was in London yesterday and brought me news of those who have recently been arrested – it might be that among those was your brother."

"My brother's name is Richard Evelyn, the Viscount St. Clare," Panthea said.

The highwayman started and she added quickly,

"You have heard of him?"

"Yes, I have heard of him," the highwayman said slowly. "Your father is the Marquess of Staverley?"

"Yes," Panthea answered.

The highwayman stood as if hesitating, and then he put out his hand and took Panthea's in his.

"Listen, little Panthea," he said, and it did not seem strange that he knew her name, "I have something to tell you that will make you very unhappy, but you must be brave and bear it."

"What is it?" Panthea asked, her voice hardly above a whisper.

She felt the strength of the highwayman's fingers on hers. They seemed to be holding her up, calming her, giving her courage she had not known before that she possessed.

"Your brother was hanged yesterday on the gibbet at Charing Cross," the highwayman said very quietly. "He died with a smile on his lips, unafraid, undaunted. As they put the rope round his neck, he said, 'God save King Charles, and long may he reign over England when the tyrant is dead.'"

Panthea gave a broken cry and then she was sobbing as if her heart would break, her face against the highwayman's shoulder, his arms around her. How long she stood there in his embrace, she had no idea. She was only aware that when the outburst of tears was diminishing, a soft linen handkerchief was being pressed against her eyes. She took it gratefully and heard a quiet voice say,

"Richard would want you to be brave, he would want you to return to your father who needs you at this moment as never before."

"But how can I?" Panthea asked, her voice still broken by sobs so that her speech came unevenly.

"I will deal with this man who has married you by lies and false promises," the highwayman said. "Wait here until I come back to you."

He smiled down at her, still supporting her – then as he released her and turned to go away, she put out her hands and clutched his arm.

"What are you going to do?" she asked.

The highwayman lifted his fingers to his lips.

"Do not worry," he said quietly. "Just wait here for me. When I come back you will be able to go home."

She trusted him without further question, but all the same, as he strode away from her, the spurs on his high boots jingling as he walked over the dry branches and fallen leaves, she wondered what would happen if he went out of her life now as quickly as he had come into it and she never saw him again. Supposing he rode away, and she was left alone with Christian Drysdale – her husband?

She felt utterly sick at the thought. She had married the Roundhead trusting to his promise that he would save her brother, and all the time he must have known that Richard was condemned to death and that no one, however powerful, could obtain his reprieve.

She felt now that she had had a premonition that Richard would die when, just over six weeks ago, he had told her what he was about to do. She had been standing in the library at Staverley looking out over the lake. It was late in the afternoon. The sun was sinking behind the great oak trees in the park, the sky was deepening into the twilight and the reflection of it was dark and mysterious in the water below the terrace.

She had a strange feeling as if she stood in a no-man's land between the past and the future, and she felt as if many of the ancestors, whose pictures graced the walls of the room behind her, were standing beside her, looking down on the lake that had, since the house was built, mirrored the history of the family. It seemed to her then as if the Staverleys filed past her in slow procession – first Sir Hubert Vyne, who had come over with William the Conqueror, then the Vynes who had won glory and honour in the Crusades, their grandsons and granddaughters who had supported the Plantagenets, and after them the members of the family who had served the Tudors loyally and with distinction.

Panthea saw them passing the honour and the traditions of the family down through the centuries, from generation to generation, until eventually she came to the present day and knew, as clearly as if she had been told so aloud, that her father had not long to live.

He had been a sick man for a long time and now, as the evening mist began to rise from the lake, she imagined that the Staverleys of the past were drawing him into their keeping, waiting there for him to join them. Then, as the pain of bereavement was an agony within her breast, she remembered that Richard would carry on the family – Richard, who loved Staverley and its splendid history as dearly as she loved it herself.

Even as she thought of her brother, she saw him come walking up the lawn towards her. As she watched him come, the mists from the lake seemed to rise and surge around him so that it appeared as if he were no longer a human being but a spirit transparent and immaterial. She had known then a sudden terror and fear, but before she could even express it to herself, Richard had reached the terrace and, seeing her at the window, waved his hand cheerfully.

She had opened the casement to him and he climbed into the room. She thought then how ridiculous it was of her to have such depressing fancies, but the expression on Richard's face told her that something untoward had occurred.

"What has happened?" she asked.

"Why do you ask me that?" Richard enquired. "What should have happened?"

"You look different," Panthea replied. "You look pleased and happy, yet there is something else. Oh, Richard, tell me."

He dropped a kiss on her cheek.

"You are much too perceptive for your years," he said. "You should be playing with your dolls, not worrying your head about serious matters."

"I am much too old for dolls,' Panthea replied indignantly, "and it is difficult not to be serious with father ill and everyone so worried."

"What are they worried about?" Richard asked quickly.

"What a silly question," Panthea replied. "You know full well that we are worried all the time. Mr. Christian Drysdale was here again today asking questions, as well as taking more money in taxes than we can possibly afford?"

"What questions did he ask?" Richard enquired.

Panthea shrugged her shoulders.

"Nothing new. If we had fugitive Royalists hiding in secret chambers. If anyone went to Mass – all the usual questions he asks every time he comes."

Richard looked over his shoulder as if he fancied someone was listening.

"I have got something to tell you, Panthea," he said. "I ought not to burden you with my secrets, but it is better for you to know the truth so that you will be clever enough to put anyone off the scent if they get too inquisitive."

"What is it?" Panthea asked.

She felt as if a cold hand clutched at her heart. She was afraid, although she did not know why.

"I am going away for a little while," Richard said. "You must not let anyone outside the house know that I have gone or else we have got to think up some really good reason for my absence."

"Why? What is it? Where are you going?" Panthea enquired.

In answer, Richard pulled her down on the sofa beside him and whispered so that his mouth was quite close to her ear.

"Our King is in England."

Panthea gave a quickly repressed cry.

"But where? How does he come here?"

"He landed in Essex a week ago," Richard said. "Now he is in London, and I am going to join him. Oh, Panthea, perhaps the tide has turned, and this is the moment when we can rise and place him on the Throne."

Richard's tone had been elated and excited, but Panthea felt curiously calm.

"Be careful," she pleaded. "Promise me you will be careful!"

"Do you think I am likely to be anything else?" Richard asked, scorning his sister's fears.

But Panthea's premonition of danger had been justified. The King, with no disguise but his hair dyed golden, which unfortunately turned a variety of colours, interviewed his sympathisers and received assurances of their loyalty. But someone betrayed him. He was driven from house to house and, only by the greatest good fortune, managed to escape back to France.

A tornado of arrests followed his departure. Being hung, drawn and quartered were the lot of those captured. Others who evaded arrest were still in hiding, hoping for a ship to carry them to France. Panthea had lived in terror from the moment the news reached her that the visit of the Royal Exile had been discovered.

When Richard did not return home, she hoped that he had found refuge in some friend's house, and then Christian Drysdale had brought her the news that her brother's name was on the list of suspects. The tax-collector had watched her face as he spoke and then, when white with misery and terror she stood silent and speechless before him, too proud to break down and cry, he had offered to make a bargain with her.

"Marry me and I will save your brother," he said. "The choice, is yours."

"And why should you want to marry me?" she stammered at last, and shrank away from the look in his eyes when he had answered. "Do you want me to tell you that I love you?"

But she had known then, child that she was, that it was not love he felt for her, yet she had no choice but to accept this offer. Her father was continually asking for Richard, for the Marquess knew only too well that his own days were numbered. He wanted to see his son and he could not understand why he should be absent for so long when there were so many things required of him at home.

There was no time to think, no time to consider. Christian Drysdale made it very clear that if she would save Richard she must act speedily and without delay. She had consented to marry him, knowing that she crucified herself but believing that nothing mattered, save that Richard should live to take his father's place at the head of the family.

Now she knew her sacrifice had been useless. Christian Drysdale had deceived her. Richard was dead, having paid the penalty of his loyalty to his King at Charing Cross. It seemed almost impossible to believe that Richard would never again walk into the great galleried hall at Staverley and call her name. And now, what of herself?

Richard was dead, but she was left married to Christian Drysdale! She wanted to shriek aloud at the horror of it, for she knew she would rather be dead than face the future as the wife of the Roundhead. And yet this stranger, a thief and an outlaw to whom she had entrusted her story, had in some curious manner of his own, given her hope.

She leant against a tree, watching the highwayman walk away from her. She could see through the bare space between the trees the coach, standing empty and unguarded, while Christian Drysdale, tied to a tree some twenty yards away, cursed and swore until the very air seemed polluted with his fury. As the highwayman came nearer to him, the two coachmen drew back. He glanced at them briefly.

"Untie the man who hired you," he said.

They looked at him in surprise, then, as they appeared too astonished to obey him, the highwayman drew his sword from his side and cut the ropes that bound the tax-collector. The freed man shook his arms to restore the circulation.

"So you have come to your senses," he snarled, "or has my loving wife pleaded with you for my freedom?"

In answer, the highwayman pointed to the sword Christian Drysdale wore at his side.

"Draw your blade!" he said curtly. "You will fight me for your life."

Christian Drysdale stared at him for a moment, then his lips twisted themselves.

"Can this be chivalry?" he enquired with a sneer. "I can assure you, fellow, that my wife will sleep the better in my arms tonight at the thought of your death."

"We shall see," the highwayman said, and began to take off his black velvet coat.

After a moment, Christian Drysdale followed him by removing his own.

"I am a noted swordsman, thief," he said briefly.

The highwayman did not answer him but laid his coat down at the foot of a tree, and standing in his silk shirt, the lace falling over his hands, he tested the steel of his blade and eyed his opponent reflectively.

Thickset, a heavier man in every way, Christian Drysdale yet had the makings of a swordsman. He was wiry and quick on his feet, and unlike the highwayman, he was not impeded by heavy riding boots. He was the taller of the two, his arm was the longer, and his muscular fitness was obvious as he stood ready in his coarse cambric shirt. He was a formidable adversary, and the smile on his thin, cruel lips was the smile of a man who intended murder.

Swiftly, and without any further words, the two men made ready. The second highwayman and the coachmen stepped back in the shadows of the trees. The horses, alone and unattended, cropped the short, snow-covered grass by the side of the road.

For a moment, all was very quiet and silent. Then the highwayman spoke.

"En garde!" he cried, and his blade flashed upwards in the moonlight.

2
1662

There were boats and vessels of every sort on the river. All were adorned and decorated so that the coloured sails, flags, garlands, arches of flowers and other such fantasies made so colourful and glittering a pageantry that the eye was almost blinded by it. People were standing on the roofs of the Palace of Whitehall, lining the waterways, massed along the muddy banks, perched precariously on scaffolding, all wide-eyed with excitement as they watched the boats manoeuvring for the best place from which they could watch the arrival of His Majesty and his Queen from Hampton Court.

The stately barges of the Lord Mayors and various companies jostled with small vessels adorned to represent symbolic devices of the Restoration or hung with coloured cloths and trimmed with ribbons as a background for pretty women and their merry young gallants who threw paper favours into the other boats. The noise was almost deafening, for besides the cheering, joking, good-humoured crowd there were a number of bands playing on shore and on the river, and volleys of artillery fire came from the vessels and from the land.

"We shall soon be too deaf to notice the Queen's Portuguese accent," the Countess of Castlemaine said laughingly to the gallants who were in attendance on her, as from the roofs of the palace they watched the pageantry below them.

"I am told Her Majesty's accent, or rather her lack of English, makes it impossible for anyone to understand what she says," someone remarked scornfully, and the

Countess gave a little cry of laughter, a sound that was, however, not echoed in her blue eyes.

She was jealous of the Queen and she made no bones about it. Her friends and those who fawned upon her because of her position at Court, were well aware that the King's return from his honeymoon would prove a crucial moment in Barbara Castlemaine's life. Would he return to her or would he remain enamoured, at least for the moment, with his Portuguese bride?

Wagers on what would happen were made by those who were highest at Court down to the lowest footman, and Barbara was well-aware that everyone was watching her this afternoon as she waited with the rest of London for Their Majesties.

She was looking exquisitely lovely. Her dark hair, which had auburn glints in it, was offset by ropes of pearls twisted among its ringlets, and her dress of yellow silk made her skin seem very white and her eyes seductively blue. She was beautiful, there was no doubt about that, but she had already borne the King two children and Charles was noted for the fickleness of his fancies.

But whatever she was feeling inside as she leant against the grey stone of the terrace, Barbara gave the impression of being absolutely sure of herself, so that those who watched her and waited became convinced that her seductive, petulant beauty would carry the day.

It was two years now since, with the triumph of twenty thousand horse and foot brandishing their swords and shouting with inexpressible joy, the King had ridden into London. The way was strewn with flowers, the bells were ringing, the streets were hung with tapestry and the fountains running with wine. At last the privations, the misery, and the poverty of those long years of exile could be forgotten and a new era was born.

It was not surprising that the King, eager for pleasure, should have been attracted by Barbara Palmer, who was openly spoken of as 'the finest woman of her age'. Her husband had prepared himself for public service as a student at the Inn's of Court, but he was completely ignorant of the raffish social life that had been Barbara's background since she had come to live in the house of her stepfather, the Earl of Anglesea. Roger Palmer's greatest virtue was his imperturbable amiability, but this was soon tested to the extreme limit by his wife's liaison with the King.

Weak and powerless to control Barbara, he could only rage against him in private, while he was forced publicly to accept the title she had earned by her infidelity.

The Earl of Castlemaine came walking now along the rooftop, elegantly dressed and wearing a curled periwig which was vastly unbecoming to his pale, rather stupid countenance. Barbara saw him approaching but took good care not to notice him until he was almost level with her. Then she glanced up, gave a start of affected surprise, and made a cold, rather mocking curtsy to which her husband replied with a courteous bow.

They had quarrelled fiercely for the last few weeks whenever they were alone together, and Barbara had already decided that Roger Palmer's usefulness to her was over. He bored her and she irritated him, so there was no point in their continuing a marriage that had grown irksome to them both, although Roger still pretended a fondness for her.

"Your Lord and Master is very smart today," a courtier sneered.

She smiled at him from under her eyelashes.

"What are you trying to tell me, Rudolph?" she enquired. "I am always suspicious when you pay anyone a compliment."

She turned away as she spoke and walked towards a nursemaid who had appeared at that moment carrying a beribboned and belaced baby in her arms.

"My little Charles," Lady Castlemaine exclaimed in tones of the fondest mother love and, taking the baby from the nursemaid, she held it for a moment in her arms, her face tender and soft as she looked down at the tiny, wrinkled face and dark hair of her son.

But the moment of tenderness passed quickly and, almost impatiently, she handed the baby back to the nursemaid and returned to the chattering group of gallants.

"We are having to wait an excessively long time," she said, glancing down at the river.

"We have waited so many years for our King to return to us that a few more minutes more won't matter," someone said soberly.

Barbara appeared not to have heard him. She was looking below to where members of the Court were assembling in small groups and converging slowly towards the Whitehall steps, up which the King would presently escort his Queen.

With an effort at cheerfulness, she took a Cavalier's plumed hat from his head and placed it on her own to keep the wind off her hair.

"I say, but I would make a remarkably handsome man," she exclaimed.

The gallants laughed.

"I prefer you as a woman," the man she had called Rudolph whispered in a low voice, which only she could hear.

As if his remark made her remember the reason she was here and the odds at stake, Barbara took the hat from her head and, unusually grave, led the way down to the terrace.

The crowds, outspoken in their comments, were pressing forward to watch the quality assemble.

"'Ere's an old 'un dug up for the occasion," a voice exclaimed.

An elderly woman had just come from the palace. She carried herself with a straight-backed dignity that, however, could not belie her years. Her skin was wrinkled and the colour of old ivory, while her patrician nose stood out like a parrot's beak. Her dress was old-fashioned and dowdy, but the jewellery she wore sparkled and glittered in the sunshine and drew Barbara Castlemaine's eyes towards it with a flash of envy. She was so intent on the old lady's diamonds that she did not notice who escorted her until she heard one of the men by her side mutter.

"Odd fish, but no one told me there was a goddess at Court."

Barbara saw then that the elderly lady was not alone. Beside her, with an air of attentiveness and affection, walked a young lady. She was not tall, almost a head shorter than Barbara herself, and everything about her was delicate and dainty, from the lovely column of her white throat to the tiny feet that peeped from beneath the laces of her petticoat.

Her hair was pale gold, hanging in ringlets on either side of her face, yet contriving as it waved gently on either side of her forehead to give her almost a spiritual air of untouched loveliness. Her eyes were enormous and unexpectedly grey, merging almost to purple in their depths, and her red lips – a perfect cupid's bow – were laughing as if something had amused her.

She was dressed in green, the soft pale green of the buds in spring, and there was something so beautiful, young and unspoiled about her that Barbara knew instinctively that the man who had called her a goddess had not exaggerated.

"Who is she?"

Barbara spoke sharply. There was no need for anyone to question of whom she spoke, for all eyes were fixed in the same direction.

"That is the Dowager Countess of Darlington," Rudolph Vyne answered. "I was told she had arrived from the country and had been given apartments in the palace. Her husband served the King's father loyally and was killed in his service, but it is surprising that after all these years the Countess should wish to return to Court life."

"I should imagine her reason is obvious," Barbara Castlemaine said sourly. "The girl is her granddaughter."

"No, she is her great-niece," Rudolph corrected Barbara turned to look at him.

"How do you know? Who is she?"

"Her name is Lady Panthea Vyne and she happens to be my second cousin," Rudolph replied.

"Your second cousin," Barbara repeated. "Why did you not tell me she was coming here?"

"To tell the truth the matter escaped my mind, though someone gave me the information a month ago and added that Panthea is an heiress. But why or how I can't imagine, for our family has been bled under the Commonwealth of everything it possessed."

"Let us make your cousin's acquaintance," Barbara said a little grimly.

She was well aware that every new face at Court was a potential enemy, provided the face was pretty enough. This was not a moment when she wished to face more rivals than was absolutely necessary. Her battle was with the Queen, but she was astute enough to realise that Lady Panthea Vyne, whoever she might be, was lovely enough to be a formidable adversary. She moved swiftly towards the Dowager and Panthea, who had paused against the stone balustrade and were watching the pageant below them.

Panthea was laughing at a little boat that was adorned with the strange masks of animals and whose crew were all dressed as monkeys.

"They must be unpleasantly warm in their furry coats," she was saying to the Countess when Rudolph Vyne, bowing before them, swept his feathered hat from his head.

"May I present myself, ma'am?' he asked of the Dowager.

"There is no need," she replied sharply. "You are my nephew, Rudolph. I should have known you anywhere from your likeness to your father. I also expected to meet you here. Your reputation has penetrated even to the wilds of Wiltshire."

"You must not believe all you hear of me," Rudolph Vyne retorted suavely, but as he kissed his aunt's hand he noticed the shrewdness of her eyes and felt uncomfortably that she was laughing at him.

"I presume you want to meet your cousin, Panthea," she said, and with a gesture of her gloved hand indicated the woman standing beside her.

Panthea sank down in a low curtsy. She was even lovelier close to than at a distance, Rudolph Vyne noticed, and then remembered that Barbara Castlemaine was waiting.

"May I present my Lady Castlemaine?" he asked, but to his astonishment the Countess drew herself up to her full height and her expression was austere.

"I have no desire for my Lady Castlemaine's acquaintance," she said coldly and turning her back, stood stolidly looking out towards the river.

To his own astonishment, Rudolph Vyne felt himself flushing. He had thought that he had been too long at Court for anything to surprise him, but that his aunt should publicly refuse to make the acquaintance of the most fêted and most favoured woman in all England was a shock which left him, for the moment, breathless and nonplussed.

He could not think what to say or what to do, and while he stood irresolute, he heard Barbara utter a furious exclamation as she turned on her heel and walked away down the terrace.

It was then Rudolph felt a hand on his arm and heard Panthea's soft voice.

"I am sorry, so sorry."

Then she too turned to stand beside her great-aunt at the balustrade and Rudolph was left alone. For a moment he hesitated whether he should join Lady Castlemaine, who was obviously in one of her bad tempers, or should try to placate his aunt. It was Panthea who decided him. He saw her glance over her shoulder, and it seemed to him that there was a look of pleading in her eyes. Instantly he crossed to his aunt's side.

"I am sorry, Aunt Anne, if I have offended you," he said.

"You have not offended me," the Countess retorted. "I am just old-fashioned enough to be particular as to whom I meet and to whom I introduce my great-niece."

"But, Aunt Anne, Lady Castlemaine is accepted everywhere."

"In London perhaps," the Countess replied, "but there are still many decent houses in the country, thank God, to which she would not be invited."

"Then they must also refuse their King," Rudolph Vyne said grimly.

"I am not prepared, Rudolph, to argue about His Majesty's principles or standards," his aunt said severely. "I am concerned only with my own. Pray heaven that when we have a Queen at Whitehall she will bring a new dignity and decency to the palace."

Rudolph Vyne sighed. He knew it was no use arguing with his aunt, but he felt that she was doomed to disappointment. The reports that had come from Hampton Court of the Queen were not particularly encouraging.

The Queen's monstrous sense of fashion had made everyone laugh, so had her attendants. The ladies, whose modesty was such that they would not wrong their virginity so far as even to sleep in sheets once touched by a man, were accompanied by a collection of very dirty and pious Portuguese monks each of whom had brought a number of relations with him. Those who went to Hampton Court to do homage to the Queen found a small, solemn little person, with lovely hands and feet and slightly protruding teeth. She was deeply in love with her jovial, charming and witty bridegroom, and reports came back to Whitehall that he was much taken with her. But would she be able to hold him, let alone change the easy pleasure-seeking court in which not only the King but everyone in England was delighting, after the gloomy austerity of Cromwell's dictatorship?

There was, however, little time to say more, for at that moment Panthea gave a cry of excitement and pointed to where, coming up the river, were the first ships of the procession that preceded Their Majesties.

There were two pageants, one of them of a king and queen with lots of courtiers grouped around them – but the crowds watched impatiently for the antique-shaped open vessel covered with a canopy of cloth of gold supported by high Corinthian pillars wreathed with flowers and festooned with garlands. Cheer upon cheer went up, as the crowd saw beneath the canopy, seated side by side and hand in hand, Charles and his dark-eyed Queen.

As the ship drew nearer and nearer to Whitehall, even the conversation ceased amongst those watching, and

Barbara Castlemaine stood in silence, her white teeth fastened on her lower lip. To the surprise of those who were watching, Barbara made no effort to push forward to greet the King and Queen Katherine as they disembarked. Instead, she stood at a distance watching the courtiers and ladies curtsying and kissing hands, and only when it was nearly time for Charles to lead his bride into the palace itself did she draw nearer and make an obeisance, with a grace and assurance that made those who preceded her seem somehow gauche and ungainly.

The Queen bowed her head, Charles' eyes rested for a moment on Barbara's face, and then they passed on into the palace and Barbara was left on the terrace with a faint smile on her lips. She was no longer worried. She had seen by the look in the King's eyes that all was well and that he would come to her in his own good time.

She walked slowly away without looking where she was going, so that she bumped against Rudolph Vyne before she saw him. He too was alone. He had been staring after his aunt and Panthea, who had withdrawn to their own apartments.

"Are you turning virtuous all of a sudden?" Barbara asked sharply, for she had not missed the look on Rudolph's face.

"Barbara, do not be angry with me," he said quickly. "It is not my fault that my aunt has such ridiculous ideas. I tried to argue with her, but she would not even listen to me."

"Do not perturb yourself," Barbara replied tartly. "Your relations are no concern of mine. They will have a dull time at court if they wish to know no one whom His Majesty favours. I'm sorry for the girl, cooped up with that old harridan."

"How kind you are!" Rudolph Vyne exclaimed, pretending to take her words literally. "Perhaps one day you will allow me to bring my cousin to meet you. She appears to be a sweet young lady."

Barbara's eyes narrowed.

"What is your game, Rudolph? Are you fortune-hunting or already in love?"

"I am in love with no one but you, as you well know," Rudolph replied. "But my debtors are pressing hard on me and she is rich, Barbara, although where in the name of heaven she gets her money from I have no idea."

"You are sure she has it?" Barbara asked.

"I shall make further enquiries," Rudolph replied, "but from the way she talked of buying horses, of acquiring a carriage and visiting the silversmiths and jewellers, I am certain that the money is there. My aunt would not allow anyone whom she chaperoned to run up debts she could not meet."

Barbara Castlemaine smiled.

"That is your idea, then, to marry money?"

"I have got to do something and quickly," Rudolph replied, "But there is something I would beg of you."

"What is that?" Barbara enquired.

"I asked His Majesty two months ago if he would appoint me to the title and estates of Staverley."

"And what stands between you and the title?" Barbara enquired.

"A cousin who must be presumed dead," Rudolph replied. "No one has heard of him for many years."

"Well, I will see what I can do," Barbara Castlemaine conceded graciously.

"You will?" Rudolph Vyne's hands touched hers eagerly. "Thank you, Barbara, you were always generous and I am ever your adoring servant, you know that."

"Do I?"

The words on her lips were provocative, and he drew a little nearer to her as if he were magnetised.

"How often must I tell you I love you?" he asked hoarsely.

"Again and again, for invariably I wonder if you speak the truth," Barbara replied.

"Can I prove it?"

Barbara shook her head.

"I am going home - and alone."

He would have argued, but he knew the tone of her voice only too well. He walked with her to her coach and saw her drive away to her house in King Street, Westminster.

Rudolph watched the coach until it was out of sight and then he turned and made his way back through the twisting galleries and courtyards of the Palace. He came at length to the apartments where the Dowager Countess of Darlington was housed. He had not realised until he came to them that they were so near to Her Majesty's, and he guessed then that his aunt was even more important than he had imagined and had come to Whitehall to wait on the new Queen.

A liveried servant admitted him and he climbed the stairs to where the windows of the lovely, long, low-ceilinged reception room looked out on to the river. His aunt was resting on the sofa, her head laid against a satin cushion, and seated on a low stool beside her, reading from a book of poems, was Panthea.

Both ladies looked up at his entrance, then Panthea rose to her feet with a smile of welcome on her face.

"It is cousin Rudolph," she said to her great-aunt, and sweeping him a curtsy drew up a comfortable armchair beside the sofa.

"Well, Rudolph, you have been quick to come a-calling," the Dowager said as her nephew bowed over her hand.

"There is so much I want to know about you," Rudolph Vyne replied, seating himself in the armchair. "I heard a vague rumour that you were coming to court, Aunt Anne, but no one told me the day of your arrival or that you would be accompanied by my cousin."

"If I had been alone, perhaps you would not have been so swift to call on me," the Countess said grimly.

But her eyes were twinkling and Rudolph felt brave enough to reply.

"Why have I been kept in ignorance of the fact that I had such a lovely relative?"

"Should we have notified you?" his aunt enquired. "I did not imagine your position in the family warranted it."

Rudolph bent forward. This was the opening he had been waiting for.

"Aunt Anne, there is something I wish to speak to you about. You are well aware that I have been out of touch with the family these past years, but it was not my fault. I was abroad until His Majesty's Restoration and since then I have found it difficult enough to live from day to day for as you well know, the little fortune my father left me was confiscated when our estate was pillaged and broken up by Cromwell's armies."

"I have heard that you have sold many of the family treasures," the Countess said.

Rudolph looked uncomfortable.

"There were not many of them," he replied, "and I was forced to obtain money by some means or another."

"Nevertheless it was a pity," the Countess remarked. "My husband's family managed, despite the privations and the troubles we have undergone, to keep our estates intact. I wish I could say the same of the Staverley fortunes."

"That is what I want to speak to you about, Aunt Anne," Rudolph said. "Two months ago I made representation to His Majesty that he should return to me the family estates and approve my inheritance of the Marquessate."

Panthea, who had been standing behind the sofa, came forward.

"You mean that you, cousin Rudolph, are the next Marquess of Staverley?" she enquired.

"I believe I have a right to your father's place," Rudolph replied, "though believe me, Panthea, I deeply regret the death of your brother."

"If only Richard had lived," Panthea said with a little sob, "how proud and happy he would have been today to see the King he loved and died for being cheered and acclaimed!"

She turned aside to hide her tears and the Countess spoke with an unexpected kindness in her voice. "None of us forget, Panthea dear, men like Richard, who died so that Charles Stuart could come to the Throne."

With a tremendous effort of willpower, Panthea choked back her tears.

"Forgive me," she said, with a little smile that was like the sun breaking through the rain clouds. "I try not to be selfish, but somehow it is hard to bear that Richard should not be here and that my father should be dead. Staverley meant so much to them – and now I believe it lies in ruins, the house empty and falling down, the gardens overgrown, the estate derelict. They loved it so deeply and they always believed that, if they could just keep it going until Cromwell was defeated, all that had been taken from us would be restored and the family would flourish again as it had in the past."

"I know what you must feel," Rudolph Vyne said sympathetically, "and that is why I want Aunt Anne to help me if she will. If the King will only acknowledge me as the fourth Marquess of Staverley - if he will proclaim me to be the rightful owner of the estates then I will restore them to what they were in your father's and my father's time."

"And how will you obtain the money to do this?" the Countess asked.

Rudolph shrugged his shoulders.

"The money will come once I am acknowledged as the rightful heir to the title."

"But are you sure that you are the heir?" the Countess asked.

"Quite sure," Rudolph replied.

"Then what of Lucius?"

There was a moment's pause.

"Lucius has not been seen or heard of for many years. At one time his name was on the list of those to be arrested for Royalist sympathies. We never heard that he was shot or hanged, but doubtless he must have been or he would have turned up before now."

"I wonder if you can be sure of that," the Countess remarked.

Panthea looked from one to the other.

"Who is Lucius?" she asked. "I seem to know the name. Is he another cousin?"

"Yes indeed! He is your second cousin as Rudolph is, and he is also my nephew," the Countess replied. "My Father, the first Marquess, had four children – myself, and I was the eldest by six years, George, who became the second Marquess of Staverley, William, who had one son, Lucius, and Arthur, my youngest brother whose eldest son was Rudolph. George had several children, but only one survived and he became the third Marquess of Staverley. He was your father, my dear," she added, turning to Panthea.

"Then my cousin, Lucius, if he is alive, should be the fourth Marquess," Panthea replied.

She was leaning forward listening to everything her great-aunt had been saying, and Rudolph, looking at her, thought he had never seen anyone so lovely. There was something so unusual in her beauty and her skin seemed to have an almost transparent look, so that once again he was reminded of his first description of her – a goddess.

"Yes, Lucius, William's son and my nephew, is the heir to the Marquessate and to the estates of Staverley," the Countess said.

"But he is dead," Rudolph interjected, "and therefore I, you must admit, Aunt Anne, am the next heir."

"That is so," the Countess conceded, "but at the same time there will be no talk of your claiming the title unless we are certain that Lucius is dead and that he left no heir."

"He is dead, I am sure of it," Rudolph repeated stubbornly.

"I wonder what makes you so sure," the Countess said reflectively. "I heard rumours, vague ones I must admit and by no means substantiated, that Lucius, when he was being hunted by Cromwell's troops, took to the road as many another Royalist did and lived as best he could."

"I too, heard that Lucius had taken to the road," Rudolph repeated grimly, "but that was many years ago. By now he has doubtless been hung up on some gibbet at the crossroads or died in a ditch with a bullet in his throat."

"What do you mean?" Panthea asked. "What did Cousin Lucius do? I don't understand."

"There was a rumour that he had become a highwayman," Rudolph explained. "It was only a rumour and I should think it to be untrue. It is not a trade to which any gentle man would stoop."

"A man who is hunted as if he were a wild animal may commit many strange actions," the Countess said. "I was fond of Lucius, and I am sure of one thing. He would do nothing dishonourable, however hard-pressed he might be."

"It depends rather on what you mean by dishonourable, Aunt Anne," Rudolph argued. "Some people have a poor opinion of thieves, whether they are on horseback or on foot."

"A gentleman may become a highwayman and be still true to his traditions and ideals," the Countess retorted. "But a woman who sells her body, even if it be to a King, is still a strumpet, however many fancy titles she may acquire."

Rudolph reddened a little under the lash of his aunt's tongue, then he spoke pleadingly.

"Help me, Aunt Anne, help me for the sake of the estate. Staverley lies derelict. You lived there once and loved it. It was Panthea's home. We can make it prosperous again and a place of which our family can well be proud."

Panthea got suddenly to her feet and walked across to the window. She stood still, looking out on to the grey river, and then she spoke quietly.

"What did Lucius look like?"

"Oh, he was quite an ordinary looking fellow," Rudolph said.

"On the contrary, he was extremely handsome," the Countess contradicted. "He was about your height, Rudolph, but thinner and more graceful than you. He rode a horse as if he were a part of it, and I have never heard anyone speak ill of him. He had a gentle, idealistic streak in him, which I believed would one day involve him in trouble, but always he was a man – a man whom a woman would trust to defend and protect her."

"Lucius was quite obviously your favourite, Aunt Anne," Rudolph said, sourly.

"How can we find out if he is still alive?" Panthea asked.

"If he were alive, he would surely have come forward now that the King is restored to the Throne and ask for his estates," Rudolph said quietly.

"How could he do that if there is a price on his head?" the Countess enquired.

Rudolph went on one knee beside his aunt's sofa.

"Listen, Aunt Anne," he said. "I respect you for your loyalty and your love for Lucius and believe me, if he were alive, I would help him in every possible way I could. Because of what the Staverleys have meant in the past and because of what they will mean in the future, I ask you now to help me, your nephew Rudolph, to obtain recognition that I am the fourth Marquess. To claim my inheritance and to return to Staverley. In order to do this, we must presume Lucius to be dead, for there has been no sign of him for so long.."

The Countess looked at him searchingly and then, as if his sincerity convinced her, she replied wearily, her voice very tired.

"Very well, Rudolph, when the opportunity occurs, I will speak with His Majesty on the subject."

"Thank you, Aunt Anne."

Rudolph's voice was warm with gratitude as he bent his head and kissed her thin fingers. Then, as he rose to his feet, he looked towards Panthea, her fair head silhouetted against the diamond-paned window. The expression on her face surprised him. She was looking troubled and her eyes were wide and anxious.

"Is there no way of making sure, cousin Rudolph, that Lucius is not still in hiding?" she asked. "Are not names of highwaymen known – at least to the authorities?"

Rudolph shook his head.

"They seldom have proper names," he said. "They are referred to as 'Blackjack', 'Gentleman Joe', 'One-armed

Bandit', or they are distinguished as 'the Velvet Mask', 'the Card', or some ridiculous title of that sort."

"Would anyone know what cousin Lucius was called?" Panthea persisted.

Rudolph's eyes shifted from hers and instinctively she was aware that he was about to lie. She did not know why she knew this, but she was sure of it.

"I have no idea what Lucius was nicknamed," Rudolph replied. "If we did know, perhaps we should be able to ascertain whether he is alive or dead. But we know nothing. After all, the supposition that he took to the road may be only a romantic legend. You know how these stories grow."

He spoke quickly and almost too easily. Panthea, watching him, was sure that he was prevaricating. Then, as she watched him say goodbye to his aunt and felt his lips against her own fingers, she thought she must have been mistaken. He carried himself well and looked like a gentle man. He sounded genuine and sincere enough in his desire to restore the family place to what it had once been, and yet there was something she did not trust, something that worried and perplexed her.

The door closed behind Rudolph and still Panthea stood by the window. She was so deep in her own thoughts that she was startled when her great-aunt spoke.

"He is a ne'er-do-well!"

"Who?" asked Panthea in astonishment.

"My nephew, Rudolph," the old lady replied. "He has a plausible tongue, a handsome face and would deceive most women, but not me. I remember him as a child, a tiresome deceitful boy for all his good looks. Lucius was worth a dozen of him, but if Lucius is dead, then Rudolph will be the Marquess of Staverley and there is nothing we can do to prevent it."

"I wonder if he is indeed dead," Panthea said.

"I wonder too," the Countess said. She sighed and added, "Come, child, we must make ourselves ready to wait on Her Majesty. She is expecting us for dinner at six of the clocks."

"I will go and change," Panthea said, and opened the door for the Dowager to leave the room for her bedchamber.

Alone, Panthea paused to set the book she had been reading back in the bookcase, then crossing the passage she entered her own bedchamber. It was a small room, but the four-poster bed that filled most of it was draped with white muslin and tied with small lover's knots of blue ribbon. This and the rest of the furniture had been brought from her great-aunt's home in Wiltshire and was therefore familiar.

Panthea had disliked leaving the country for London. She had wanted to come to Court, but at the same time she had not wanted to leave the home that had been hers these past four years since her father died. Yet now that she was here living in the palace, she found it had a thrill of its own.

She was, of course, bewildered by the warren of galleries, apartments and gardens that housed not only the King, but the ministers of state, courtiers, chaplains, ladies, servants and all the countless company that encompassed the Throne. Already Panthea had gaped with the public in the long Stone Gallery, which was open to all comers and where hung the fine pictures that Charles I had collected and which had been partly reassembled. She had been shown the magnificent, perfumed Banqueting Hall and been allowed to peep into the Withdrawing Room, where the King would sup, talking – she was told – wittily and without restraint to those around him. Beyond was the bedchamber, where the most secret affairs of State were transacted, and off which lay the King's closet, containing

His Majesty's prized collection of enamelled clocks and model ships.

Everywhere, Panthea thought, there were treasures and wonders such as she had never imagined in the simplicity of country life. The Chapel Royal with its cloth of gold on the Communion Table was very different from the plain stone church in which she and her great-aunt had worshipped on Sundays. The scarlet and gold of the Palace, the fringed hangings of crimson brocade, the gilt mirrors from France, the marbles, mosaics, polished woods and priceless tapestries left her breathless when she compared them with the unpretentious decorations of the houses she had known previously.

It was all very exciting, and yet at the same time rather frightening. In the midst of so much grandeur, Panthea felt young and inexperienced and above all quite unable to cope with the difficulties of social life, such as that moment this afternoon when her great-aunt had refused to meet Lady Castlemaine. Although she had always known that a court was full of intrigue, gossip and small personal vendettas, she had not expected to be involved in the latter so quickly. But she had seen the expression on Lady Castlemaine's face when her great-aunt turned her back upon her, and she knew they had both made a bitter enemy.

Lady Castlemaine was beautiful, Panthea thought, and yet there was something threatening and overpowering about her. She stood for a moment in her bedchamber and wished she was back in Wiltshire. There she could be running in the garden with the spaniels, riding her horse over the park land, feeding the goldfish in the waterlily pond or sitting peacefully in the orangery, listening to the song of the birds.

Life there had all been quiet and uneventful. This was tumultuous and frightening, a world in which she was half afraid to breathe for fear that she would do the wrong thing.

She crossed to the dressing table and stared at herself in the polished surface of the gold-framed mirror. It showed her the reflection of her own loveliness and she was quite unaware of it. Instead she saw the heavy-eyed beauty of Barbara Castlemaine, the magnolia whiteness of her skin, the sensuous crimson of her full mouth, the heavy-lidded eyes that seemed to glitter with a strange fire.

A voice from behind made her jump.

"'Tis time to change, my Lady."

Panthea turned. Marta, the maid she had brought with her from Wiltshire, was smiling at her from beneath a mob cap of starched whitelinen. Marta was a buxom, apple-cheeked woman of some thirty summers and no one would ever have mistaken her for anything but country born. She had fair flecked skin and russet-brown hair that matched her warm brown eyes, and when she entered the room she seemed to bring with her a fragrance of newly turned hay and sweet purple clover.

"How you startled me, Marta! I did not hear you come into the room," Panthea exclaimed.

"You were deep in thought, my Lady," Marta replied. "Was it the handsome gentleman who called just now that you were thinking about?"

"That is Mr. Rudolph Vyne, my cousin, Marta. I had no idea I had a cousin called Rudolph until he introduced himself today on the terrace, just before Their Majesties' arrival."

"He is as handsome a gentleman as I have seen for a long time, my Lady, but doubtless there will be many more of them calling here now that you have come to London. I have been busy all this day finishing your new gown and you will turn the heads of everyone when you wear it tonight."

"You need not worry about that," Panthea said with a smile. "No one will look at me, Marta. You have never seen such lovely ladies as there were on the terrace. The clothes they wore made Aunt Anne and I look as if we had come out of the ark."

"Don't you believe it, my Lady – you are lovelier than all those grand ladies with their paints, their powders and lip salves. I'll wager they don't look their best in the morning, not after their parties with wine, dancing and cards, which do not finish until the sun has risen."

"I shall not look my best either if those are the hours we must keep," Panthea smiled. "Help me change, Marta, for I must not be late."

Marta came towards her and started to undo her gown. Panthea picked up a comb and ran it through her fair curls.

"Marta, have you ever heard of Mr. Lucius Vyne," she asked suddenly, "another cousin of mine?"

She looked in the mirror as she spoke, and she saw Marta's face over her shoulder as she unhooked her gown. To her astonishment, the woman's face was suddenly white and strained, a look almost akin to terror in her eyes. And then, after a moment's pause which Panthea knew she would not have noticed had she not been watching Marta's face, the woman replied.

"I think I have heard of him, my Lady."

"Tell me about him, Marta, tell me everything you know," she commanded.

Marta hesitated and again there was a kind of terror in her eyes.

"I know nothing, my Lady," she said. "Nothing at all! Indeed you will not have heard me mention him."

"But, Marta, you are trembling," Panthea said incredulously. "What is this? What have I said to upset you?"

"Nothing, it is nothing – nothing at all, my Lady," Marta repeated. "I know naught, I promise you that."

"You are lying, Marta," Panthea said. "Come, you can't pretend to me after all these years we have been together. Why, Marta, you are frightened about something. What have I said that should frighten you? We are speaking only of Lucius Vyne, my cousin. They say he is dead. Why, then, should his name perturb you?"

Marta opened her mouth to speak, then she shut it again. The woman was badly shaken, Panthea could see that. Her face was white and her hands were trembling. She would not look up but twisted the hem of her apron in her fingers, staring at it as if she had never seen a piece of linen before.

"Tell me, Marta," Panthea coaxed. "Please tell me what you know."

"I cannot, my Lady, I cannot! *I dare not!*"

"Then you *do* know something," Panthea said. "And there is something to know. Oh, Marta, trust me! There is nothing you could say to me that would possibly do any harm to anyone. Tell me, please tell me."

Marta still looked down at the hem of her apron.

"What is it you want to know, my Lady?" she said at last.

Panthea chose her words carefully.

"I have heard, Marta," she said, "that my cousin Lucius is a highwayman. Is that true?"

A shudder seemed to go through Marta's body and her hands closed convulsively on her apron then, at length, in a voice barely above a whisper, she spoke.

"It may be so! I have heard talk of such things!"

"And his name, Marta? By what name is he known, for I am well aware that he would not use his own?"

Marta swallowed convulsively but did not speak.

"Tell me, Marta, please tell me," Panthea pleaded. "It can do no harm. I swear that I will tell no one."

Marta swallowed again.

"I have heard tell, my Lady,' she began at length. "I have heard tell that he is called . . . White Throat."

Panthea put her hands to her breast and checked the cry that rose to her lips. She had known it, she had been certain of it almost from the first moment, she thought. Of course it had been Lucius who saved her. Who else could it have been?

3

Panthea stood speechless for a long moment, her thoughts racing through her mind, while Marta bent down to unfasten her shoes with fingers that trembled so obviously that Panthea knew it was but an excuse to be doing something. She bore Marta fumbling with her silver buckles for a few seconds, then she put her hands under the woman's arms and drew her to her feet to stare into her face with questioning eyes.

"Marta, you have got to be frank with me," Panthea commanded.

But Marta twisted herself from her grasp.

"I pray you, my Lady, question me no further. There is naught that I can tell you, I promise you that. I have already said more than I should. I beseech you, let me be, for it is none of my business."

Marta's voice suddenly broke into a sob and to Panthea's astonishment, she turned and ran from the room. The door banged behind her and Panthea was alone.

There was something here that she could not understand. In all the years that she had known Marta, she had never known her behave so strangely before. The daughter of the head gardener at Staverley, she had come into the house when she was quite a young girl to wait on the nurseries, and on the formidable old nanny who had ruled Richard and Panthea with a rod of iron.

When Nannie had retired to a comfortable little cottage in the village to live out her remaining years in being autocratic and dogmatic to the villagers, Marta had stayed on as personal maid to Panthea. She was a willing, good-tempered girl and Panthea had grown very fond of her. When she moved to Wiltshire to live with her great-aunt, she had been grateful that Marta should accompany her there.

She had indeed found her more of a companion than a maid, for although Marta was older than her young mistress, she was still young enough to play with Panthea and they found much in common in their love of pretty things and their delight in the simple pleasures of the countryside. Now they were both thrilled with London.

Panthea thought she would never forget her first impressions of the walled City. The fields and meadows grew right up to its walls, and so the rich earthy smell of the fruits, flowers and beasts lay all about it. But once they had passed through the gates, the streets, crowded with hackney carriages, waggons, sedan chairs and the glass coaches of great lords and ladies, had left both Panthea and Marta wide eyed and open-mouthed. Lady Darlington had laughed at them and said that they looked like gaping yokels and indeed the City was not nearly so fine as it had been in her young days.

But Panthea had not listened to her great-aunt. To her everything was exciting, from the ladies' fashionable attire of short, slit and beribboned sleeves, low-necked bodices, full skirts of satin and brocade, to the monstrous swinging signs along the roads leading to Charing Cross, or the bell men crying, "Past one o'clock and a cold, frosty morning!"

Yet when they came to the Palace of Whitehall, lying for nearly half a mile beside the river, Panthea had felt glad that Marta was with her, for the place seemed almost frightening in its pomposity and grandeur. Although Lady Darlington took it as a matter of course having stayed there so often in the past, Marta was as awed as Panthea was, and it was pleasant to have someone with whom one could exclaim over everything that occurred and discuss every strange person and object that one saw, with excitement and interest.

If Panthea had been told a few days earlier that Marta had any secrets from her, she would have been astonished and surprised and she would, without doubt, have repudiated the suggestion as ridiculous. Now she was astounded not only at Marta's behaviour, but that for the moment she seemed a complete stranger – someone withdrawn in an unfriendly and secretive manner into some private fortress of her own where Panthea could not follow her.

What did White Throat mean to Marta and why should the mere mention of his name perturb her?

Panthea sat down at her dressing table, puzzled and perplexed – and then the memory of that night five years ago came flooding back to her. She could see him walking towards her through the trees. She had not been able to watch the fight between him and the man to whom she had been married but a few hours earlier. She had heard the sound of steel striking steel, then she had known that she dared not look, she could not.

The whole evening had been one of horror, culminating in that stricken moment when he had killed the dog and she knew him for the brute he was. She had always suspected that he was cruel, known it in the way he had come to Staverley to torture her, known it when he had driven his hard bargain in demanding that she should marry him or else he would not save Richard.

But she had never before in her soft and sheltered life, encountered deliberate brutality – a man who will use his cruelty and strength against the defenceless, and who could with a single blow destroy the animal she loved.

She could not watch the fight, could not see the man who had befriended her, who had come to her rescue at the moment when she most needed help, lie wounded at the feet of the man she loathed and hated. She felt despairingly that there could be no other end to the duel.

Christian Drysdale appeared so immeasurably bigger and more powerful than the highwayman. Perhaps it was her own fear of him which made him seem so prodigious, perhaps it was just the utter despair in her heart that made it impossible for her even to hope that she personally might be saved.

She had sunk down on her knees, her satin dress billowing out over the dried leaves and twigs that lay beneath the trees. The ground was damp, but she did not feel it stain her dress. She could only kneel, her face in her hands, and pray a childlike prayer in which the words were meaningless, but in which her whole spirit cried out beseechingly.

She heard the clang and crash of their swords. Occasionally there was a muttered oath or a guttural sound as if an animal snorted, and then the clash of steel sounded again. How long she knelt there she did not know, for suddenly it seemed to her there came a strange silence – a silence that was all the more frightening because her ears were strained to hear it. She knew then that the end had come.

Slowly, trembling in every limb, she raised her head and opened her eyes. It was then she saw him coming through the trees, the moonlight shining on his uncovered head, the lace at his throat very white against the darkness of his coat.

He had laid his sword aside. His hands were empty as he came towards her, and he stretched them out and caught her as she tried to run towards him, only to stumble and fall into his arms. She had clung to him for a moment speechless, still too possessed by her terror to know that there was no longer any need for it. And as he looked down at her white, tearstained face, he seemed to understand, for holding her warmly and comfortingly, as a brother might have done, he spoke quietly.

"It is all right, my dear. It is all over! Now you can go home."

"Home?" she questioned, the word coming stupidly from her lips as if she did not know what it meant.

"Yes, home," he said quietly. "The nightmare is over. You can go back to Staverley, little Panthea. But first tell me who knows of your marriage?"

She could not answer his question for suddenly the full realisation of what he had done for her swept over her in an overwhelming flood. She felt the wonder of it seep into her like the warmth of the sun and she hid her face against his coat.

"H-he is dead?" she whispered at last.

"He will trouble you no more," the highwayman said gently. Then as he looked over his shoulder, he added, "Come and sit down for a few minutes. There are things to be done which it would be best for you not to see."

But she had already seen what was happening. The coach men were digging a deep hole beneath an oak tree and a body lay still, the arms flung forward, on the downtrodden earth of the clearing.

"Come and sit down," the highwayman repeated, and he drew her to a fallen tree beside the stream.

He brushed the snow from it with his hand, and when she had seated herself, he asked again the question she had forgotten to answer.

"Who knows of your marriage?"

"No one," Panthea replied. "I crept from the house after everyone was asleep. He drove me some miles to a church on the outskirts of the forest. A blind priest officiates there. H-he married us."

"Why such secrecy?" the highwayman enquired.

"H-he told me," Panthea said, "that it would not be good for him if it were known that he had wed a Royalist. He said that he would keep me hidden at his house in the country. He would not inform his friends of the marriage until this last visit of the King had been forgotten. I was glad when he suggested such concealment, for I was ashamed that my friends should know that I had married a Roundhead."

"I am not surprised," the highwayman replied. "Did you not realise what he was like?"

"We were always afraid of him. When he came to collect the taxes, my father said he extorted every possible penny from the estate. He was cruel and unjust, but there was nothing we could do. We dared not refuse his requests."

"He has done the same everywhere," the highwayman said grimly. "Now you must forget about him. I am going to take you back home. Perhaps no one will have noticed your absence. If they have, you will have to make some trifling excuse, but you understand that you must tell no one of what has occurred this night. I want you to forget it yourself, to forget that you have ever been married, to forget that you have been widowed."

Panthea looked up at him.

"I shall never forget you – or what you have done for me," she said softly.

She thought that the highwayman's eyes behind his mask were tender, but he replied almost brusquely,

"You must forget me too. This whole night must seem to you like a bad dream, one from which you have awakened to find it all a fantasy."

"But I shall never forget you," Panthea repeated.

She felt somehow that it was important that he should know this.

"Then if you must remember me," the highwayman said, "pray that when I come to die I shall do so bravely, and with the same courage as your brother showed."

"But you must not die," Panthea cried. "Can you not come back with me? My father will hide you. There is room at Staverley for you – there are secret passages. You would be safe there at least for a little while."

"Thank you, my dear," the highwayman replied, "but your father has enough troubles of his own. As your brother has been hanged as a traitor, doubtless vengeance will be taken on your family and on the estate. There will be more taxes to be paid, but at least there will be another tax-collector."

"But you? What will you do?" Panthea asked.

"What I have done in the past," the highwayman said with a sudden smile. "Rob those who deserve it. I am not so wretched as you might think. I have my friends and they never fail me. I have my horses and they mean more to me than I can tell you."

"But always you are in danger," Panthea said. "There must be a price on your head. Men are hunting for you. There might be even people who would betray you for what you have done tonight."

The highwayman shook his head.

"By tomorrow I shall be far away from here. You are not to worry about me. Go home and grow up into a woman. You are only a child, Panthea, a child who should not have her pretty head worried by the hardships and difficulties of life."

"Even tonight, when I left my bedchamber to creep downstairs, I did not realise quite what I was doing," Panthea said in a low voice. "Then in the coach I began to understand, but before I could die from the horror of it, you came and saved me."

"Forget it," he said urgently. "Forget all that happened, then and now. Go home, little Panthea. You are tired and it is long past your bedtime."

She put out her hands impulsively and clutched his arm.

"You will take care of yourself? Promise me?"

~53~

"I promise," he said lightly after a moment's hesitation. "After all, who knows you might need me one day in the future? If you do, I will always be ready to serve you."

"But how shall I find you?" Panthea asked earnestly, her serious tone in vivid contrast to his jovial, laughing one.

"Perhaps fate will make our paths cross once again," the highwayman said.

"But supposing I need you," Panthea persisted. "Why, I do not even know your name."

It was then she had thrown back her head to look up at him and he saw her face full in the moonlight. She was very innocent as she pleaded with him, her eyes raised to his, the sweet oval of her little face and the pale gold of her shining hair vivid against the shadows of the trees. He looked at her for a long moment and then abruptly he rose to his feet.

"I have told you to forget me," he said harshly. "Go home, Panthea. Staverley is waiting for you."

Slowly Panthea rose to her feet.

"He called you WhiteThroat," she said. "Is that the name by which you are known?"

"Yes, that is what they call me," the highwayman replied. "WhiteThroat because I place a bunch of lace at my chin, and those who follow my trade are usually not so reckless as to offer a target for the marksman. It is a name given to me half in jest and half in respect for being foolhardier than the majority of those who play the same dangerous game."

He spoke bitterly, then his mood changed and he was smiling as he put an arm round Panthea's shoulder and drew her through the trees towards the clearing.

"Can you ride pillion?" he asked.

"Of course," she answered. "Father used to take me round the estate that way when I was very little."

"Then that is how you will travel back to Staverley tonight," the highwayman said.

They had reached the clearing by now. There was no sign of Christian Drysdale's body, but the coachmen were moving away from a mound under the oak tree. As the highwayman appeared, they stood looking at him as if waiting for further orders.

He took some coins from his pocket and threw them in their direction.

"Get home as quickly as you can," he said, "and forget tonight's work. If anyone asks you what occurred, you will say you were dismissed from the tax-collector's service after you had driven him about five miles. Two other men took your place, but you knew not who they were or where they came from. He paid you well and you have the money there to prove it. He appeared to be on some errand of great importance and on which he travelled alone. I repeat he travelled alone. Is that clear?"

"Aye, sir."

The older of the coachmen touched his forelock.

"Neither of you wish to involve yourselves in trouble," the highwayman continued. "If you talk, you will undoubtedly be arrested and who will believe the story that you have to tell? Say nothing, keep silent. I am certain that neither of you has any desire to be questioned by the military."

"Us'll not talk, sir, ye can be sure o' that," one of the men said.

"Good! Now get off – right away."

The men hesitated.

"But the coach, sir, and the horses?"

"They are none of your business. Hurry now! If you step out, you should be back at your village before dawn."

The men pocketed the guineas and started off sturdily down the road. The highwayman watched them go and then turned to his companion waiting in the shadows.

"Unharness the horses, Jack," he said, "and let them go."

Jack did not question his orders. He stuck the pistol that he held in his hand into his pocket, and walking across the road began to unharness the two big grey horses that had drawn the coach. Panthea watched, wondering what plan the highwayman had in mind. To her surprise, he opened the door of the coach. She saw him feeling beneath the seat and then, when he found nothing there, he ripped up the upholstery. She moved across the roadway and watched him.

"What are you looking for?" she asked at length.

"Money," the highwayman replied.

"Do you think he kept it in the coach?" she asked, and as if in answer to her question, the highwayman gave an exclamation as he tore a shred of cloth from the ceiling with a sharp movement.

There was a sudden trickle of coins on the floor of the coach and the highwayman dragged down from the roof two large bags. Panthea let out a little exclamation of astonishment.

"His month's takings," the highwayman remarked as he carried the bags from the coach out into the moonlight, and Panthea saw the guineas glittering. "Mr. Drysdale made a tour of this district every month. He was returning home and arranged to pick you up on his way. He sent his regular coachmen ahead and hired two village men so that the people in his house would not know who you were. He doubtless had some plausible lies ready on his tongue and you would have found yourself belonging to an acknowledged family of Roundheads and forced to conceal your own name."

"I would not have obeyed him in that," Panthea said hotly.

The highwayman looked at her and the words died away on her lips. She remembered Christian Drysdale's strength. She remembered the way he had disposed of Bobo who had defied him. Would she have been able to stand up against him? She knew the answer and flushed with the shame of it.

The highwayman tied the mouths of the bags together again.

"This is yours," he said quietly. "You are entitled to it because the man to whom they belonged was, if only for a few hours, your husband. I want you to take it and guard it very carefully. Tell no one what you have, keep it for emergencies. They may punish your father because his son was hanged as a traitor – they may inflict new and terrible taxes upon the estate for the same reason, but this money will safeguard you. I wish it were more, but at least it will be some security against anything the future may hold."

For a moment Panthea could not find words to answer him, then she cried out.

"But why are you doing all this for me? Why should you? You need the money yourself. If you meant to rob him, why should you give it away now?"

She searched his face as if to find an answer to her question, but it was hard to see anything behind the black mask. Instead, he smiled down at her and put the bags of money into her arms.

"One day, perhaps you will find an answer to these questions. At the moment, this is not the time nor the place to answer them."

He took Panthea's cloak from the coach and wrapped it round her shoulders, then he whistled a low but clear note and his black stallion, which had been cropping the grass contentedly, came trotting up to him. He lifted Panthea on to its back and swung himself into the saddle.

"I will be back as quickly as I can, Jack," he said to his assistant who, having freed the horses from the coach, was watching them trotting away down the road.

"Shall I wait for you here, sir?" Jack enquired respectfully.

"Yes, and set fire to the coach. Burn every stick and rag in it until there is nothing left to identify it."

"I will do that, sir," Jack said.

The highwayman gathered up the reins, and they started off in the opposite direction to that which had been taken by the horses freed from the coach.

They had not gone far before the highwayman turned off from the road. They crossed fields, forded a stream and came in a surprisingly short space of time to the woods which bordered the Staverley Estate. He seemed to know the way and never once did he hesitate or check his horse. He rode forward determinedly and with the air of one who follows a familiar path.

When at last he drew in the reins, Panthea saw they were standing on high ground and Staverley lay below them. The moon was sinking in the sky, but it was still bright enough to turn the lake to molten silver and reveal the beauty of the great house, encircled by its terraces as if by a jewelled necklace.

It was a vista of unsurpassed loveliness, but it seemed to Panthea that there was something sad and shuttered about her house with its darkened windows and encompassed by the silence of the night. The place might be empty and no longer inhabited.

As she looked at the silver water, she remembered her sudden premonition of disaster but a few weeks ago when Richard had come to tell her that he must go to London.

She shivered, and as if the highwayman felt it, he turned his head to her.

"You are cold?"

'No," Panthea answered. "My cloak is warm."

She could not explain to the highwayman what she felt. She could not even put it into words to herself, but she knew that strange emotions were rising within her, a feeling of sadness and of parting, a feeling that she was losing something, that this was a moment in her life she would always remember.

"It is time you were abed," the highwayman said, and spurring his horse they trotted downhill.

They came to rest at last at a gate which led into the garden, and which was closest to the door by which Panthea had left the house. The highwayman jumped to the ground and lifted her gently from the back of the horse. She was stiff and cramped from the long ride and when he set her down, she clung to him for a moment, in fear that she might have fallen.

"Good night, Panthea," he said.

"But how can I thank you?" she asked.

"You cannot! You are to do nothing of the sort," he answered.

"But I must," Panthea said.

She dropped the heavy bags of money which were occupying her hands and reaching out her arms as naturally and as sweetly as any child might have done, she put them round his neck.

"Thank you, thank you," she said. "I shall never forget what you have done for me – and please don't forget me, for I shall always remember you."

She spoke feelingly and in a spontaneous manner which showed that the words came straight from her heart and held her face up to his. He kissed her cheek and put his arms round her, holding her close. His lips were very gentle on her cheek – then quickly as if he feared to stay, he put her from him and leaped into the saddle.

She had a bemused memory of her own voice calling out to him before, with a flashing smile, he was gone, galloping hard across the park as if the devil himself were at his heels. She watched him until he was out of sight, and when he was, she realised that the tears were streaming down her cheeks. She did not know why she cried except that the night had been such a full one.

She collected the bags of money and crept into the house with them. When she reached her own bedroom, she realised that everything was exactly as it had been when she crept away earlier in the night. No one knew she had gone. Her note for her father was where she had left it, propped up on the dressing table. She tore it into a thousand pieces and flung herself face downwards on the bed. And then she began to cry, deep tempestuous sobs, the sobs of a child who has been frightened but still goes on crying when the danger is past.

Panthea, looking at herself now in the mirror, could remember how those tears had passed into a dreamless, exhausted sleep. She had been roused from her sleep hours later by the dogs barking, and awakened with a start to realise where she was and that she was still in her best satin dress and fur lined cloak. She jumped off the bed and hastily undressed herself. She had hidden the bags of money in the bottom of her wardrobe and was lying back on the pillows looking much as usual, when Marta came in with her morning chocolate.

All through the day that followed, Panthea remembered, she had moved as if in a dream. The morning had brought her the bitter realisation of her brother's death, and yet she could not speak of it to anyone. She could not answer how she knew that he was dead until the tidings should be brought to them officially.

On the following morning, something strange occurred. A boy, a half-witted youth in his early teens, came to the kitchen door and demanded to see her. The servants tried to extract from him what his business might be, but he had refused to say anything, save that he must speak with Lady Panthea Vyne.

When eventually Panthea had been fetched to him, he took her on one side and pressed a crumpled piece of paper into her hand. Before she could ask him anything further, he was gone speeding like a startled hare down the drive.

She opened the note. It contained but a few words.

'Look in the grotto when you are alone'.

She stared at it in perplexity. The writing was educated and well-formed, and suddenly a flush spread over her face. She guessed from whom it had come. Perhaps he was waiting for her, perhaps he wished to see her again. She felt herself tingle with a sudden excitement but, remembering that she might endanger him by not doing exactly as she was told, she moved back into the house, ignoring the curious stares of the servants who were wondering why the boy was so intent on seeing her.

She went about her usual tasks until she was quite certain she was unobserved, then sped as quickly as she could through the gardens to the little grotto.

It was a small stone edifice built on the side of the lake opposite to the house. A flagged path led to it, which in the spring was banked with flowers, and it stood amongst rhododendron and azalea bushes and the graceful trailing branches of a weeping willow. But at this time of year, the tree was leafless and the path was slippery with ice, so that Panthea had to pick her way carefully.

Even so, she could not prevent herself from hurrying, only to feel the sudden stab of bitter disappointment when she found the grotto was empty. The damp dripped down the walls and the seat on which one could sit with such pleasure in the summertime was dark and slimy. There was a smell of decay about the place, but as Panthea looked around her with a feeling of emptiness, she saw that there was a heavy wrought-iron box laid in a corner. She crossed to it and could see, lying on the top of it, a piece of paper like the piece she had received before.

'This also is yours. Keep it safely'.

She read the note several times before she inspected the box. She recognised it as the kind that her father used for the safe keeping of money. It had a lock and a key in it. Having turned the key and raised the lid she saw that the box was full of coins. She stared for a moment and then she understood. This was more of Christian Drysdale's money. The highwayman must have stolen it from his house and carried it here for her. There was more money in the box than in the bags he had given her previously, in fact more than she had seen in her life before.

And yet she had felt defrauded. She had expected something very different to be waiting for her in the grotto than a box of money.

*

But all the money that Panthea possessed had not been enough to prevent the seizure of Staverley and the expulsion of its owners by Cromwell's men. Her father had been dying when the soldiers turned him from his home and from his bed, and he died as the coach carried them away down the drive.

He would not have wanted to live in a small uncomfortable house that was the only one available to them on the far edge of the estate. Panthea fortunately had spent only a short while there before, with Marta to accompany her, she went to live with her great-aunt in Wiltshire.

If Lady Darlington was surprised at the enormous fortune that Panthea brought with her and which had to be put into safekeeping, she did not ask many unnecessary questions. Perhaps she thought that her nephew had been wise enough to foresee the inevitable seizure of the estates and to prepare against the emergency. Perhaps she thought that Panthea, knowing so little of money, would not understand her questioning, but whatever the reason, she had accepted the fact that Panthea was a considerable heiress and had deposited the gold with a reputable goldsmith, save for the small amount that Panthea expended yearly on her apparel.

The money had acquired interest and had increased in the years in which she had owned it. Panthea wondered now whether it would be possible to buy a pardon for Lucius, her cousin, from whatever crimes he might have committed. He was alive, she was sure of that, just as she knew that Rudolph coveted the estates and was presuming on Lucius' death for his own ends.

Her first thought was to tell her great-aunt the truth, but then she hesitated. She had kept silent all these years. Was it wise to speak now and on such a slender pretext? Supposing her great-aunt said something inadvertently that would enable Rudolph to denounce his cousin. It suited his purpose to presume that Lucius was dead – it would suit him even better if it was an accomplished fact. Supposing he contrived that Lucius should be hanged. Panthea was suddenly resolved and determined with a strength of purpose she had not known she possessed. Somehow and in some way, she must restore Lucius to his rightful place. How she could do this she did not know. She only knew that, as once he had saved her, so now she must save him.

~63~

She thought how stupid she had been not to realise before that the highwayman who had come to her rescue was one of the family. He had known her name – he had spoken with such assurance and familiarity of Staverley.

Looking back now, she saw herself trusting Lucius with that instinct which children and animals have for someone who is utterly sincere and completely trustworthy. She had questioned him so little. She had known from the first moment when he had spoken to her, that he was there to help her. She had thought of him every day in the years that had followed, but never for one moment had she been astute enough to guess who he might be. It was not surprising, for she had not known that he existed.

Her great-aunt had always been curiously reticent about the Vynes. Panthea had not understood it until she stumbled on the truth after she had lived with her for a long time.

Lord Darlington had been a difficult, overpowering man with an exceptionally jealous nature. He disliked his brothers-in-law because his wife was fond of them, and with a possessiveness that was in some ways flattering, he had kept her entirely separated from her family and had done everything he could to make her forget their very existence. Panthea learned that it threw him into a rage if she so much as mentioned her brothers, or the life she had lived at Staverley before she married, and after fifty years of what had, in many ways, been an extremely happily married life, she had grown out of the habit of talking about her relations.

It was fortunate that Lord Darlington was dead when, lonely and orphaned, Panthea went to make her home with her great-aunt. Had he been alive, there was no doubt that he would not have tolerated her in his household. His had been a strange character, and yet he had made her great-aunt happy. She mourned him sincerely, although on his death she had become all the things he had prevented her from being during his lifetime, and she always spoke as if without him life was a dismal and almost insupportable existence.

Actually, Lady Darlington enjoyed her widowhood. Outspoken and of a decided strength of character, she found that without a husband there was no one to curb or correct her, no one to force from her an obedience which she instinctively resented, no one to be jealous and possessive, so that she must hide even the most natural affections.

The Countess had been delighted at the thought of coming to London again and there was no question of her being invited to be in attendance on Her Majesty. She intrigued, plotted, schemed and pulled strings until that position was offered to her, not spontaneously, but because she had manoeuvred herself into a position to command it. Now that her husband was dead, there were few people who could withstand the Dowager Countess when she made up her mind.

Panthea watched her great-aunt's manoeuvres with amusement. At the same time, she was slightly afraid of her. So were a number of other people. Lady Darlington usually said what came into her mind, however uncomfortable it might be for the hearer. It would not be wise, Panthea decided, to confide in her about her ideas of Lucius. Besides, when she came to think of it, what was there to confide?

She knew nothing save that Lucius was the highwayman who had saved her from a brutal husband, and that the mention of him made Marta shiver and tremble and run from the room to hide.

4

Barbara Castlemaine sat in the bedchamber of her new apartments. There was a look of triumph on her face as she glanced round the elaborately furnished room and looked out of the windows, which afforded a view of the Privy Garden. She might have been a General smiling over a victory, won against overwhelming odds and snatched, as it were, from the very teeth of the enemy.

Barbara knew that everyone, including her greatest friends, had expected her to retire from the field of battle, if not vanquished at least incapacitated. Instead, the last defences had fallen before her onslaughts and the citadel she had set out to capture had surrendered abjectly.

In her own heart she knew that she had been luckier than she had dared to hope, even while her air of assurance told the world that she had never expected anything but victory.

She looked round her bedchamber again and threw out her arms in a little sensuous gesture of abandonment. Yes, she had won. She was here in the Palace of Whitehall with apartments specially allotted to her as Lady of the Bedchamber to Queen Katherine of Braganza.

No one would ever know what she had felt when she heard that her name had been crossed off the list of ladies submitted to the Queen. No one would ever know the fury she had experienced when she learned that the Queen had even vowed she would return home to her parents, rather than submit to including her husband's mistress among her own entourage.

And yet Barbara had won! It had been a battle of wits between two women. One the inexperienced, young and unsophisticated girl from Portugal, who had little knowledge of how to handle the attractive, winsome and unstable man she had married – the other Barbara, with her flashing, sparkling beauty, and boundless ambitions, who had held the heart of the most fascinating man in Britain captive at her feet for over two years.

Yes, Barbara had won despite the bitter enmity of the more respectable and straitlaced ladies of the Court, despite the intrigues against her by many of the King's own personal advisers. She had won – and now that her enemies were discomfited, she planned that they should suffer, one and all, for having dared to raise their voices against her.

Moving about her bedchamber in her lace petticoats, a white negligée thrown over her bare shoulders and her dark hair undressed, Barbara looked younger than years. She was perhaps lovelier now than she had ever been in her whole life, and it was hard for any man to resist her flattery, let alone Charles who not only had a weakness for any pretty woman, but who was soft-hearted enough to find it difficult to refuse any request made to him by a woman who had borne him a child.

Yet what surprised everyone was that Charles, whose susceptibility was well known, should be faithful for so long and should find such continual beguilement in Barbara, when there were younger, fresher and less turbulent beauties languishing for a glance from his eyes. Already those at Court were whispering that Barbara had some strange magic that held Charles by her side, or used some hitherto unknown sorcery to keep him faithful. These whispers were to grow louder and stronger as the years passed and history was to hint at many hidden and peculiar vices, while never actually giving them a name.

But the truth was quite simple. Barbara was no monster, no exotic, unnatural creature – she was a woman to whom passion came as easily as breathing and who was at her very best when being loved and making love. She was not different from other women, save perhaps in the exceptional quality of her skin, which was soft, smooth and as silky to the touch as the petal of a magnolia blossom.

Her attraction for Charles lay in the fact that there was a magnetism between them that aroused one another as a fire is kindled from timber. They had only to look deep into each other's eyes to feel that mounting flame which, burning, aspiring, consuming, made every nerve in their bodies tingle with an inexpressible exhilaration.

It was not love, for Barbara had loved but one man in her life and that was the notorious rake, the Earl of Chesterfield, who had seduced her before she wed. A good swordsman and the greatest knave in England, she had loved him with the whole force of her heart and soul, and, as she had said once a little sadly, to the very last drop of blood in her body.

She had loved him, but while he had found himself attracted and fascinated by the young woman that Barbara was, he had married elsewhere and his heart had never left his own keeping.

From the moment when she finally lost him out of her life, Barbara was never to love anyone else. She was amused, and even at times infatuated, by the men who crowded around her, but her interest in them lay only in that they could arouse her desires. Once satiated, she would throw them away and forget their very existence.

It was only Charles who had for her other interests, other attractions, in that her power and prestige rested entirely in him, and should he fail her she knew all too well how quickly she would be hounded from Court and from Society. But at the moment, triumphantly basking in the Royal favour, conscious that her position at Court was second to none, Barbara was supremely happy and completely confident in herself and her future.

Her thoughts were disturbed by a knock on her door. Without looking round, she called out, "Come in", then hearing a step behind her, she turned quickly. She had expected the King for this was about the hour of the day when he usually visited her, but it was Rudolph Vyne who advanced across the room. Barbara raised her eyebrows at the sight of him.

"I was not expecting you this evening," she said.

"Forgive me, but I had to see you," Rudolph said.

He bent over her to plant a kiss on her white shoulder where the wrapper had slipped away to reveal the beauty of her swelling bosom and the lovely firm column of her neck. It was a kiss of easy familiarity, the kiss of a man who has possessed a woman and who has for her an almost proprietary affection.

At his caress Barbara did not move, and passing on, he threw his feathered hat down on a chair and seated himself on the day bed which was set across the foot of the great four-poster.

"Barbara, I am worried," he said, and looked at her almost beseechingly.

He was a fine figure of a man in his velvet embroidered coat with slashed sleeves of crimson satin and knee breeches edged with silver lace. He wore his own hair curled and waved by the most fashionable Parisian *coiffeur* in St. James's Street, and the gold buttons on his coat glittered as he moved.

"What is worrying you now?" Barbara asked.

Her eyes rested critically for a moment on Rudolph's face. It was handsome enough, indeed he was one of the most handsome men at Court, and yet there was something lacking. She was not quite certain what it was, but she was invariably conscious in Rudolph's presence that he failed in some way to be as good-looking as one expected.

"I want you to help me, Barbara," he said.

"Again?"

Barbara's red lips curved a little disdainfully. She despised weakness in a man, wishing always to be the recipient rather than the benefactor.

"I have but this moment come from the Lord Chamberlain," Rudolph began. "I spoke to him about my claim to the Marquessate of Staverley. He said – and the words seemed strange to me – that His Majesty is strangely reluctant to act in this matter. Now what does that mean?"

Barbara picked up an emerald and diamond bracelet from the dressing table and clasped it round her wrist.

"I spoke to the King," she said at length, "and he said much the same to me. I did not press him to explain his hesitation. It would not have been wise for him to think I concerned myself too deeply in your affairs. He is inclined to be jealous, as you know."

"I am sure you did your best, and I am grateful," Rudolph said, getting restlessly to his feet and walking across the room to drum his fingers on the windowsill, "but I cannot brook this delay. It is impossible!"

"Your creditors are getting restless, I suppose?" Barbara queried, yet knowing the answer even while she asked the question.

Rudolph nodded.

"Restless is putting it mildly," he answered. "If I cannot persuade His Majesty to act soon, I shall have to flee the country."

"Is it as bad as that?" Barbara asked. "You must have been very reckless, Rudolph."

"God knows I have tried to economise," he replied, "but what is the use of talking? Only His Majesty can save me. Can you not force him to act?"

Barbara smiled and pouted her red lips.

"For your sake, I will endeavour to persuade him."

"Bless you for those kind words," Rudolph said, and moving across the room he pulled her peremptorily to her feet and held her closely in his arms.

"No man could refuse you anything," he added a little thickly, as he looked down into her eyes.

She stood passively enough, a faint smile at the corner of her lips, the heavy dark-fringed eyelids dropping until there was only a gleam of blue to tell him that she was watching him.

"Ye gods, you drive me mad," he muttered as he kissed her mouth and felt a sudden tremor go through her.

"What about your rich cousin?" Barbara asked softly. "Haven't you managed to get your hands on her moneybags as yet?"

The words acted like a *douche* of cold water. Rudolph released Barbara and turned abruptly on his heel. He crossed the room and back again before he replied.

"Curse the jade! She is as elusive as the sunshine in a November fog. I court her, but she pretends to think that all I offer her is a cousinly affection. She seems friendly enough but manages to create a barrier between us which one would have to be an acrobat to scale."

"Do you mean that she has not fallen for your handsome features and glib tongue?" Barbara asked mockingly.

"You know full well she has not," Rudolph growled angrily.

"I know nothing of the sort," Barbara retorted. "I am not interested in your cousin or your prudish aunt. They pretend they do not see me when I enter the Banqueting Hall, and when I come into the Privy Garden they look the other way. But wait, sooner or later they shall suffer for every word they have not spoken to me, for every look they have not given me, for every discourtesy they have committed. Lady Darlington was behind the Queen's refusal to appoint me to the Bedchamber. She is responsible for many of the accusations the Queen made against me to His Majesty. I have not forgotten, and I shall not forget. One day she shall pay, and so shall that stupid, pale-faced creature whom you would make your wife."

As she was speaking, Barbara had gradually worked herself up into one of her celebrated furies. Her eyes were flashing, her hands were clenched until the knuckles showed white, her bosom heaved, and the words seemed finally to spit forth from her twisted lips as poison might be spat from the fangs of a snake. In a rage, she quivered and sparkled with the volubility which had a fascination all of its own.

Few women can be angry and not look ugly. Barbara in a rage contrived to become almost breathtakingly beautiful. Rudolph, watching her as he had watched her so often on similar occasions, hardly heard what she said. There was something exciting in her anger, something that drew a man as seductively and surely as he might fall for the soft whispered languishing of another woman.

As he watched her, Barbara tore the white wrapper from her shoulder and flinging it on the floor stamped on it and then, half naked, her lace petticoats whirling around her, she cried out.

"They shall suffer, I tell you! I will stamp on their stupid faces as I stamp on this! I will fling them from court as easily as I fling this brush to the ground."

Barbara snatched up her hairbrush from the dressing table as she spoke and flung it across the room. Of gold set with coloured jewels, it flashed through the air, travelled through the open casement, and disappeared. For a moment both Barbara and Rudolph stared after it, and then they both hurried towards the window and looked out. Below them in the Privy Garden the ladies and gentlemen of the court were taking the evening air.

The hairbrush had caught an elderly man on the head and knocked off his hat. As Barbara and Rudolph reached the window, he had just bent down to pick it up and was staring at it in perplexity while his hat lay on the ground and his wig was pushed awry on his bald head. They both looked out, then at each other, and simultaneously burst out laughing.

Barbara's anger was gone as a thunderstorm flashed across the summer sky. Now the sun was shining again, and her laughter pealed forth as she regarded first the unfortunate victim below, and then Rudolph's convulsed face.

"Lord save us, but I should not be surprised if he brings an action for assault," Rudolph exclaimed.

Barbara giggled and put her hand up to touch his cheek.

"You are too nice to be wasted on that stupid country wench with her innocent air and simpering ways," she said. "When you become a Marquess, I might even marry you myself."

The laughter faded from Rudolph's face.

"The question is when that will be," he said ominously.

"I will do what I can about it," Barbara promised. "You had best go now. If the King finds you here it will be no help to your cause."

Even as she spoke, they both heard a voice outside the door. She glanced at Rudolph and hastily he looked round the room. There was no other exit. For a moment he hesitated and then he looked at Barbara. Her naked shoulders seemed almost aggressively bare and her white wrapper, trampled on the floor, seemed as abandoned as the tresses of her dark hair hanging loose against her face.

Barbara saw the expression of consternation on Rudolph's face and before she realised what he intended to do, he had taken one quick stride and swung himself over the windowsill. She gave a little hysterical but hastily repressed cry as he lowered himself until only the tips of his fingers could be seen, and then before she could move or even breathe, they too had vanished.

She heard the door open behind her. She did not turn her head. Instead, she stepped forward and looked out of the window. Rudolph had fallen on to the grass of the Privy Garden. Unhurt, he was picking himself up, while staring at him in abject amazement was a small fat man who was holding in his hand the jewelled hairbrush.

"What is interesting you so mightily?" a voice asked.

Barbara pulled the casement shut and turned back into the bedchamber.

"There is a crowd in the garden tonight, Sire," she answered. "I would not have them overhear the sweet things that we say to each other."

"I am glad they are to be sweet," Charles said with a whimsical air. "Last night you berated me mightily because I would not give you the country excise on ale and beer."

"It was paltry of you, Sire, to refuse me," Barbara said.

She moved a little nearer to him. Charles' eyes were on her white skin. She stood with her back to the window and the glow of the evening sun seeming to envelop her, as if with the tongues of fire. He raised his eyes to her lips. They were parted and, it seemed to him as he looked at them, that they quivered a little as if with a sudden ecstasy.

"Suppose I make amends for my meanness," Charles said softly. "Suppose I say that – if it please you – you can have the excise?"

"Would you say that, Sire?" Barbara asked. "Would you?"

At last, their eyes met and held each other. They were both breathing a little quickly, yet still neither of them moved, deliberately anticipating the delight that was to be theirs within the passing of a few seconds.

*

Outside, Rudolph brushed the grass and dirt from his coat. It was then he remembered that he had left his hat behind in Barbara's bedchamber. For a moment he felt stricken. She would find it difficult to explain away such an object! Then he shrugged his shoulders. There was nothing to tell anyone it was his hat and tomorrow, when he got it back, he would have the feathers changed for those of another colour.

He was just about to walk off when the small fat man, who had been regarding him with considerable surprise remarked,

"Do you usually enter the garden in such a way, sir?"

"Why not?" Rudolph enquired. "To come in through the gates is so prosaic, do you not think so?"

The fat man scratched his head.

"I have not thought of it in such a light."

"The whole art of good living," Rudolph went on with the air of a philosopher, "is the unexpected. I can see, sir, that I am speaking to someone who has already found that. For what do you carry in your hand? Not a cane, sir, nor a sword, nor even a stick, but a jewelled hairbrush. A brilliant and original idea which must commend itself to all those whose minds are not too commonplace to accept a new innovation."

The fat man cleared his throat uncertainly.

"You – you think such an action is to be commended?" he asked hesitatingly.

"I am sure of it," Rudolph replied. "Let me be the first to congratulate you, sir." He bowed as he spoke. "May I introduce myself? My name is Rudolph Vyne, at your service."

The fat man returned the bow.

"Delighted to meet you, sir. I am Sir Philip Gage, Justice of the Peace."

"I am delighted to meet you, sir," Rudolph exclaimed.

"And I you," Sir Philip replied, not to be outdone in courtesy. "I am new to Court and know few people here. The Lord Chancellor, an old friend, asked me to attend on His Majesty with a view to advising him on how the thieves and rogues who flourish in the City and in the vicinity, might best be brought to justice."

"Are there so many of them?" Rudolph enquired.

His interest was wandering. He glanced towards the people perambulating through the gardens and hoped he might see a friend, thereby finding an excuse to break off the conversation.

"Many?" Sir Philip echoed. "If I gave you the numbers, dear sir, of the vagrants and misdoers known to the authorities, you would be astonished, yes, astonished. Take the case of highwaymen alone. In the past two months, there have been no less than three hundred reported cases of robbery of travellers approaching our City. Three hundred cases! Is that not a disgrace in these modern days when we pride ourselves on having a civilisation that is both enlightened and intelligent?"

"And what do you propose to do about it?"

Rudolph stifled a yawn.

"Do? *Do?* What do you expect me to do?" Sir Philip spluttered. "Catch them, of course, catch these dastardly highwaymen and string them up from the nearest gibbet, or from a tree if there is not a gibbet handy."

"Highwaymen? Did you say highwaymen?"

Rudolph's interest was piqued.

"It was of these rogues I was speaking, sir," Sir Philip said pompously.

"Then you are just the man I am looking for," Rudolph said. "Come, Sir Philip, will you not repair with me to a tavern? I have several things I would like to discuss with you."

"Delighted, my dear sir, delighted," Sir Philip said. "But the King? Maybe he will send for me! I should not like to be absent should His Majesty require me."

"His Majesty will not be requiring you for an hour or so," Rudolph said positively. "You can be certain of that. Come, sir, a glass of wine. I am sure you are in as much need of it as I am."

"Well, since you mention it, I am indeed thirsty," Sir Philip said.

He set his hat squarely on his wig, glanced down in perplexity at the jewelled hairbrush he still carried in his hand, and followed Rudolph across the Privy Garden and out into Downing Street.

Panthea, coming into the Privy Garden from the bowling green, saw them disappearing along the path lined with trees.

"Look!" she said to her great-aunt, "There is cousin Rudolph. He is walking without a hat and talking with a funny little fat man I have never seen before."

The Dowager raised her quizzing glass to her eye.

"I see Rudolph," she said, "but I have no idea who he is with."

"I can tell you who he is," Lord St. Vincent said.

He had accompanied Panthea and the Dowager to the bowling green. He was a rather boring young man who had attached himself to Panthea since he had heard rumours of her fortune, the size of which had grown with the telling, until a quite outrageous sum was whispered to be her dowry when she bestowed her hand and heart on some fortunate young man.

The only asset Lord St. Vincent had, as far as Panthea was concerned, was that he was a mine of information about everything and everybody at court. He was not only a gossip, but also an authority on the history of the Palace and though as a suitor Panthea would have dismissed him easily and without another thought, however as a guidebook and an informant, she found him so interesting that she was willing to endure his companionship for several hours a day.

"Well, who is he?" Panthea asked now, watching Rudolph and his companion draw steadily away from them, so intent on their conversation that they had no idea they were being watched.

"That is Sir Philip Gage, the Justice of the Peace, who has been sent for by the Lord Chancellor to advise the King on how to create a law-abiding community. He will find it hard enough when there is as much corruption and robbery in high places as in low."

"If he can advise the King how to disperse the pickpockets round the playhouse, it will be something," Lady Darlington said. "Lady Sears, in Waiting on Her Majesty, had a gold bracelet taken last night from off her arm, and two gentlemen of our acquaintance had their pockets picked between stepping from their coaches and entering the portals of the theatre itself."

"It is a disgrace, I agree with you," Lord St. Vincent said, but I doubt if Sir Philip will be much use in ridding us of pickpockets or thieves. There is only one thing in which he is really interested and that is the abolition of highwaymen. The story goes that he had his family jewels stolen by one when he was conveying them to London for the Coronation. Anyway, whether it be that or something else, he certainly loathes the sight and sound of a highway robber. It is reported that he has hanged more highwaymen these last eighteen months than any other Justice has got rid of in ten years."

"A good thing too, for they are a menace to peaceful travellers," Lady Darlington exclaimed. "I vow when we came to London from Wiltshire, I never closed my eyes the whole way for fear I should open them again to see a pistol pointing through the window at my heart. Do you remember, Panthea, how nervous I was?"

She glanced round as she spoke and realised that, while she and Lord St. Vincent had walked on over the smooth lawns of the garden, Panthea was still standing just inside the entrance and was watching Rudolph and Sir Philip Gage, although they were almost out of sight.

"Panthea," the Dowager called, "come along, dear. We must be getting back for it is almost dinnertime."

Panthea gave a start, realised she was being called, and joined her great-aunt and Lord St. Vincent. She said nothing as they moved across the lawns and entered the Stone Gallery. After bidding farewell to their escort, they moved upstairs to their own apartments.

"I find that young man surprisingly interesting," the Countess said as she went towards her own room. "If he was not so foppish in his dress, I vow I should think twice before I allowed you to refuse him."

Panthea laughed.

"He is all right to listen to, Aunt Anne, but one must not look at him. His style is scarcely a quality one could find enviable in a husband."

"Go and change, you naughty child," the Dowager said affectionately. "Heaven knows, I have no desire to lose you as a companion, but at the rate you are refusing the offers of marriage that are made to you, you will die an old maid."

"I will risk it," Panthea smiled, and reaching up kissed the old lady on the cheek. "I am far too happy with you to want anything else for the moment," she added, then turned and went to her own room, while the Dowager, with a smile of pleasure on her thin lips, retired to hers.

Alone in her bedchamber, Panthea closed the door behind her, and her face was serious. She did not need to ask herself what Rudolph was doing with Sir Philip Gage. She knew. She was well aware that her cousin was desperate to have himself acknowledged as the Marquess of Staverley and to be allowed to lay claim to the house and estate. From the first day when he had come to call and had pleaded for his aunt's help, Panthea had sensed Rudolph's impatience and had known, as the weeks passed, that his impatience was growing in urgency.

It was difficult for him to be in the Dowager's company for long without returning to the subject. Panthea did not know whether Lady Darlington had spoken to the King or not. She seemed to watch her nephew with shrewd eyes and yet she said little to Panthea on the subject.

Since that first strange occasion when Panthea had found out from Marta who Lucius was, she had never been able to drag any more information from the girl or persuade her to return to the subject. For the first time in her life, where Panthea was concerned, she had become surly and uncommunicative.

"I know nothing," she would repeat again and again. Panthea had realised that she had managed to place a guard over herself and her emotions, so that never again could she wring from her an admission concerning the highwayman White Throat.

It seemed to Panthea as if she were up against a brick wall where information regarding Lucius was concerned, and yet at the same time some inner premonition told her that gradually she would learn more. She watched Rudolph, encouraged him to talk, tried to catch him out in some admission, or induce him to give her some clue to what he knew about her cousin. But he was too clever for her. However much she plied him with questions, he managed to circumvent the more penetrating ones, and would only reiterate, over and over again, that poor Lucius was most certainly dead, either hanged or lying shot in a ditch.

It had been difficult for Panthea to play her part in trying to extract information and at the same time not to let Rudolph guess at her curiosity regarding Lucius. Only by pretending a deep interest in his future could she persuade him to talk about himself and therefore learn a little of his plans. At times, she felt so inexperienced and so ineffective that she could have cried at her own helplessness.

She had a feeling that something was about to happen, something tremendous, and yet there was nothing tangible to which she could put a name. She could only grope, as it were, through a fog, trying to find her way, trying to see what was happening. Here, she was sure, was something new. Why should Rudolph be interested in Sir Philip Gage except for one reason?

They were walking away together, and she guessed they might be going to a tavern or to Sir Philip Gage's lodgings. There they would talk. Was there any information that Rudolph could give Sir Philip with regard to one highwayman whose arrest and death would benefit him more than anything else?

Panthea put her hands to her face. What could she do? There must be something she could do in the matter. Her thoughts went over the information Lord St. Vincent had given her. She remembered him saying that Sir Philip's family jewels had been stolen by a highwayman when he was coming to London for the Coronation. Panthea gave a little start. Jewels would mean that Sir Philip had a wife! Here was one approach at any rate. She must persuade her great-aunt to call on Lady Gage the following day. Women were more talkative than men. Perhaps here was a way she might learn of Rudolph's plans.

Delighted at her idea, Panthea rang the bell for Marta and started to change her dress. She and her great-aunt were dining at about six o'clock in the great Banqueting

Hall. It would be a convivial scene tonight, as it was most nights, and Panthea, putting on her dress of white satin over a petticoat of blue taffeta embroidered with pearls, felt excited at what lay before her.

There was something about the majesty and splendour of the Banqueting Hall that never failed to thrill her. The trumpeters and kettle-drummers, with scarlet cloaks faced with silver and their trumpets hung with taffeta ribbons and banners of gold, always seemed to her like something out of a fairy story. The music of the King's fiddlers made her feel as if she were a princess, and as the lords and ladies of the Court went in procession into dinner, the scent of the flowers and the French perfume that the King loved made the air fragrant and sweet.

There would be that sudden pregnant hush when the King and Queen entered the room. There was something about His Majesty, too, that made Panthea feel as if he were a hero of romance, so tall, slim and dark, a glint of irony between his tired smiling eyes. Even now, after two years, she would see that look of exaltation in the eyes of his Cavaliers as they viewed him, their King, whom so many had secretly toasted, dreamed of and dared to mention only in bated breath. He was their King, this man who had suffered and yet retained his sense of humour. A man of extraordinary generosity and kindness, a man who loved animals and had a passion for his own children, who took a delight in dancing, music and the theatre, who liked to talk of astronomy, architecture, chemistry and gardening and had an endless repertoire of stories, which were nearly always witty but not always refined.

It was little wonder that many of the more prosaic Englishmen found their King an enigma. Perhaps they understood best his love of sport – his prowess on the tennis court, where he would be at play before six o'clock in the morning, his hunting and his rides to Hampton

Court in the cool of a summer morning, and the delight he took in boating so that his barge lay always off the piers that jutted out from the Palace wall.

A strange, unaccountable, cultured man of exceptional good manners and tremendous virility – a man who looked every inch a King as he entered the Banqueting Hall, followed by his court of brilliant men and lovely women, while a French boy sang love songs in the gallery.

Sometimes Panthea would feel the tears fill her eyes as she watched him seat himself, this man who had suffered poverty and privation, exile and misery for so many years – and then as she watched the little Queen look up at him with adoration in her eyes, she would see Charles' eyes wander down the table to where Barbara Castlemaine flaunted her dark, outrageous beauty.

It was then Panthea would feel sad. The fairy story was not ending the way it should. Charles should have come to the Throne and lived happily ever afterwards. But there was Lady Castlemaine, to twist the tale from its happy ending. And suddenly, the illusion of ethereal loveliness was gone and instead Panthea could see the human feelings, emotions and heartbreaks underlying all the glamour.

The Queen was anxious and worried lest she lose even her husband's kindness – Barbara Castlemaine grasping and greedy, demanding more of everything, more of the King's attention and time, more from the Privy Purse, more presents of money and goods, which he afforded her so generously.

Their faces would swim before Panthea's eyes, and with them the worried look of the Lord Chancellor, striving to keep a balance between the King and Parliament, the lewd eyes of the wicked Duke of Buckingham, whose entanglement with the Countess of Shrewsbury was the scandal of the Court, the coarse plebeian countenance of

General Monk, whom no one remembered to call by his new title of the Duke of Albemarle, and his ill-looking, ill-natured wife, who had been his seamstress, laundress and mistress, and who was always referred to as 'The Monkey Duchess'. There were so many other faces, all stamped with their own individual thoughts and feelings, their desires, and hungers, and occasionally, across the room or beside her at the table, Panthea would catch sight of Rudolph's face and wonder what he was thinking. Sometimes he would be smiling at her, striving to attract her attention, but at others he appeared to be watching Barbara Castlemaine. Sometimes she thought there was another expression in his eyes, one she feared and hated.

For a long time, she would not put a name to it, even to herself – then at length she knew the truth for what it was. She had seen it glint there in Rudolph's expression when he first talked to his aunt of his ambitions and Lady Darlington had told him that Lucius was the rightful heir. She had seen it not once, but many times in the days that followed, although she had been unable then to see his face, Panthea was sure it was lurking there behind his eyes as he talked to Sir Philip Gage.

There would be, too, desperation, anxiety and that ever growing impatience to get what he wanted, to achieve his ambitions. But behind all this, as menacing as a coiled snake, was the desire to kill – to kill and know there was no longer the shadow of a highwayman between himself and his heart's desire.

5

The two old ladies' heads nodded together.

"They say that the Earl has gone to France to enter a monastery."

Lady Darlington made a sound with her lips that expressed her disapproval all too clearly.

"It is not surprising," she snorted, "that he is disgusted with his wife's behaviour."

Lady Gage, who was thin and cadaverous and had a face not unlike a horse, bent a little nearer.

"'Tis whispered that she is again with child."

"That would not surprise me," Lady Darlington said grimly. "It is a national calamity that such a woman should hold the position she does at Court."

At their side, a piece of embroidery in her lap, sat Panthea. It seemed to her that no one had anything else to talk about except the misdemeanours of Lady Castlemaine. She had heard it before, not once but a hundred times, but all such talk got the gossips nowhere. Lady Castlemaine continued her triumphant progress with the King completely in her power.

She had even been clever enough to become on friendly terms with the Queen. How this had been achieved no one knew, but there was no doubt that the Queen not only had accepted the inevitable, by having Lady Castlemaine as a Lady of the Bedchamber, but was apparently determined to make the best of a bad business and accorded her public favours, which was galling to her other more respectable Ladies in Waiting.

It was a sad setback to those who had advised Her Majesty not to accept her husband's mistress on any terms whatsoever. That they were discomfited was to put it mildly, for they had lost face, and it was obvious that only a very few were prepared now to stand by their guns and continue to ostracise the triumphant Countess.

The younger members of the Court, who had been half hearted at the beginning, had all drifted away, leaving but half a dozen angry, impotent and helpless old ladies to whisper and gossip amongst themselves and be utterly powerless to do anything more.

Lady Gage, a newcomer to court, was unwise, Panthea thought, to let herself be drawn into this bitter controversy on the losing side, for it was obvious that her feelings where Lady Castlemaine was concerned were aroused only by jealousy – the bitter jealousy of an ugly woman of one who is supremely confident of her charms and her ability to gain anything she wants by their use.

"I hear that the Lord Chancellor is in despair at the money she is taking from the Privy Purse."

"There is a rumour that the King has promised to buy her Berkshire House in St. James's for five thousand pounds."

"She is insatiable in her demands. The Lord Chancellor declared yesterday, 'That woman will sell everything'."

Panthea got to her feet and went softly from the room. The old ladies took no notice of her departure. Their hooked noses, like parrots' beaks, seemed to grow more pronounced than ever, as their withered lips mouthed and repeated the latest scandals.

It got nobody anywhere, Panthea thought a little wearily as she went along the passage that led to her bedchamber. She personally could not help but admire Lady Castlemaine. She was so cheerful, she laughed so easily, she made the tempo of every party rise when she came to it. Had things been different, Panthea thought that she would have liked to be friendly with the beautiful, if notorious, lady. But such a course was impossible. Her great-aunt had offended the woman who held captive the King's affections and whose power at court was unassailable, so the Dowager was branded as Lady Castlemaine's bitter enemy and she, Panthea, perforce was relegated to the same category.

She wondered often enough how Barbara managed to hold men so securely and so abjectly at her side. Panthea was well aware that, although Rudolph made love to her with his lips, his eyes often wandered in Lady Castlemaine's direction, and there was a look in them such as she had seen in other men's eyes when they gazed at that lovely petulant face with its drooping eyelids. It made Panthea realise all too clearly that there were many sorts of love.

Yet this unceasing gossip and talk and whispering against Barbara Castlemaine disgusted her. She felt as if there was something primitive and savage in the way the older women delighted in any new slander about her, and Panthea knew that they would, if they could, hurl filth and dirt at the object of their enmity with their hands rather than their tongues. There was, in fact, little difference between the fine ladies of the court who spat poison in the privacy of their closets, and the crowds who jeered and spat at the women beaten naked at the pillories, or who watched with amusement the poor lunatics fighting amongst themselves in Bedlam.

It was a fine afternoon, the September sun warm and golden, and only a breath of wind was coming from the river to move the flags on the palace roofs and ruffle the ribbons of the ladies walking on the Embankment.

It would be a nice day for riding, Panthea thought, and calling Marta, she told her to order her horse from the stables and help her change into her riding habit of sapphire blue velvet. Her aunt, she knew, would not be requiring her for some hours now that Lady Gage had come to call.

Panthea often regretted that she had ever instigated this new and ardent friendship when she had asked her great-aunt to call on Sir Philip's wife. Her hopes that such a course might lead her to learn more of Rudolph's business with Sir Philip were doomed to disappointment. From the very beginning, Lady Gage had made it clear that her husband's activities bored her to distraction.

When Panthea tried skilfully and diplomatically to question her, she shrugged her shoulders and declared that she was in complete ignorance as to what her husband was engaged upon at that particular moment.

"All men are bores on the subject of their own particular hobby," she declared, "and I assure you, dear child, that Sir Philip is no exception. Some men find their sport in shooting, cockfighting, or bullbaiting, but Sir Philip, I declare, has made the pursuit of thieves and vagabonds as much a sport as any hound that enjoys pulling down his hare. But such things are of little interest to me. When Sir Philip talks of his arrests and hangings, I close my ears and think of other things."

Lady Gage would be no help, Panthea decided quickly, and she even found it in her heart to be sorry for the stout, good-humoured Sir Philip when she realised that Lady Gage was that most obnoxious creature, a woman who despised her husband and who was not even prepared to pander to his interests by hearing about them.

What was still more unfortunate was that while Lady Gage became a close friend of the Dowager, she made no attempt to bring her husband with her on her many visits, nor did they find Sir Philip at home when they called at the house in Charing Cross where the Gages were lodging. It was quite obvious to Panthea, therefore, that she would have to find another approach to Sir Philip, and she searched her brain day after day to discover in what manner, and by what means, she might contrive it, but unfortunately without result.

Rudolph managed to be extraordinarily uncommunicative when she tried to question him.

"I saw you with Sir Philip Gage the other evening," she said. "Her Ladyship has become a dear friend of Aunt Anne's, but I have not yet managed to meet Sir Philip."

"He would not interest you," Rudolph Vyne replied, but she thought that he glanced at her curiously out of the corner of his eye.

"Why not?" Panthea enquired innocently. "I hear he is a very able man at his job and the King thinks a great deal of him."

"It is not a very thankful task, bringing men to justice and striving to keep law and order in a land which wants only to forget the privations and shackles of the past years."

Rudolph spoke pompously and Panthea guessed he was repeating a speech made by Sir Philip himself.

"Are things so lawless?" she enquired. "I have heard talk of robberies, but do they amount to much?"

"I have no idea," Rudolph replied. "You will have to ask Sir Philip when you meet him."

Panthea realised that he was deliberately evading a discussion and there was nothing she could do about it. She knew she must be careful not to arouse Rudolph's suspicions that she was in any way personally interested in highwaymen and their doings. So, reluctantly, she was forced to talk of other things, and because she was for the moment absentminded, it gave Rudolph another opportunity to press his suit.

"To look at you sets my heart a-beating, cousin Panthea," he said in a low voice. Then before she could reply he added, "You know that I love you. Will you not let me tell you how much?"

Quickly, Panthea had risen to her feet.

"We are cousins and friends," she said. "Do not let us spoil the relationship. I am thrilled to be at Court, and I am content to live with Aunt Anne. It is far too soon in our acquaintance to talk about other matters."

"But I love you, Panthea, and I want you for my wife," Rudolph insisted.

Panthea shook her head.

"You must not say that to me as yet," she said. "We have known each other such a short time. Love is not a thing to be declared lightly or on an impulse."

"At least consider me as your suitor," Rudolph pleaded, but once again she shook her head and smiled at him so that he could not really be offended by her refusal.

She was well aware that her elusiveness irritated and annoyed him, and she managed, by a tremendous effort of will, to keep him her friend, even while she would permit him to come no closer. And yet, Panthea told herself a little sadly, such methods were getting her nowhere, nor was she finding out anything about Lucius.

When Marta had finished dressing her, she set her hat of black velvet trimmed with a long curling ostrich feather on her fair hair, picked up the silver-mounted whip and, holding her full skirts in her hands, ran down the stairs, along the galleries and out into the courtyard where her horse was waiting.

Harry, the groom they had brought with them from Wiltshire, was astride a fine chestnut mare that her great-aunt had purchased since coming to London. He was wearing the livery of the Darlington family and his black hat was ornamented with gold lace. A boy was holding Panthea's horse. It was a graceful thoroughbred creature, white as the December snow, and she had ridden it for the last five years. The horse, Socrates by name, whinnied a little with pleasure when Panthea appeared and thrust its nose into her hand to eat the apple she had brought him.

She mounted and trotted away over the cobbles, old Harry following her at a respectful distance. Panthea turned her horse's head towards the St. James's Park. There were crowds of people there enjoying the sunshine, and inspecting the King's improvements on the Canal which had been started soon after he came to London. His Majesty had recently introduced on the lake a number of ducks and strange birds, which he delighted in feeding every morning.

It had caused great comment and much excitement that the King, who loved all animals, should make his park a home for them. Wildfowl were not the only living creatures that had been housed there. Beyond the lake there were deer of all kinds, antelopes, goats, elk and an Arabian sheep, and everywhere the King had planted flowers, walks and trees, making a green paradise around the grey walls of Whitehall.

Panthea rode through St. James's and came to Hyde Park. Here there were many coaches driving around with fine gentlemen and ladies taking the air. As Panthea expected, amongst the riders was the King himself, for Charles was indefatigable and not only managed to keep fresh and alert until the early hours of every morning, but also insisted on his exercise, being often abroad at dawn, sometimes upon the river in his pleasure barge, at others playing tennis, at which game he managed to beat most of his friends, including many men younger than himself.

As he came riding towards Panthea now, a little cavalcade of courtiers and cavaliers surrounding him, Panthea thought how well he looked. His skin was naturally sallow, but there was nevertheless a glow of health about it and when he was laughing, as he was at the moment, his eyes lost their cynical tiredness and the look that made Panthea think sometimes that his illusions had been shattered one by one and that he was left only to smile at all the world, himself included.

As she rode towards the King now, she got ready to bow, expecting him to do little more than sweep his broad brimmed hat from his dark head, but to her surprise he reined in his horse and drew alongside her.

"You are riding alone, Lady Panthea," he said. "What has happened to all the gallants at Court that there is no one here to escort you?"

"I sometimes prefer to be alone, sire," Panthea replied.

"That is where the lowest subject in the land is more fortunate than I," the King replied, "for I can never be alone."

There was something in the way he spoke, or perhaps in his pretended woebegone expression, that made Panthea laugh.

"Indeed, Sire," she said, "you speak the truth when you say you are never alone. Cupid rides pillion wherever you go."

The King threw back his head and laughed.

"A pretty idea, Lady Panthea, but I think you flatter me."

"On the contrary," Panthea retorted.

It was not often she felt so at ease with the King. Today, however, it was perhaps the sunshine, or the fact that she was alone and not chaperoned by her great-aunt, that made her feel strangely light-hearted.

"Come ride with me," the King said, "and we will see if Cupid is astride your horse as well as mine."

Panthea knew that the courtiers were watching her, and the look in their eyes suggested that yet another favourite had come to court. But all the same, it was not unpleasant to see the admiration and envy on people's faces as she rode beside the King, underneath the hanging branches of the great trees through which in the distance one could see the silver gleam of the Serpentine.

"Tell me what you think of London," the King said as they moved forward together, "for I believe you have lived in the country most of your life."

"I find London a place of enchantment," Panthea said, "but sometimes I am homesick for Staverley, my home until my father died."

"I remember your father," the King said.

"And do you also remember my brother, Sire?" Panthea asked. "He was hanged after Your Majesty returned to France."

"I recall him well," Charles said. "He was betrayed, as I was, by someone we trusted."

Panthea said nothing for a moment. She was remembering Richard as she last saw him, his eyes alight with excitement, his heart aflame with loyalty.

"Tell me," the King said suddenly, "what do you think of your cousin Rudolph? Are you fond of him?"

Panthea wondered for a second whether she should tell the truth. Should she say she did not trust Rudolph? Should she make a confidant of the King? But before she could make up her mind, before she could answer the question he had put to her, she saw Sir Philip Gage coming towards them and riding at a sharp trot.

The King had not noticed his approach, for his eyes were on Panthea's face, waiting for her answer, but watching she perceived Sir Philip see the King and determine that, as the Royal Head was turned away from him, he should none the less be recognised. He drew up his horse on its haunches and with a loud, "Your servant, Sire," took off his hat.

The King turned at the sound of his voice. Sir Philip was but a few feet away from him and it would have been impossible for him not to acknowledge the greeting.

"Ah, Sir Philip," he said with a lazy smile. "I see you are enjoying a short holiday from the worries of your department."

"On the contrary, Your Majesty," Sir Philip replied, "I am at this moment but returning from the pursuit of duty. I have news for Your Majesty, which I was about to bring to the palace and crave an audience."

"Let us waive such formalities," the King said. "Good news should never be allowed to grow cold by waiting. Ride with us, Sir Philip, and tell us what this news may be."

Flushing with pleasure, Sir Philip turned his horse and drew it alongside His Majesty's black charger. The courtiers and gentlemen behind pressed forward eagerly, for they were keen to hear the good news which Sir Philip had brought. But he lowered his voice so that in moving his horse forward at His Majesty's side, only the King and Panthea were able to hear what he said.

"Ever since you commanded my presence at Court," the little man began pompously, "I have been engaged in trying to fulfil Your Majesty's command to clean up the environs of this City. Today I have taken an important step in the right direction, and I have, I believe, stumbled upon a clue that will lead to the arrest of one of the most notorious highwaymen, a man who plagues the travellers coming from and going to the north."

"That is indeed good news," the King said.

"All I ask of Your Majesty," Sir Philip went on, "is a company of soldiers at my disposal for the next twenty-four hours?"

"They are yours, Sir Philip," His Majesty said good humouredly. "But may we not hear more details? Is this some notorious gang you expect to apprehend?"

"A gang, Your Majesty, and one that has affronted authority too long, led by a highwayman whose deeds of daring have become almost a legend these past four or five years."

"Indeed," the King said, with an amused smile, "and have I heard of him?"

"Everyone has heard of White Throat, Sire," Sir Philip said. "There are many tales about him, too many for me to relate and they would undoubtedly bore Your Majesty. But to my own personal knowledge, he has recently released no less than three rogues from prison by one device or another. He stopped a hanging at Charing Cross only last month, and galloped away with the prisoner astride his horse before anyone could prevent it."

"I remember hearing of that," Charles said. "Was not the lad in question on the verge of being reprieved?"

'The reprieve would have arrived too late," Sir Philip replied, "but that surely is not the point, Sire. That a hanging should be prevented by such cutthroat methods is surely a disgrace to our laws. If every vagabond who thinks injustice is being done chooses to interfere, our authority will be at an end."

"Yet it was a case of injustice," the King said.

"On this particular occasion," Sir Philip agreed. "But the other men he has rescued from prison have all been convicted by the magistrates on charges of robbery or poaching. The last lad he brought away from Newgate was due for transportation the following day."

"And what has this buccaneer, White Throat I think you called him, done with all these rescued criminals?"

"That is where we are in ignorance, Sire, but we imagine they must be banded together. They are dangerous men, Your Majesty, dangerous and armed, and that is why I must request that I be given at least a company of soldiers if we are to capture them, either alive or dead."

"I see," the King said. "And where is their hiding place?"

Panthea held her breath. Sir Philip looked over his shoulder.

"With Your Majesty's permission, I would keep that a secret until the arrests are made. The slightest suspicion, the slightest word that we are on their track, and they will be gone. White Throat has not evaded capture all these years for nothing."

"I see!"

The King spoke reflectively, while Panthea could have cried with vexation.

"Well, Sir Philip, we must possess ourselves in patience until you next report to us."

"Thank you, Sire, and I may have the soldiers?"

"Speak with the Captain of the Guard and tell him that it is my wish that you are accommodated in this matter."

"Thank you, Sire, thank you."

Sir Philip, looking absurdly like a fat, good-humoured Humpty Dumpty, bowed low over his horse's neck, then knowing that his audience was at an end, he galloped away. The King was silent for a moment and then Panthea spoke.

"You said, Sire," she said quickly, "that you had heard of this highwayman, White Throat. What do you know of him?"

"I am trying to recall that very thing," the King replied. "There is something about him that eludes me, and I cannot remember what it is."

"He might, Sire, be one of your supporters, someone who had sacrificed his life and security in the old days to serve your cause."

"He might be," replied the King, "and yet I doubt it. Those who served me have been only too quick to come to Whitehall to petition for the return of their possessions, titles, and money – in fact all they had lost. I would to God that I could satisfy them all, and yet it is impossible."

The King sighed and Panthea, remembering the crowds of Cavaliers, penniless yet hopeful, who hung around the Audience Chamber, day after day, knew that the people who said the King had forgotten those who served him were being unjust.

Not all the wealth of the Indies could have met the needs of an impoverished and defrauded generation. The Royalists had suffered bitterly, but lands had, in some cases, passed through a dozen hands since they had first been sold by their bankrupt owners. Houses that had originally been seized from those who owned them had been acquired by several successive families, all of whom had spent money on them, and whom it would have been sheer injustice to displace.

There were many grave responsibilities, Panthea knew, for those who must decide such difficult and delicate matters, and she felt a sudden warm sympathy for the King who rode beside her and whose generosity must be questioned where he himself most wished to be generous. Yet this was no time, Panthea thought, to think of anything, save that somehow she must help the man who had once saved her from a degradation and a horror that even now she could hardly contemplate without terror.

Urgently, she turned towards the King.

"I have reason to believe, Sire," she said, "that this highwayman, White Throat, is no ordinary person."

She would have said more, but the King put out his hand and checked the words on her lips.

"I have a feeling," he said, "that you are about to interfere in the cause of justice. There are many favours, Lady Panthea, that I would delight to give you if you would permit me, but do not ask me for something that it must be my stern duty to refuse. Sir Philip has been empowered by my ministers to take action against what appears to us to be a growing evil. This man, White Throat, is but one of many ruffians who defame and make ugly our countryside."

"But, Sire," Panthea cried passionately, "did you not hear Sir Philip himself admit that the boy whom White Throat rescued from the scaffold had been unjustly committed? There was a reprieve for him, but it would have come too late had he not been saved just in time."

"I heard that," the King said, "but the law must not be mocked. My people are high-spirited, and unless a strong hand is kept upon them, who knows what might happen? And now, Lady Panthea, let us talk of more cheerful things."

It was a command, and Panthea, with her heart sinking and feeling a dryness in her mouth, was forced to obey it. It was with almost a sense of relief that she saw, a little later, a carriage drawn up beneath the trees and noticed the King's eyes wander towards it. She was indeed so relieved that she might take her *adieu* of the King and turn for home that she did not notice the dark angry glances directed towards her by the occupant of the coach. Nor, as she galloped away through the park towards St. James's, did she hear the low, warm voice of Lady Castlemaine speaking to the King.

"What, Sire, are you doing with that little serpent whom I have vowed, before many moons have passed, shall feel my heel upon her head?"

Panthea indeed felt nothing, heard nothing, saw nothing, save two eyes looking down into hers through a black mask and a gentle mouth that comforted her when she cried because her brother had been betrayed and hanged. She had got to save him, *she must*. She knew that she would rather die herself than know that he had died with a rope around his neck.

All the happiness of the past five years she owed to him, every garment she had put on her back, every purchase she had made, every penny she had spent was due to his generosity, his kindness. She wondered now how she could have remained so long in Wiltshire, content just to grow older without wishing to seek him out, to find him and to thank him.

She had indeed thought of him every day. She had prayed for him, prayed that he might remain safe and unhurt, and she knew now that the thought of him had coloured her days and that somehow the future, in some strange manner, held him too.

Panthea rode so swiftly that she reached the courtyard long before old Harry. She had dismounted and had turned into the gallery that led to her great-aunt's apartment before he came thundering into the yard.

He muttered crossly to himself as he came, and wiping the sweat from his brow, told the second groom sharply to take the horses into the stable and rub them down.

"Kings and cities ain't for the likes of you and Oi, lass," he said to his mare a moment later. "I wish to God we were safe back in the country, where naught unusual happens."

Panthea sped up the stairs to her bedchamber. In the salon she heard the murmur of voices and knew that Lady Gage was still there, still talking with her great-aunt. Then she hurried into her room and pealed the bell.

Marta came hurrying at the impetuous summons. As she waited for her, Panthea dragged the riding gloves from her hands and pulled off her hat. She was standing in the centre of the room, tapping her shoe impatiently on the floor, when Marta came through the door. The girl was smiling, her rosy cheeks aglow as if she had just been sparring good-humouredly with one of the footmen or enjoying a game with some of the giggling maids who hung about the passages of the palace, exchanging confidences about the liveried menservants.

When she saw Panthea's face her smile faded.

"Shut the door," Panthea said in a voice that was suddenly vested with authority.

Marta did as she was told, and Panthea stepped forward and put her hands on the girl's shoulders.

"Listen, Marta," she said, "listen attentively, for this is of the utmost importance. For weeks now you have refused to speak of the highwayman, White Throat. I have begged and pleaded with you, I have commanded and bullied you, but nothing I can do or say can make you tell me what you know. But now you must speak, and quickly, for there is no time to be lost."

Panthea's fingers tightened on Marta's shoulders. The maid's face had grown white, her eyes had darkened, but she had not cried out. Instead, it seemed to Panthea, that her expression had grown stony and that look of obstinacy she knew only too well had dropped over it like a mask.

"If you do not speak now," Panthea said, "then in the future there will be no need for me to question you, for, Marta – and listen to this carefully – I have just come from the King. His Majesty has given Sir Philip Gage a company of soldiers so that he may lead them to where White Throat lies in hiding. He knows his hiding place, and I have with my own ears heard him say so. If you do nothing, if you persist in this silence, then White Throat will be arrested within a few hours – he and all those who are with him."

For a moment Marta swayed as if she must faint, then with a cry that was almost a shriek, she put her hands up to her face.

"Oh, my Lady, *,"* she moaned, and collapsing on to the floor, crouched at Panthea's feet, crying over and over again the same words, "Oh, my Lady, my Lady."

Panthea watched her for a moment and then, kneeling down beside the moaning girl, pulled her hands from her face.

"In God's name, Marta," she said, "tell me what you know."

With a tremendous effort Marta managed to speak.

"You are sure of this, my Lady?" she asked in a voice that seemed almost strangled in her throat.

"I swear to you I am speaking the truth," Panthea said. "I was with His Majesty riding in Hyde Park when Sir Philip approached us. He told the King that he knew White Throat's hiding place and that he was sure he could arrest him and his followers."

Marta gave a convulsive sob.

"Oh, Jack, Jack," she muttered, "if they get you this time, there is no hope for either of us!"

"Jack?" Panthea questioned. She remembered now, remembered the servant who was in attendance on White Throat, the man who had been left to set the coach on fire. The highwayman had called him Jack.

She put out her hand and turned Marta's face up to hers.

"Yes, Jack will be captured with him too," she said. "He will be hanged as White Throat will be hanged, unless you tell me how I can save them both."

"But I have sworn, my Lady, I have given my oath. I have laid my hand on the Bible and sworn by everything I hold sacred. I cannot speak, I dare not."

"You would rather that they should die, murdered by your silence?" Panthea said passionately.

Marta began to cry again, the weak helpless tears of a woman tortured almost beyond endurance.

Panthea suddenly took her by the shoulders and shook her.

"You have got to tell me, Marta, you have got to," she said. "What does your stupid oath matter beside White Throat's life, and Jack's, and perhaps a dozen others?"

The shaking took Marta by surprise. Her head jerked back and her mouth flew open and then, as if a decision was jerked from her, she spoke.

"I will tell all I know, my Lady. I will tell you and God help me."

"Quickly then," Panthea commanded, and stood while Marta, on the floor and still crying, poured out her story in broken, sob-racked tones.

"Jack was courting me, my Lady. We had loved each other ever since we were children. I used to creep out and meet him even when I first came to Staverley, and I was in terror that Nurse would catch me. Then one night, as he was going home he heard a hare squealing in a trap. He was always fond of animals, Jack was, and he could not have hurt the hair of any of them. Hearing this poor creature, he could not go on and leave it in its agony, so he bends down to set it free. It took him a moment or two to undo it, for the trap was caught in its foot. Then he stood up with the hare in his hand, and he sees them watching him."

"Who?" Panthea asked, for Marta seemed to be overcome.

"The soldiers, my Lady. Those who were on guard at Staverley, those who used to come sneaking round the house at night in case his Lordship should come back from London.'

"This was when we were at Staverley," Panthea said, "and Richard – Richard had gone to meet the King?"

"Yes, that's right, my Lady."

"And what happened to Jack?" Panthea asked.

"They took him, the soldiers did, before the magistrate. If Mr. Warner, the gamekeeper, had found him, he would have said nothing. He knew Jack was a good boy and would not kill anything on the estate, not even if he had been starved. But the magistrate sentenced Jack there and then to transportation. He was shut up for the night and the soldiers were to take him to London the next day. We were all in despair. I crept out of the house that night and went down to his home. His mother was crying, as were many of the neighbours, but there was nothing they could do about it. I was that desperate, my Lady, I felt as if I could lay down and die myself. Better death, I thought, than a life without Jack, knowing that if he were sent to the galleys, he would never come back alive. And then, while we were all crying in the kitchen, Jack's father comes to the door.

"'Come here, Marta,' he says to me. 'There's someun waunts to see you.' Wondering a little, I goes outside. It was dark. He points to the gate at the end of the garden. There was a man waiting there, I could see him quite clearly and for a moment I thought I was dreaming, then I saw who it was. It was Jack, my Lady, Jack, free and alone. I runs towards him and he takes me in his arms. 'This is just to say goodbye, Marta girl. I didn't want to leave you worrying and I'll send you a message whenever I can.'

"'But Jack, Jack, what has happened to you?' I asked, and then he tells me, my Lady.

"He tells me that he has been rescued from the prison by Mr. Lucius. 'When they comes for me in the morning, they will find me gone,' he says, and he laughs. I could hardly believe that he was really laughing after all we had feared for him. He kisses me, my Lady, then he slips away into the darkness. I stands there, bewildered and hardly knowing if I am on my head or my heels. It was then Jack's father came up to me, he takes me round the back of the house and puts a Bible in my hand. He makes me swear, there and then, that I would never tell a soul what had happened or who had rescued Jack. All the village people think as how he has gone for transportation, and they wondered how we could be so brave about it."

"And it was Lucius – Lucius, my cousin, who saved him?" Panthea asked quietly.

"Yes, my Lady. We had known about him being on the road for some years. The soldiers had come questioning us after it was known that he had helped the King to escape to France. He had said then to Jack's father, 'I might as well give them a run for their money. I have hunted over this country for years and know every stick and stone of it. There's many a fox got away from the hounds, and what Roundhead has the intelligence of a hound?'

"It was, of course, after Jack joined him that his father, Harry, told me this. Before that none of us ever spoke of Mr. Lucius for fear we might say something which would give information to them pestering Roundheads."

"Harry?" Panthea said in a questioning voice. "Harry? Is old Harry Jack's father?"

"Yes, my Lady."

"Do you or Jack's father know where he is now?"

"I think Harry does, my Lady. Sometimes he brings me a message from Jack and sometimes he sends me a flower or a ribbon which tells me, as sure as if I could hear him saying it, that he still loves me."

"Then I must go to Harry at once," Panthea said.

"But, my Lady, have you forgotten the dinner tonight? It is already time to dress."

Panthea looked at the clock by her bed, an expensive pretty toy which she had bought in a fit of extravagance after she came to London.

"It is a quarter past five," she said, "and we dine at six with Their Majesties. I must be there, for there is no excuse I would make at this hour that would be acceptable. I must wait until the banquet is over. Then I'll get my chance – then I will be able to go."

"Go where, my Lady?" Marta asked bewildered.

"To warn White Throat," Panthea replied, then added softly, "my cousin Lucius."

6

Panthea thought the banquet would never end. On any other evening she would have been thrilled with the luxury and beauty of the crowd in the great Banqueting Hall, but tonight she found it difficult to concentrate even for a few minutes on the conversation of the gentlemen who sat on either side of her, or on the food over which a French chef had spent hours in preparation. Cow's tongue, powdered beef and trifling tarts tasted like sawdust.

Even the latest addition to the King's musicians, a French boy who sang love songs in the gallery with the voice of an angel, failed to thrill her. It was only when at length she could withdraw unobserved, the eyes of His Majesty's guests being concentrated on the gamblers at a basset table, that she felt she could breathe again, and the frustrated sense of being fettered which had oppressed her during the banquet passed from her.

Lady Darlington was surprised at Panthea's impatience to leave, but she was not loath to enjoy an early evening, for far too often of late they had been forced to be in attendance on the Queen until the early hours of the morning.

"Are you ill, child?" the Dowager enquired as they climbed the polished oak stairway to their apartments.

"No indeed," Panthea said quickly, then remembered that such an excuse might explain her desire to leave the party so early. "I am well enough," she added hastily, "but the room was so hot that I felt a trifle faint."

"You are overtired, I expect," her great-aunt said kindly. "I should ask Marta to bring you a hot posset to drink before you blow out your candle. They say it is the best protection there is against the plague."

"I am not sickening for anything so horrible, so you must not worry," Panthea said as she bent to kiss her aunt's withered cheek. "Sleep well, ma'am, and I hope nothing disturbs you tonight."

"Nothing disturbs me once I am asleep," the Dowager replied, as she passed into her bedchamber.

Marta was waiting for Panthea in her own bedroom. Her riding clothes lay ready on the bed.

"Quick, Marta, unlace my dress," Panthea commanded. "I thought the evening would never end. Have you spoken with Harry?"

"Oh, my Lady, I have not been able to find him to tell him that you will be needing him and the horses. I went down into the yard, but there were a lot of footmen wandering about there, and they began to tease me and asked what my business was at the stable. You told me to be careful and so I dared not linger, but came away before I had seen Harry."

Panthea made a little sound of impatience, then spoke kindly.

"It cannot be helped, Marta. I am sure you did your best, but there is no time to lose."

"Oh, my Lady, suppose you cannot find him?"

"Even if he is out, he will come back sooner or later," Panthea replied confidently. "Does he sleep over the stables?"

"Yes, my Lady, the grooms all have rooms over the loose boxes."

That her horse would not be ready for her was a setback which Panthea had not anticipated. She had left Marta with instructions to tell Harry that she would want him and the horses and to warn him to be as discreet about it as possible. That the first step of the desperate adventure should have gone wrong was discomfiting, but she was determined not to be cast down by it. She saw that Marta was in a nervous state and she felt that at all costs she herself must remain calm.

It took her a little time to change, discarding her gown of satin and lace for her velvet riding habit. She had no thought for her appearance, but when finally she was dressed she caught a glimpse of herself in the mirror and realised how perfectly the material of her habit, being the deep blue of an old stained-glass window, set off the pale fragility of her skin and the soft glowing gold of her hair.

Panthea picked up her riding gloves and whip, and turned to the worried, white-faced maid.

"Keep guard on this door, Marta," she said. "Let no one know that I have left the Palace. Pray too that I may be successful in my quest. The men I go to save have need of your prayers."

Marta answered her with a sob that seemed to come from the very depths of her being.

"God guard you, my dear mistress," she said, and bending down she kissed Panthea's hand.

In answer, Panthea raised her finger and laid it against her lips, then very cautiously she opened the door. The passage outside was lit only by three guttering tapers, held high on the wall in a silver sconce. Everything was very still and silent. Panthea knew that she must avoid the night watchmen going their rounds, and the servants who would be waiting for the return of their masters and mistresses from the Banqueting Hall.

Fortunately the old palace was full of dark corners and deep shadows where one might hide from the prying eyes of a passerby, or avoid the flickering gleam of a lantern held by those who perambulated through the passages. Panthea slipped from shadow to shadow.

Once William Chiffinch, the King's Page of the Back Stairs, passed her so closely that his sleeve brushed against her coat. Well fed and silky, with pouches of dissipation under his eyes, he was sought after and well bribed by those who wished to enlist his help in the belief that he had the King's ear when it came to personal and individual matters. But Panthea knew it was also gossiped that he was in the pay of Lady Castlemaine and was reported to have acted as her spy on more than one occasion.

She was well aware that, should he see her, he would make it his business to find out where she was going but fortunately Chiffinch had dined well that evening, and was humming under his wine-laden breath as he walked unsteadily down the passage.

Panthea waited until he was well out of sight before she slipped from her hiding place. A few minutes later, she had reached the stable yard where the horses of the court were housed. There was a smell of hay and of polished leather, and the sound of an animal neighing in the darkness. Instantly its challenge was answered by a dozen others.

There was the clatter of hooves as a groom came into the yard, and from the distance there was the lilt of a fiddle playing a country melody, perhaps for the entertainment of some of the stableboys.

Panthea knew her way. She frequently came to the stable to feed Socrates, and as she moved across the yard now she thought he must have recognised her step, for he threw up his head and she could hear him jangling against the side of the manger the ring to which his halter was attached.

She came nearer, peering into his stall to see if there was anyone about and then, as she searched the darkness, Harry appeared from a stall on the other side of the stable.

He carried a lantern and was wearing only his breeches and a shirt, collarless and open to the waist. His hair was streaked with grey and, looking at him as if for the first time, Panthea saw that he was an old and tired man. He always appeared so spick and span in his uniform that she had grown used to thinking of him as an automaton rather than as an individual.

He was always there when she needed him. He was as respectful and obliging as he could have been ever since she could first remember him when, one spring morning, he had brought her father's big chestnut stallion round to the front door at Staverley and lifted her out of the nurse's arms to perch her high in the saddle.

Almost as if it were yesterday, she could hear her nurse saying, "You be careful of her Ladyship. She will fall off that great beast and be frightened to death."

"Her Ladyship won't fall off," Harry replied in his quiet voice. "The sooner she learns to ride the better. You can't start 'em too young, that's what I says."

"Stuff and nonsense – her Ladyship's far too young to think about riding as yet," the nurse had said. "Give her back to me at once. The idea of the child risking her life on that treacherous monster! It gives me the shudders."

Obediently Harry had lifted Panthea down, but to his delight she cried and asked to be put back again.

"I want to wide, I want to wide a horse," she had cried as her father came down the steps and stopped to enquire the reason for her distress.

When he learned the cause for her tears, he seemed as pleased as Harry had been.

"What is bred in the bone comes out in the flesh, eh, Harry?" he said. "Get her Ladyship a pony – a quiet one, of course. You can take her out for an hour every morning except on hunting days."

During those rides Panthea would chatter to Harry of her own interests, telling him her thoughts and fears, her joys and disappointments. Then gradually she had grown older, and when she could ride as well as Harry himself if not better, it seemed as if he relinquished the post of recipient of her confidences and became again the well-trained servant, as punctilious as a machine and as inhuman as one.

Yet now Panthea remembered what those rides with Harry when she was a little girl had meant to her. Impulsively, she stepped towards him, her hands outstretched.

"Harry," she exclaimed, "thank heaven I have found you!"

He stared at her for a moment in bewilderment, as if he could hardly believe his eyes, then as her hand touched his bare arm, he spoke.

"Lord save us, your Ladyship, but you gave me quite a start."

Panthea looked over her shoulder.

"Can we be overheard?" she asked in a low voice.

In answer Harry drew her into the loose box from which he had come. She saw it was empty, and she had barely left the yard before a bunch of stableboys came running over the cobbles. They were shouting and laughing at the top of their voices, chasing one of their number who had an armful of cheesecakes, which he had evidently filched from a supper table. It was impossible for the moment to speak above the noise and bustle of their passing, but when they had gone Panthea looked at Harry, and she could see in the dim light of the lantern that his face was grave.

"You are in trouble, my Lady?" he asked.

"Grave trouble, Harry," Panthea replied. "I learned this afternoon that a member of my family is likely to be captured within the next few hours, unless I am able to warn him."

"A member of the family, my Lady?"

"Yes, Harry, and only you can tell me where to find him," Panthea replied. "A company of soldiers has been detailed to arrest the notorious highwayman, White Throat."

She saw Harry start so violently that someone might have pricked him with a sword, then as his hand went up to wipe the sweat from his brow, she continued before he could speak.

"There is no time to be lost. You know where my cousin Lucius is hidden. Take me to him, so that I may warn him."

"But, my Lady, it is not safe! You, you must stay here," Harry stammered.

"I am coming with you, Harry," she said. "Saddle the horses. I will tell you more as we go."

For a moment she thought Harry would refuse her, but the habits of a lifetime asserted themselves and he obeyed her command. Five minutes later, they swung out of the stable yard and were trotting down the narrow streets in which the lights of the linkboys often revealed the evil faces of thieves waiting to rob drunken revellers, staggering home from the taverns and bawdy houses.

It was impossible for Panthea to talk to Harry until the town was left behind and they were riding in the open countryside. They were heading north, Panthea realised, and she was glad when the young moon climbing up the sky lightened their way. It was a glorious night, the sky strewn with stars, and the air clear and fresh after the sultry heat of the afternoon.

Harry never paused or hesitated as to the way among the labyrinth of lanes and tracks, but his horse kept up an even, unhurried pace and Panthea had difficulty in holding the faster and more spirited Socrates in check.

They were about two miles from London when Harry at last spoke.

"Was it Marta, who told you, my Lady, that I should know where to find Mr. Lucius?"

"You must not blame her, Harry," Panthea replied. "She said as little as she could, but I forced an admission from her when she realised that Jack's life was also at stake."

She heard Harry sigh above the clatter of their horses' hooves.

"Jack were a good boy, my Lady," he said, "until this trouble came upon him."

They came to a straight piece of the road with grass on either side. It was firm and sweet. The horses broke into a gallop, and there was no need for Panthea to put into words that every moment saved might be a crucial one. After about an hour's hard riding they reached the edge of a thick wood, and here Harry reined in his horse.

"Will you wait here for me, my Lady," he asked, "while I go forward alone?"

"No, Harry, I am coming with you. There are many things which I alone can tell my cousin."

"Very well, my Lady," Harry agreed, "but I must ask your permission that I may bind your eyes. I have given my word, my Lady, that I will not reveal the place of hiding of Mr. Lucius to any living soul. Your Ladyship will understand."

"Yes, I understand," Panthea replied, and taking a handkerchief from her pocket she held it out.

"Tie my eyes if it please you, Harry, but I will keep them closed at the same time. I have not come here to spy."

Of delicate cotton, the handkerchief was edged with a border of fine lace. Harry's clumsy fingers had difficulty in tying the knot behind Panthea's head, and finally she had to help him. At last it was done, and she spoke in a voice which had a sudden note of joy in it. "I am as blind as the one-legged beggar who stands at the entrance to the pit. What happens now?"

"I will lead Socrates, my Lady," Harry replied, and she felt him take the bridle from her hands and start both horses forward at a slow walk.

There must have been a ride through the woods that Panthea had not perceived when they drew rein. She could sense that there were trees on either side of them, and she could hear the quick scurrying movements of animals and birds that can only be heard in the quiets of a wood at night. An owl hooted far away in the distance, a pigeon fluttered from a nearby tree, disturbed from its roosting. Panthea felt her heart begin to beat faster, a delicious sense of anticipation began to rise in her throat so that her lips were warm and dry.

They went on for what seemed to her a long time. Harry did not speak, neither did she, and they appeared to move very quietly. The horses' hooves were deadened by the soft grass, and only the jingle of their crested silver harness betrayed their presence.

At length, they came to a standstill. Panthea heard Harry dismount and she guessed that he was tethering the horses to a railing or a post. She felt his hands at her waist.

"Will you dismount, my Lady?" he asked in a very low voice.

She lowered herself carefully, feeling as helpless as a baby in the darkness and half afraid to move for fear she should fall. Harry's arm guided her forward and then, putting each foot cautiously before the other, there came to her nostrils a sudden overwhelming fragrance – the scent of roses, ambrosial, exotic and sweeter than any other perfume she had ever known.

Instantly she knew where she was. There was only one place in the world where the roses smelt like that. She could remember from her babyhood being entranced by the aroma of the white roses which climbed in profusion over the terraces at Staverley.

She was home! That was where Harry had brought her. She thought then that she might have guessed that Lucius would be hiding in the family house, the place that was his by right of inheritance, the one spot where it was unlikely that anyone would come to look for him.

Panthea said nothing, but she could feel the excitement rising within her, making her breathless. She felt as if every nerve in her body was tingling, and she no longer walked cautiously for her feet knew the way along the terrace. Harry stopped and she knew they were outside one of the long windows that led into the library. She guessed that he was listening, for he hesitated and then knocked three times on the wooden shutter.

There was a pause and then he knocked again, twice this time. For a moment there was no answer and then there was a gentle creak as if someone opened the window inside. Harry tapped for the third time – a single knock, his knuckles sharp against the wood. There was the sound of a shutter being unlatched and then she heard a voice, which Panthea knew she had been waiting to hear for over five years.

"Zounds, Harry, but I was not expecting a visit from you this night."

"My Lord, I have someone with me."

There was anxiety and almost a note of pleading in Harry's voice. Panthea stood very still. She could not see, but she was certain that Lucius was staring at her. She could almost feel his eyes burning through the handkerchief that bandaged her eyes, but before he could speak, Harry did. "Her Ladyship has news to impart to you, my Lord, news of the utmost importance, which concerns your safety."

"Then why has she been blindfolded?" Lucius asked. "If she comes as a friend then she is welcome to our hospitality, poor though it may be."

Panthea would have put her hands up to the handkerchief to take it from her eyes, but she was forestalled. She felt his hands swiftly and skilfully untie the knot, and then her eyes were free and she could see. He was standing close beside her, although she had not heard him approach. She thought as she looked up at him that she had forgotten how tall he was, then she realised something else.

She was seeing him for the first time without a mask. He was handsome, she thought, more handsome than she had ever imagined him to be. There was a look of Rudolph about him, and yet what a difference there was even in the likeness! His eyes were grey and very gentle, and his lips were curved in a charming smile.

"Welcome to Staverley," he said quietly. "I wish I had known that you were coming – we could perhaps have made the place more presentable for you."

She hardly heard what he said. Her eyes were taking in every detail of his face and expression. He had not expected her to visit him and yet he was dressed as if he had come straight from the Banqueting Hall in Whitehall. His black coat was embroidered with silver, and his breeches were of satin. At his chin was the well-remembered knot of priceless lace, laundered until snowy and spotless, and it seemed almost luminous against the darkness of his coat and of the sky behind him.

His clothes were elegant and dandified and yet one could sense the alert fitness of the body beneath them. The years of living in the saddle, of a life without luxury and without comfort, made other men seem soft beside the hard masculinity of him. He took Panthea's hand in his, and at the warm strength of his fingers she quivered and felt as if the touch ignited some flame within herself.

"You have not grown very much, little cousin," he said softly, and she saw that he was smiling at her as he drew her gently by the hand, in through the window which lay open behind him.

It led, as she had known, into the library. To her astonishment, the room was furnished and warm from a fire blazing on the hearth. There were big armchairs on either side of the fireplace, just as she remembered. There was a desk in the window, and the chair before it was awry as if Lucius had risen hastily at the sound of Harry's signal on the shutter. Panthea looked around her as in a dream, then she heard Lucius speak.

"You will find Jack in the kitchen, Harry."

The door closed softly behind the groom. They were alone and Panthea, pulling her hat from her head, felt as if she were moving in some entrancing dream. Free of her hat she put her hands up to her flattened hair and shook her curls loose. The deep waves fell like fairy gold on either side of her white forehead, and her eyelashes, long, dark and curling upwards at their ends, swept her faintly flushed cheeks. She dared not look up, for a sudden shyness held her spellbound and she knew he was watching her and waiting.

Still her fingers trembled over her hair, until at last they fell to her sides. She was very still. She could feel him commanding her to look up. For a moment she resisted him, afraid of her own surrender to his will, and then, almost as if she were mesmerised into obedience, she raised her eyes to his.

He looked at her for a long, long moment and then he spoke quietly.

"You are as lovely as I dreamed you would be when you grew up, and yet I think the little girl in the wood has not quite disappeared."

His words made her remember why she had come, and that in wasting time she endangered his life.

"I – I have come to warn you," she stammered quickly. "You must leave here at once. You are in danger, grave danger. A company of soldiers is being sent to apprehend you."

It seemed to her as if Lucius had not heard what she said, for he still stared down into her face, taking in the widening fear in her big eyes, the quiver and tremble of her lips, the sudden agitated little movement of her hands towards her breast.

"Yes, you are lovelier than I remember," he said very quietly.

Now she could look at him no longer, dropping her eyes again.

"You must listen to me, cousin," she pleaded. "I was with the King today when Sir Philip Gage told him that he had been informed of your hiding place."

"And who told him that, I wonder?" Lucius asked slowly, and it seemed to Panthea without much interest.

"It was Rudolph, I am sure it was Rudolph, for he hates you and is eager to be assured of your death," Panthea replied.

"The devil he does!" Lucius exclaimed. "And what have I done to offend the fellow? I have not seen him for over ten years."

"Can you not understand that he wishes to inherit the estate and the title?" Panthea asked. "He has already petitioned the King to have Staverley restored to him. He has begged my great-aunt, Lady Darlington, to intercede on his behalf with His Majesty. He is scheming all the time to be acknowledged as the head of the family and the fourth Marquess of Staverley."

Lucius threw back his head and laughed.

"Does it mean so much to him?" he enquired. "Well, why not? I am dead to all intents and purposes, dead to the world I know, to the world in which Rudolph wishes to live. It would be inconvenient to move and find another hiding place as comfortable as this, but if it means so much to my cousin, I will remove myself instantly. The house is his!"

His voice seemed to ring out round the room, and then he saw that Panthea was confronting him, no longer with shyness but with a sudden anger that appeared to sharpen her voice as she spoke.

"How can you speak like that? How can Staverley mean so little to you? Or your rightful place as the head of the family? To my father, this house and all it stood for in the history of our family meant more than I can ever attempt to tell you. He died heartbroken that his son could not inherit, but towards the end he said to me, 'If Richard had to die, Panthea, I am content that he died serving his King loyally and faithfully, as the Vynes have done since the very beginning of our family history. Richard is dead, but the Vynes will live on. I have not, I think, betrayed my trust to those who will follow me.'"

Panthea's voice broke on a sob, then fiercely she continued,

"His trust is handed to you. You are now, whether the world acknowledges it or not, the Marquess of Staverley. You stand in my father's place. You shall not treat that lightly or refuse your birthright."

She was trembling now with the intensity of her feeling, and when Lucius moved to her side she did not anticipate what he was about to do. To her astonishment, he went down on one knee and taking her hand laid his lips against it.

"Forgive me," he said. "I have grown used to laughing at things that are most sacred, simply because if I contemplate them in any other way I must cry. Staverley means as much to me as it means to you, as much as it has meant to all our family. I love it, and I will, if need be, die for it."

His lips pressed her hand again and then he rose to his feet.

"Thank you, little Panthea," he said.

"For what?" Panthea asked wonderingly.

Her anger had gone from her now, and in its place there was another and very different emotion which had seemed to palpitate through her at the touch of his lips.

"I am thanking you," he answered, "for making me believe, for just a few moments, that I am still of importance, not just an outcast and an outlaw, a man exiled by his own actions from his friends, society and all civilised form of life."

"But that is not true," Panthea said. "You are a highwayman and there is a price on your head, but what you have done you have done with a reason. Marta told me that it was your loyalty to the King that made you a fugitive. Now that the King is restored to his Throne, can you not ask his pardon and obtain a reprieve as many others have done?"

Lucius shook his head.

"A charming idea," he said, "but quite impossible. There is a price on my head, little cousin. A thousand guineas, I am told, for my crimes are a legend, and I add to them every day. I have too many enemies who would make sure that my petition for mercy never reached His Majesty, until it was too late."

"I will take it to the King with my own hands," Panthea said, but again he shook his head.

"I would not have you dirty yourself with the mud that stains me," he said.

"But you do not understand," Panthea said. "You must be pardoned. We must find some way in which the King will understand and forgive you, for otherwise . . ."

Her voice seemed to die in her throat.

"Yes, otherwise?" Lucius prompted.

"I believe that Rudolph will contrive to have you taken by the military. If he fails this time, he will try again. I have seen by the look in his eyes, I have known without being told in so many words that this has been his intention for a long time. Only you stand between him and Staverley, and to help him in the pursuit of you he has all the might and majesty of the law."

"They have still to catch me," Lucius said lightly. "It is five years ago since you and I first met, and yet I am still alive, still pursuing my nefarious game of robbing those who well deserve it and helping those who have no one else to help them."

"I heard you saved three men from being hanged or transported," Panthea said eagerly.

"Let us not talk of my exploits," Lucius answered quickly. "Let us speak rather of you. Tell me about yourself. Are you happy?"

"Owing to your kindness, I have had many things that I could never otherwise have afforded," Panthea said. "May I thank you now for the money you left for me in the grotto. It was a vast sum, so vast that I was afraid questions would be asked as to where I had obtained it."

"That old skinflint, Christian Drysdale, had a fortune tucked away in his house," Lucius answered. "Had I had time to search further, I dare say I would have found much more. As it was, I was forced to leave behind the gold and silver plate he had collected from royalist families, and the jewels he had snatched from bereaved mothers and widowed wives."

"I cannot think of him, even now, without shuddering," Panthea murmured.

"Forget him," Lucius said quietly. "He has passed from your life. All you have to do is be happy, and doubtless there are a thousand gallants only too eager to make you so."

It seemed to Panthea there was a sudden bitter note in his voice as he said the last words, and she thrilled a little, as women always must at the idea that a man is jealous of them. But she had never learned the tricks of prevarication and of teasing a man to intensify his affection.

"I have had many offers of marriage," she said frankly, "but I have thought that most of those who made them have been more interested in my money than in myself, and I have never as yet cared for any man."

Even as she spoke the last words, she knew them to be a lie. There was one man she had cared for ever since she had first seen him. She knew now that it was her memories of him that had made all the other men lifeless and uninteresting. It was his voice that had held her captive since he first spoke to her, his lips that had been unforgettable because they had pressed themselves against her cheek.

She felt as if her secret were written on her face, and try as she would, she could not meet his eyes.

"So many men have offered for you!" he said reflectively. "And is cousin Rudolph amongst them?"

The blood rose to her cheeks.

"He desires my money," she said quietly. "If he loves anyone, I believe it is my Lady Castlemaine."

Lucius turned away from her abruptly, and she wondered miserably what she had said to offend him. He walked across the room and stood with his back to her.

"Rudolph wishes to marry you! You had best accept him and come back to Staverley. I would like to think of you living here as a reigning Marchioness."

Panthea said nothing. She did not know why, but his words seemed to bring her a sadness and misery almost beyond expression. She felt he was relinquishing everything – not only Staverley, but also herself.

"You will entertain in the Silver Salon," Lucius continued. "I can see you arranging the flowers there. Red roses against the grey walls. You will walk in the herb garden and fill the stillroom with pots and bottles of healing potions and balm for every type of ill. You will sit at the head of the dining room table and look down it at your guests as they eat off the gold dishes, and drink from the crystal goblets engraved with the family crest. And from these very windows in this room, you will watch your children fishing in the lake, or playing ball on the lawns while the puppies run and bark beside them. That is the future I can visualise for you."

"But not with Rudolph, *not with Rudolph!*"

The words seemed to burst from Panthea's lips, almost uncontrollably, and as she spoke them she saw him swing round to face her. There was an expression on his face she had never seen before.

For what seemed an eternity, they stared at each other across the room – then swiftly in a single stride, he was beside her and had taken her in his arms. She was trembling as she felt herself drawn against his breast, but her eyes never left his. Her lovely lips were parted as if inviting his kiss. For a long, long moment he looked down at her exquisite face, alight now with an inner radiance that made her more compellingly beautiful than she had ever been before. At last, in a voice broken and hoarse with emotion he spoke. ,

"Oh, my dear love, how can I let you go? I love you so."

Then his mouth was on hers and they were locked together in an embrace that seemed to unite them, one with the other, until they were indivisible. His kisses were those of a man who has almost died of thirst and suddenly feels the healing drops of water touch his lips. They clung to each other desperately, an ecstasy so glorious, so wonderful, sweeping over them that they felt as if they were consumed by a divine flame and carried away into a golden paradise. And yet at the same moment, the fear and terror of separation was present in both their minds. They clung to each other, knowing their need for one another and yet aware that danger hung like a sword above their heads.

"My darling – my love," Lucius murmured brokenly, and then his lips were on Panthea's shining eyes, on her flushed cheeks and rounded chin, then searching in the softness of her neck until she felt she must swoon into unconsciousness at the joy and ecstasy of the feelings he awoke within her.

"My sweetheart, my love, the woman of whom I have dreamed for so long," he murmured again and again.

And now at length, her arms crept up to his neck and she could feel the springing virility of his hair beneath her fingers and the hard warmth of his skin.

"I love you! Oh, darling . . . I . . . *love you!*"

She whispered the words against his mouth, and then once again their lips were joined together.

How long they stood there spellbound by their love, Panthea had no idea. For a moment, the world was forgotten, Whitehall was far away as if it had never been. Lucius had swept her into an enchanted land where he and she were alone, and there was nothing else save their love and their desire for one another.

A log falling in the fireplace awoke Panthea to reality. She moved in Lucius' arms, then pushed him away from her.

"Darling, you are in danger! At any moment the soldiers may be arriving. I could not come to you when I first learned of what Sir Philip intended to do because I had to attend a dinner in the Banqueting Hall this evening. It will not take them long to march here if they are guided by someone who knows the way. You must go. Warn your men and saddle the horses."

"I cannot go now," Lucius said. "What does danger matter to me now that I know you love me?"

"Oh, my darling, be sensible," Panthea pleaded. "If you are arrested then I shall plead with them to arrest me too. If you must die, then I shall die with you."

Her words seemed to rouse him at last to a realisation that the danger of which she spoke was not so far away. Once again, he swept her into his arms but the kiss was a quick one, before he turned towards the door, and opening it shouted through the darkness of the hall.

"Jack, come here."

There was the sound of footsteps on the bare boards and then Panthea saw Jack standing in the doorway. He was not unlike his father, save that he was bigger built and his hair was a dark russet brown curling closely over his head.

"Warn the others we must leave here immediately," Lucius said. "Cover our traces as much as possible. We want them to think that the house has not been used."

"But the fire?" Panthea asked. "If there have been fires in the rooms they will know someone has been here."

"We must risk it," Lucius replied. "The horses, Jack."

"Very good, my Lord."

Jack turned and ran across the hall. Lucius looked at Panthea without speaking.

"Of what are you thinking?" she asked, knowing the answer, but womanlike, wishing to hear him say it.

"I am thinking," he answered softly, "that no man is more fortunate than I, no man luckier."

Her hands went out towards him, her face alight with happiness at his words, and then as she moved towards him, she was frozen into a sudden immobility, as cold and as stiff as if she had been turned to stone.

They both heard it at the same time – the sound of marching feet coming down the drive towards the house.

7

For a moment it seemed as if Panthea and Lucius could neither of them draw in their breath – then Panthea spoke first in a voice vibrant with fear.

"It is the soldiers! Go, *go quickly!*"

"And leave you here?" Lucius asked.

She saw that he had decided not to leave her. Urgently, she put out her hands as if to force him from her.

"But of course! What does it matter if they find me! This is my home! I have come here to reminisce on the old times. It will explain the fire, the fact that the place has been lived in."

Still Lucius hesitated, and she added, "Oh, go, my love, go quickly!"

She saw the expression on his face change and knew that she had but half convinced him.

"Think of Jack," she urged. "It will kill Harry if he is taken now. Think of the others too! They will not go without you."

The appeal for assistance for those who looked to him for leadership did not go unanswered. Lucius picked up his hat and riding whip, which lay on a chair as he must have thrown them down when he entered the room, and then, though it seemed to Panthea that the footsteps of the marching men were growing terrifyingly near, he turned and swept her into his arms.

For one ecstatic moment their lips were joined. and she could feel his heart beating against her breast. Then he was gone. The library door closed behind him and she could hear his footsteps hurrying over the polished floor, then growing fainter and fainter until she could hear them no more. Still she stood listening, conscious at the same time of the advancing force outside the window.

A command rang out and although she could not hear the words, she guessed that the soldiers were dispersing round the house. She began to pray then, as she had never prayed before.

Would Lucius be in time? Would he reach his horse? The stables lay at the back of the house and she guessed the way he would go to them, passing down one of the long galleries where she and Richard had played as children and that ended in the servants' quarters. From there a door led directly into the big, square stable yard, above which towered the dovecot, on which the birds, white against the sky, would coo seductively the whole day through.

It would take a man who knew the house well but a few seconds to reach the stables, to take a horse from the loose box and, leaving the yard by the northern gate, gallop away into the darkness of the trees that grew thick and verdant on that side of the building.

Yet even if she had planned it in her mind's eye, she saw so many things that might prevent Lucius from escaping. The body of soldiers might have been sent to occupy the stables first. It would have been a wise move, for without their horses it would be hard for the highwaymen to escape. Perhaps their horses were not saddled and it would take time to buckle the girths and fasten the bridles over their heads. Perhaps Lucius had been unable to warn all his followers and she had the feeling that he would not leave any one of them behind. He would be captured himself rather than sacrifice any of those who trusted him.

There were so many things that might happen, dangerous, disastrous things, and they passed through Panthea's mind as she prayed, her hands clasped, her lips moving, with the effort of concentration.

~128~

There was the sound of movement on the terrace outside. Swiftly, she remembered that she had a part to play and that the shutters of the window of the library had been left open. Quickly, she picked up a book from the table by the fire and, settling herself in an armchair, opened it on her lap. She was only just in time. A second later she heard a window crash open and turned to see two soldiers with their muskets to their shoulders.

She screamed then – the startled, astonished scream of a woman who had been surprised by something she never expected to happen. Even as the sound echoed round the room, the door of the library opened and Rudolph Vyne entered, followed by Sir Philip Gage.

Panthea had never seen a man look so astonished as Rudolph when he saw her sitting there by the fire, her hands gripping a leatherbound volume of Latin prose which she clasped to her breast as if for protection. His mouth literally dropped open and his eyes seem to protrude from his head.

As for Sir Philip Gage, his astonishment made him look more like Humpty Dumpty than ever, and on this occasion a deflated one.

Rudolph found his voice first.

"Cousin Panthea!" he exclaimed. "Can I believe my eyes?"

"Indeed," Panthea said pettishly, "I do not know what this is all about but get these ferocious soldiers in the windows to lower their muskets. I am sadly afraid of having my head blown off."

"What are you doing here, ma'am?" Sir Philip Gage spluttered. "Have you seen anything of the man we seek?"

Panthea opened her eyes very wide.

"What man?" she enquired.

"A highwayman – White Throat he is called," Sir Philip exclaimed. "I am credibly informed that he makes this house his hiding place."

Panthea gave a little laugh.

"Why, Sir Philip, you don't believe that nonsense, do you? I promise you it is but an old wives' tale. Ever since I was a child there are supposed to have been monsters of some sort or another hiding in the woods or lurking in the secret passages of Staverley. I promise you I have not seen so much as the shadow of a highwayman or the ghost of one."

Sir Philip scowled and his eyes turned towards Rudolph. The latter advanced slowly into the room to take up his stand on the hearthrug, his back to the fire. His glance travelled over Panthea seated in the armchair, at the writing desk where a long quill pen had been freshly dipped in the ink, his eyes flickered over the chairs and the tables arranged round the room, and Panthea knew that he noted there was no dust on them. Then finally his glance rested on her again.

"You have not yet explained, my dear cousin," he said, and his voice was silky, "what you are doing here."

"Surely that is obvious," Panthea said. "I am sitting by the fireside reading a book."

"And why?"

Panthea gave a little sigh.

"Isn't that obvious too? I was homesick, as I often am for my home, the house where I was brought up, the place where my father died. No one seems to have a thought for Staverley these days and so, whenever I can creep away, I come here. It brings me comfort and a happiness I cannot begin to explain to you."

Rudolph said nothing as she finished speaking but she thought that his expression had altered a little, although his eyes were still watchful and suspicious. There was a sudden commotion in the hall outside, and then a Sergeant came through the open doorway saluting.

"We have a captured a man in the kitchens, sir," he said to Sir Philip Gage.

The latter started and said quickly,

"Bring him in, bring him in!"

Panthea felt as if the blood was drained away from her heart, and then into the room, escorted by two soldiers, came Harry. She almost cried aloud with the relief of it, and it was with a genuine smile of amusement that she turned to Sir Philip.

"I assure you, sir, that this is no highwayman but only my groom, a most respectable, sober man, who has accompanied me here from London. He has been in my father's employment for over twenty-five years, and now is in the service of my great-aunt, the Dowager Countess of Darlington, and myself. I assure you it would be difficult to find him capable of any crime save of pampering his horses.'

The amusement in her voice, and the sarcasm of her words, made Sir Philip tighten his lips as he blew out his cheeks like an enraged bullfrog.

"Release the man," he ordered sharply, "and search the house from garret to cellars."

"Very good, sir."

"I will show you round if you like," Harry said, as he rubbed his freed hands to restore the circulation.

"The soldiers have no need of your help," Rudolph snapped suddenly.

Harry's honest blue eyes appeared pained as if he had been unjustly accused, but he raised his finger respectfully to his forelock.

"Can I wait with the horses then, Mr. Rudolph?" he enquired.

"No, don't go outside, Harry," Panthea said before her cousin could reply. "We must be getting back to London in a short while and there will be the fires to quench, both here and in the kitchen. As I have so often said before, we must be very careful not to set the place alight."

"Very good, my Lady," Harry said. "I will wait in the hall."

His eyes met Panthea's meaningly, and she knew that he understood what she had tried to convey to him.

"The place must be searched thoroughly," Sir Philip said, and he turned to the soldiers still standing at the window. "Go all round the house and see if you can perceive anything unusual."

The soldiers withdrew, and after a moment's hesitation Sir Philip, who had seemed about to say something to Rudolph, followed them. Almost before he was out of earshot, Panthea spoke.

"What is all this commotion about? I beg you to let me into the secret of this sudden invasion of Staverley."

Her voice and expression were one of complete innocence, and she met her cousin's eyes fairly and squarely.

"Ye gods, but I'm not certain how to answer you," Rudolph said. "I can scarcely credit your story of coming here to sit by yourself and think of your childhood. It is a long way to come, Panthea, and a journey that few women would wish to undertake at night alone."

"Why should I be afraid?" Panthea enquired. "Besides, Harry was with me."

"And whom did you meet when you arrived here?" Rudolph enquired.

"Whom should I expect to meet?" Panthea parried. "Fie on you, cousin Rudolph, surely you don't believe Sir Philip's ridiculous story of a highwayman and the like?"

Rudolph drummed his fingers on the mantelshelf.

"These stories are not so ridiculous. Sir Philip has reason to believe, and so have I, that this house is being used as the headquarters of some nefarious scoundrels."

"The highwayman, White Throat," Panthea said. "Well, if reports are to be believed, he is not such a scoundrel as all that, but rather a knight errant helping those in need and making only those who most deserve it disgorge their ill-gotten gains."

"What do you know about him?"

She was not prepared for the sudden savagery of Rudolph's question. His face was suddenly contorted, and she saw that she had driven him far enough and it would be wise to tease him no further. She rose to her feet and crossed the room to put the book she held down on a distant table.

"You can rest assured of one thing, cousin Rudolph," she said. "I am not particularly interested in highwaymen or their like. I am more concerned with Staverley, with seeing it restored to its former glory, and that it shall hold once more the head of our family."

"I am the head of the family," Rudolph said. "Perhaps if you speak with His Majesty, he will listen to you."

"And what of our cousin Lucius?" Panthea asked.

She spoke the words lightly, but at the same time she could not prevent herself from asking the question, the temptation was too great. She saw Rudolph's face darken – his eyes narrow.

"He is dead!" he shouted at her. "Or, if he isn't, he soon will be."

He turned on his heel as he spoke and strode from the room. She heard him go running up the broad oak staircase, shouting to the soldiers who were tramping in and out of the rooms upstairs, to make their search a really thorough one.

There was the sound of doors being slammed, of furniture being pushed around, of curtains being torn back, of walls being thumped in case they concealed a secret closet. Panthea suddenly felt cold. The elation of sparring with Rudolph was passing and now she could only remember that the man she loved had gone, was riding away into the forest a fugitive, an exile from his home and from those to whom he belonged.

The fire was dying down in the grate, but Panthea held out her hands to it. As she stood there, Harry came through the doorway.

"Shall I put out the fire, my Lady?"

She nodded. Harry bent down as if to quench the flames. As he did so he whispered to her,

"They got away, my Lady."

"Thank God!"

Panthea's reply came from the very depths of her heart. Harry straightened himself.

"We had best be getting home, my Lady."

"There is certainly no reason for us to stay here," Panthea replied.

She walked from the library into the hall. At the head of the stairs she saw a soldier smashing in the linen panelling with the butt of his musket.

"Stop that at once!"

Panthea's tone was imperious. The man turned to gape at her.

"Them's my orders," he said a little sullenly.

"I care not what orders you have received," Panthea said angrily. "You will stop that destruction."

"Is anything the matter?"

Sir Philip's fussy, slightly high-pitched voice came from the balcony overlooking the hall. Then, slowly placing each foot carefully before him as if he feared to slip, he began to descend the stairs. Behind him, Rudolph came from one of the bedrooms and stood looking over the balustrade.

Incensed beyond endurance, Panthea lost her temper. There was something about both men that enraged her beyond all restraint. There was Sir Philip, fat and pompous, ordering the soldiers to smash up her home, and Rudolph using him for his own ends, hunting for the the man who was its rightful owner, ready to stain his hands with the blood of his own kith and kin so that he might gain by it.

"There is a great deal the matter," Panthea said in a clear voice.

She looked very small as she stood there, with only the light of a few tapers to illuminate her fair uncovered head and small velvet-clad figure. But even so, she seemed to shine from the darkness and there was a live vitality about her that made it impossible not to listen to what she said.

"You and these soldiers have come here," she said, "on some absurd pretence that cannot be substantiated. You are encouraging these men to wanton destruction of a house that, through all the difficult and miserable years of the Commonwealth, remained loyal and true to His Majesty. My brother, who should at this moment be reigning here as head of the family, was hanged because he supported our King when he was in exile.

"My father died here, loyal with his last breath to the Stuart cause, and what thanks does this bring, what do we receive in return for these years of suffering and privation? Only this, that without reasonable excuse or explanation, you force your way in and, without permission or authority, do more damage in a short space of time than Cromwell's armies dared to do in all the years we lived under the yoke of his tyranny. I am disgusted and ashamed that such things should take place now and in the name of our King. His Majesty shall hear of this, I promise you, and I cannot believe that he will countenance such acts of violence and wanton destruction."

As Panthea finished speaking there was no doubt of the consternation on the fat face of Sir Philip or on the faces of the soldiers who had been listening. Only Rudolph's face seemed twisted as if in a sneer, as he came slowly down the stairs in Sir Philip's wake.

"My dear young lady, I beg you not to distress yourself in this matter," Sir Philip said. "Very little damage has been done, I assure you. We have but searched the house following the information we had that it had become the hiding place of miscreants. There is, I admit, no trace of them and I must therefore apologise to you for having disturbed or upset you. Let me make it quite clear that I did not enter this house without permission or authority. That was generously offered me by your cousin, Mr. Rudolph Vyne, who I understand is claimant to the estate and can therefore be assumed to be acting, at least for the time being, for the rightful owner."

"My cousin Rudolph has left no one in doubt as to his belief that he should inherit this house and estate," Panthea said, "but until he does so, until the King honours his petition, I suggest that his permission to damage the family property is as valueless as your search itself has proved to be."

"But really, my Lady, I must protest," Sir Philip began to stutter, but Panthea stopped him with a scant curtsy.

"Good night, sir," she said.

She walked from the hall without a backward glance, either at Sir Philip or at Rudolph. She entered the library, picked up her hat from where she had placed it on the chair and, going through the window on to the terrace, saw that the horses were where Harry had tethered them. She heard footsteps behind her and thought that Harry had followed her.

"Let us get away, Harry," she said, and now that her anger was passing her voice trembled.

She felt a hand on her arm and, realising it was not Harry who had followed her but Rudolph, she swung herself round to face him. By the light of the moon she could see that he was scowling.

"You shall not go like this," he said, "to make trouble for me with the King."

"And how will you prevent me?" Panthea asked, striving to free herself from the grip of his hands, but he was too strong.

"There is something strange about all this," Rudolph muttered. "I swear that you came here to meet that cursed fellow."

His fury was making him indiscreet, and instantly Panthea felt cool and calm.

"What fellow?" she enquired.

She saw Rudolph bite his lip. As he did not speak, she continued.

"You will please unhand me, cousin Rudolph. I am surprised at your behaviour tonight, and this does not make me feel any sweeter towards you."

Still Rudolph did not release her, his fingers seemed to bite deep into the flesh of her arms, and now she was afraid of the expression on his face.

"Curse you for a meddlesome jade," he said. "I am certain that you brought him warning. It was not for you that the fire was lit, that beds had been slept in, that the spit in the kitchen was thick with grease. You were at the banquet tonight and yet you contrive to come here ahead of us. There is something behind all this and I am not deceived by your play acting."

"Let me *go!*"

Panthea's voice was as sharp as a whip.

"And if I don't?" Rudolph asked.

"Do you wish me to scream for the help of some of your incompetent soldiers?" Panthea asked. "They may be oafs, but they may also have enough decency in them to protect a woman who is too weak to help herself."

"You drive me mad," Rudolph said thickly. "You had best marry me, then you can do as you like with the damned house."

He drew a little nearer to her as he spoke and Panthea was suddenly afraid of him. With a quickness and strength she had not known she possessed, she made a sudden movement that took him by surprise, and twisted herself free. Before he could prevent her, she ran down the stone steps which led from the terrace and reached her horse's side.

To her relief she saw that Harry was there before her. The horses were untied and without pausing to question her hurry, he swung her into the saddle and a second later was astride his own horse. As Socrates reared a little and stamped the ground, eager to be off, Panthea looked up at the terrace and saw that Rudolph was standing there watching her.

She pulled at the reins and called up at him so that her voice floated clear and loud over the night air.

"You may be certain of one thing, cousin Rudolph," she said, "I would not marry you if you were the last man on Earth."

She did not hear his reply if he made one. She let the reins go and touched Socrates with her whip. The horse broke into a canter, and with Harry following behind her, Panthea sped up the drive, the dust and gravel of the roadway flying from behind her horse's hooves.

It was not the fear of pursuit which caused her to ride away from Staverley as if all the forces of hell were behind her. She forgot that Harry's horse was slower and could not keep up with hers. She delighted at feeling the wind whipping up the colour in her cheeks, her hair blowing back from her tiny ears, she let Socrates have his head. There was something exhilarating and yet soothing in feeling the horse move quickly beneath her, the ground seeming to be swallowed up by each great stride he took.

The fury of her pace seemed somehow to relieve the ache within her breast, the throbbing questions that overshadowed her mind. For the moment she could forget everything in the physical relief of being free, knowing that she, like Lucius, had escaped, if only for the moment.

She knew the way back to London, and it was only when she had gone a mile or two that she realised that Harry was left behind and she was travelling alone down a lonely tree-bordered road. She looked over her shoulder, pulling in Socrates as she did so. He chafed a little because she checked his speed, for he was as fresh as when he had left the stable earlier that evening and delighted in the opportunity of stretching his legs in the country, rather than having to perambulate politely in the park as had been his lot for the past month.

"Steady, boy, we must wait for Harry," Panthea told him, quietening him by patting his neck as he pulled against the bridle.

It was then, as she wheeled and turned in the road, that she saw someone ahead of her come from the shadows of the trees. Instantly she knew who it was, and her heart leapt as the joy of it ran through her body, making her thrill with a happiness she had never believed possible. She rode towards him and they met under the branches of a great oak tree. He put out his hand and laid it on hers.

"You are safe, my darling?" he asked. "I have been almost distraught with worry."

"You need not have troubled yourself about me," Panthea answered, but her eyes told him she was glad he had done so.

"They did not insult you?" he asked.

She did not bother to answer the question.

"Rudolph is certain that you were there and that I came to warn you," she said. "But he cannot prove it."

"We should not have been taken unawares in such a way," Lucius said, and his voice was self-condemning. "I have grown careless. It has been so comfortable and easy living at Staverley and no one has suspected, until now, that the house was occupied by anything save rats and bats."

"Where will you go now?" Panthea asked.

"The woods have always proved a shelter for me," Lucius answered, "and I am fortunate in that I have many friends. They are humble people – they live in cottages, not in palaces – but all that they have they will share with me, and I can trust them completely, even with my life."

"But how shall I find you?" Panthea asked, "for I must see you again."

"It is unwise, and it might do you harm," Lucius said.

"Do you think I am afraid?" Panthea asked. "I must see you again, you know that."

"Do you not think I want to see you?" Lucius enquired tenderly. "I shall be thinking of you every moment, every second that we are apart, and yet I know that this is wrong. I am of no use to you, my beloved. I love you – God knows that I love you with my whole heart and being, but what use is it to a man who is outlawed? Do you realise that any good citizen of this country should consider it his duty to shoot me and leave me for dead? And what is more, he would be well rewarded for doing so."

"Oh, Lucius!"

Panthea's cry was that of a child, overwhelmed suddenly by fear and misery.

He leant forward from the saddle and, putting his arms round her, held her for a moment close, his cheek against hers.

"Do you remember how, the last time we met, I carried you pillion home to Staverley?"

"I never asked you how you should know the way or wondered that you should call me by my name," Panthea said. "It all seemed so natural, so right."

"Oh, Lucius!"

Panthea turned to hide her face against his neck. After a moment Lucius turned his head.

"I can see the faithful Harry in the distance," he said. "I must leave you now, dear heart, but I shall be thinking of you, you know that. Give me something of yours, that I may wear it against my breast."

Panthea drew from her pocket the handkerchief with which Harry had bandaged her eyes. It was scented with essence of jasmine and he pressed it against his lips before he placed it in an inner pocket of his coat. He drew her close to him once again and his mouth was on hers as he murmured.

"I love you! I love you so much, my lovely Panthea, that I believe now that I would die willingly because the world cannot hold a greater happiness than this."

He kissed her before she could answer him and then, as Harry came trotting up the road, he was gone. The trees were very dark and close just there. One moment he was with her and the next he had vanished and she remembered now, when they had first met, he had contrived to move very silently.

"There you are, your Ladyship. I was half afraid you would not wait for me," Harry exclaimed, breathless with the speed at which he had been travelling.

"I am sorry, Harry, but Socrates wanted to stretch his legs and I forgot that your horse could not keep up with me."

"There's few that can keep up with Socrates, my Lady," Harry said.

They moved forward together slowly, and after a moment Panthea spoke.

"How many men were with him?"

He did not need to ask of whom she spoke.

'Three, my Lady, and my son Jack," Harry replied.

"Five of them," Panthea said in a soft voice. "I am glad he is not alone."

"There is nothing they would not do for his Lordship," Harry said. "He saved their lives, every man jack of them, and they would all die for him willingly enough."

It was then that Panthea knew the answer to the question she had put to Lucius. This was why he would ask no reprieve or pardon for himself. He would not leave the men he had rescued, and who without him would be leader less and doubtless easily captured. Although Panthea felt the tears rise in her eyes at his chivalry, she felt a sudden hopelessness and a sense of dismay. How now could she obtain her heart's desire?

The joy that had made all her senses tingle at his presence gradually ebbed away from her. The road back to London was long and she was suddenly very tired. There seemed nothing to look forward to, and the future was dark and empty. Slowly, the tears began to flow down her cheeks. She made no attempt to wipe them away but rode blindly on into the night.

8

Barbara Castlemaine, sitting in the window of her crimson salon, made a lovely picture. The sunshine glinting through the thick diamond-shaped panes of glass sought out the auburn glints in her dark hair and revealed the flawless purity of her white skin, which had passed unscathed through the terrible scourge of smallpox and left her perfection unimpaired.

Her gown of shimmering oyster satin was cut low enough to cause even the least prudish of the Queen's ladies to raise their eyebrows, and with it she wore a necklace of blood red rubies which the King had given her after a stormy scene in which her greed had triumphed over his hope for economy.

The room in which she sat was as fabulous as its mistress.

Pictures from the King's collection, furniture that belonged to the Royal Palaces and a priceless carpet of Aubusson needlework all made an expensive if appropriate setting for the most extravagant woman in all Britain.

In strange contrast to this luxury, was the sweating, frightened Corporal whom Barbara was interviewing. His red tunic was faded, stained and threadbare at the seams, his boots badly in need of repair and his crossbelts almost falling apart with old age.

If he had been asked about himself, he would have related that his pay was long overdue, as was that of the majority of those serving with him. The food in the barracks was excruciating, and most of the weapons of war with which the military were issued were out of date and badly in need of repair.

The Army was desperately in need of money and its plight was no worse than that of the Navy, whose ships were left rotting at the quays, because the Admiralty could not afford to fit them out so that they might go to sea.

But Lady Castlemaine, the recipient of so much of the King's bounty, was not interested in the personal life or feelings of the unhappy Corporal. She was forcing from his reluctant lips the story of what had occurred the night before, and the man himself was only an instrument which she could use to further her own ends.

"Go on," she prompted as the Corporal's voice faltered into silence. "What happened then?"

"Us goes in thro' the open window, ma'am . . . I means, my Lady . . . and us sees no highwayman, but a lady sitting there."

Barbara's eyes widened.

"A lady!" she exclaimed. "What did she look like? Describe her."

She did not really listen to the Corporal's halting and inadequate description, for she had already guessed who had been waiting in the library at Staverley. Her spies were efficient and there was very little that went on in the palace which she did not know – and when she was informed early that morning that Panthea had been seen riding from the stables in the darkness of the night with only a groom to accompany her, and had returned when dawn was breaking, she had immediately set the machinery of her espionage in motion.

It had not taken a great stretch of imagination to connect Panthea's absence from the Palace with the strange accounts that were brought to her of Rudolph and Sir Philip Gage's ill-fated expedition in search of a notorious highwayman.

Barbara was far too shrewd not to have suspected from the very first that Rudolph's interest in the capture of miscreants had an extremely personal side to it. She had long realised that he was hiding something when it came to a question of his claim to the Marquessate. Her vast experience of men had taught her to know, all too clearly, when a man either lied or evaded the truth. Rudolph's protestations that he was the only surviving member of the family rang false, and Barbara guessed that there was in fact another and more direct claimant, should he care to come forward.

This, however, was of little interest to Barbara and she would not have interfered with Rudolph's plans or made the slightest effort to prove him a liar, had she not resented his growing interest in his cousin Panthea. Barbara had vowed vengeance on the Countess of Darlington and her great-niece and was determined to avenge herself for the insult the Dowager had offered her on the day of the King's return to Whitehall.

Barbara was well aware that the Countess's refusal of an introduction had been overheard and noticed by some in the court. The story had lost nothing in the telling, and though the King's attentions had restored her to the position of power and importance that she had held before his marriage, she knew there were many who desired her downfall and were only waiting for the day when they too could turn their backs upon her.

It was a trifling incident in itself, yet it was the first time it had happened in actual court circles and, as such, it had left a deep scar that was not likely to be forgotten. But Barbara was well prepared to bide her time, knowing that sooner or later something would happen which would put either the Countess or Panthea in her power.

She had learned from bitter experience that there was always something in everyone's life that they wished to keep private, or of which they were ashamed, and she had not been surprised when the footman she had bribed to watch the Countess's apartment brought her the information that Panthea had crept from the palace the night before. She had let him tell his story and then rewarded him liberally.

"Keep a closer watch than ever," she instructed him. "Make love to her Ladyship's maid if need be. Women are always the best source of information."

"I'll not let anything escape me, my Lady," the footman promised.

He was not prepared to tell Barbara that he had already tried to make love to Marta and had had his ears boxed for his pains. He was a good-looking lad and it had been a blow to his pride, so that he was prepared to watch Panthea, not only for what he might obtain for it but also for a frustrated idea of "getting even" with the households. Barbara was not surprised that Rudolph and Sir Philip Gage had failed in their search for White Throat. She had no great opinion of Rudolph's powers of organisation, and she thought that if Sir Philip had been successful in the past in tracking down his prey, it was merely because they were even more stupid than he was.

She could imagine nothing more absurd in a world where news travels quickly by strange methods, and even stranger messengers, than for Sir Philip to tell the King of his plans before they were put into operation. There was always likely to be some servant who, learning of such matters from his master, would relay what was to be done to the other servants below stairs, any of whom might be in league with the thieves, cutthroats and pickpockets who frequented the town and waylaid the travellers in the countryside outside the walls of the City.

It was therefore not surprising that the highwayman whom Rudolph and Sir Philip sought should have eluded capture. What was unexpected was that Panthea should have been the person to warn him. As the Corporal told her what had occurred, finding it difficult to choose the right words, Barbara could see all too clearly that scene in the library – Panthea pretending to be at her ease, then screaming at the sudden intrusion of the soldiers, Rudolph and Sir Philip's disappointment in finding that their bird had flown, doubtless through the back door, and Panthea's final attack on Sir Philip and the discomfiture of those who listened.

She could see the great house being ransacked and fruitlessly searched by the soldiers and thought that only a pompous old fool like Sir Philip would have believed that his quarry would still remain in the house once he and his escort had forced the doors and windows.

She could well imagine Sir Philip, defrauded and downcast at the failure of his plans, collecting his men together again and marching them away down the drive, quite oblivious of the fact that as soon as his back was turned, those he had failed to find could return at their ease. The whole expedition had obviously been mismanaged and badly executed, and the only result of the midnight march had been to make both Sir Philip and Rudolph look ridiculous.

At the same time, from Barbara's point of view, some valuable information had come to light, first and foremost that the highwayman, White Throat, had some personal connection with Rudolph, and secondly that Panthea was interested enough in the man, whoever he might be, to risk her reputation, if not her life, in undertaking an extremely dangerous ride in order to warn him.

The Corporal's stammering voice finished its story, and he wiped his forehead with the back of his hand. He had told Barbara all that he knew, and she was well aware that he was like a sponge that she had squeezed dry and there was no more to be obtained from him. She therefore took three guineas from a silk purse that lay beside her on a table.

His eyes gleamed with excitement at the immensity of the sum. When Lady Castlemaine's Major Domo approached him and promised that, should he give the information that her Ladyship required, he would be well rewarded he had calculated that he might get a guinea at the most, perhaps less if what he had to tell was not as valuable as what was anticipated. He had never in the whole of his life possessed so much money at one time and, remembering his long-overdue pay and a pretty barmaid at the Three Horseshoes, he felt almost light-hearted with excitement at suddenly becoming so rich.

As Barbara paid the Corporal, she smiled at him. It was the mechanical, easy smile of a woman who is used to making herself pleasant to men and who automatically exudes charm in the presence of one, whether he be of high or low degree.

It was that smile that, combined with the guineas held tightly now in his hot hand, completely bowled the Corporal over. He, like most of his mates, considered Barbara to be a fine figure of a woman, for all that they called her 'The King's Whore' amongst themselves and made lewd jests about her, as did many of the citizens of London.

At the same time the Corporal, like many other men of England, was all for their King enjoying himself. He had suffered for long enough on the other side of the Channel, and now that he was come to power, England was a very different place from what it had been under the iron rule of Cromwell and his grim-faced Roundheads. It was merrie England again, and why, his subjects argued, shouldn't the King make merry himself if he wished? If he wanted a mistress, let her be the prettiest and finest woman obtainable, and Barbara was undoubtedly both these things.

There were those, of course, who were shocked at the easy pleasure-loving court and condemned the King, along with the rest of the nobility. But the Corporal was not amongst them, and when Barbara smiled at him, he felt his heart give a sudden bound and he flushed with the intensity of his emotions so that his face was crimson, right to the roots of his curly hair.

It was indeed part of Barbara's power that she made men wish to serve her, and at that moment the Corporal would, if the necessity had arisen, have gladly died on her behalf. He wanted more urgently than he had ever wanted anything in the whole of his short life, to do something for her, to please her so that once again she might smile at him with that slow, beguiling and completely captivating smile.

"Thank you, Corporal, you can go now," Barbara told him. "If there is anything else I wish to know I will send for you again."

"Thank you, ma'am, I mean, my Lady, thank you, thank you," the Corporal said, bowing awkwardly as he tried to walk backwards towards the door, aware that the interview was at an end.

He had reached the hall outside and a footman was directing him towards the servants' quarters, where a tankard of ale was ready for him, when he stopped, an unusual expression on his face. He was thinking. It was not an exercise in which he indulged very often, for in the army a man obeyed orders and was seldom required to use either initiative or intelligence, even presuming that he had any. But now the Corporal's brain was working, and as an idea came slowly to his brain, he put out his hand and pointed at the doors through which he had just come.

"I've got ter go back."

"What for?" the footman enquired suspiciously. "She paid you, didn't she?"

The Corporal nodded.

"Then you've finished, see? She doesn't pay until there's nothing more she requires. Come on, I can't wait about here all day for you."

But the Corporal refused to move and, planting his big feet in their worn boots firmly on the polished floor, he repeated it.

"I got ter go back! I got somethin' more ter say."

The footman argued with him, but without avail. Now that the decision was made, he was tenacious and obstinate as a mule. He had something more to say and nothing would move him until he had said it.

Exasperated and defeated, the footman went towards Barbara's door and knocked on it tentatively.

"Gawd help you if it ain't what she wants to hear," he said ominously as in response to Barbara's command he entered the room.

She was seated at her bureau writing a letter and she was by no means pleased at the interruption.

"More to say?" she repeated. "I could swear he had nothing left to relate, but if he insists, bring him in."

She turned her writing chair sideways as the Corporal came back into the room. This time there was no smile on her lips as she spoke sharply.

"Well, Corporal, I am told you have something else to tell me. Speak swiftly, for I have little time to attend to you."

But as the Corporal began to stammer all over again, Barbara's air of impatience vanished and instead she bent forward, listening eagerly. The Corporal had not been mistaken. He had something of interest to tell her Ladyship and he was well gratified with the way she received it.

"The Sergeant was drunk, you say?" she asked.

"Not proper drunk as us knows it in the army, my Lady," the Corporal corrected, "but he'd had a powerful lot o' ale down his throat and he wanted ter talk. Certain he was that this 'ere highwayman, White Throat they calls him, were not so fierce and dangerous as were made out by them as was out ter capture him."

"What else did he say?" Barbara encouraged.

The story did not take long to tell, for the Corporal had no flowery adjectives with which to garnish the tale. He could only repeat what the Sergeant in his company had said to astonish those who had listened to him in the bar of the Three Horseshoes.

It was a somewhat garbled tale as well as sounding very improbable. A secret wedding at midnight, a duel beside a lonely wood, the two men who had acted as coachmen walking back to their village with a handful of guineas, and the coach and horses left behind.

"The Sergeant, he swears that the lady as was at the house yestereve were the same he seeds that night five years ago," the Corporal said. "Us didn't believe him, but I thought as how, ma'am, I'd tell you what he said, seeing you were that interested in the lady."

"You were quite right to tell me, Corporal, quite right," Barbara Castlemaine said, reaching for her purse again. "I must see your Sergeant – I would like to speak to him, but it would be best for you not to say you have been here and not to know aught of the matter if anybody asks you about it. I will send my own man to talk to him."

"Yes, ma'am, I mean, my Lady, that'd be best," he said. "The Sergeant, he'd half kill me if he thought as how I had been talking about him."

"You shall not be implicated in any way, Corporal," Barbara said soothingly, and she dismissed him.

He had no sooner left the room than she summoned her Major Domo. He was a fat, bald-headed man with an impassive face and gave a casual observer the impression of being rather stupid. Actually he was both astute and intelligent. He had been Barbara's servant for only about a year, but already she found him invaluable, and in the many years he was to serve her he was to grow increasingly irreplaceable.

By the name of Oakley, he had a natural aptitude for intrigue and though he had served good masters and his references were impeccable, he had grown tired of the easy, undemanding life of a great house in Sussex and had craved the excitement and the perils of service at Court.

He had been recommended to Barbara by her first lover, the Earl of Chesterfield, to whom Oakley had once rendered a small service. As it had been a case then of rogue appealing to rogue whatever the difference in their class, Oakley, with the presumption of a man to whom a debt is owed, had asked Lord Chesterfield to obtain for him a place at Whitehall.

The Earl would not have bestirred himself on another's account had not he thought that to place Oakley in Barbara's household might, in some way, be advantageous to himself. Barbara, however, had suspected his motive, and on engaging Oakley had made it very clear that if there was any spying to be done it would be on her behalf and not on anyone else's.

Oakley's reply had been characteristic.

"My loyalty, my Lady," he said, "is to the one who pays me."

She had known then exactly the type of man with whom she was dealing, and she paid him enough to make it very unlikely that anyone would overbid his salary and thus divert his attention into other channels.

Oakley had the unusual quality of being able to persuade others to espionage. It is not easy for an Englishman to intrigue or scheme, or above all things to spy on his own race, yet Oakley could charm the most straitlaced and honourable character into accepting a bribe for information. He could persuade servants who had been loyal to their masters and mistresses for years to talk against them. He could extort information from the most unlikely people and those who, in other circumstances, would have gone to the stake rather than reveal what they knew.

His influence at times appeared almost brutally overbearing, whilst at others he had the fascination of a snake so that the willpower of his victim was snapped, and he could learn what he wanted without the slightest difficulty.

It was Oakley, of course, who had chosen the Corporal out of the whole company of men who had gone with Sir Philip Gage to Staverley, because he had known from the very look of him that everything that he knew could be drawn from him as easily as one might empty a basin of dirty water into a slop pail.

When Barbara told him now about the Sergeant and what the Corporal had repeated of the talk in the Three Horseshoes, Oakley looked pensive. In repose, his face had the expression of a pontifical Bishop, and with his white hair and rotund stomach it was hard indeed to realise that the man was at heart a master spy, the type who, born in different circumstances, might have been the head of a system of international espionage.

"I know the Sergeant, my Lady," he said, as Barbara finished speaking. "It will not be as easy to deal with him as with the Corporal. If he talked last night, it must have been in exceptional circumstances. He is not talkative as a rule."

"The exceptional circumstances were, I believe, the quantity of ale he drank," Barbara said a trifle sharply. "If drink will loosen his tongue, it should not be difficult with a cellar stocked with wine."

"I think, my Lady," Oakley said, paying, it seemed, no attention to her last remark, "that the Sergeant will talk easier to me than to you. With your permission, I will endeavour to extort the story from him by one means or another."

Barbara's eyes met his. Oakley's means of obtaining information varied. There were some, to say the least of it, which were extremely unpleasant, and she preferred to know nothing of them.

"Very well, Oakley," she said, "but I want the whole story and as soon as possible."

"I will do my best, my Lady, as you well know," Oakley said quietly.

He bowed, and his face was almost saintly in the sunshine which came through the window.

Barbara returned to her desk, but when she was alone, she found she had no further interest in the letter she had been writing. Instead, she moved restlessly across the room, her mind turning over and over again the information she had obtained.

It was past three o'clock when she realised that Rudolph had not called on her. She felt a sudden wave of anger envelop her. Three months ago, never a day had passed but he was at her door, waiting for hours, if need be, in the antechamber until she could see him. She had been sure of his devotion, taking it indeed for granted as from most of the men she knew, yet Rudolph had rather a special place in her affections.

She liked handsome men, and he was by far the most handsome of any who sought her favour. She did not love him, and if he had died she would have given him no more than a passing thought, but he had not died. Instead she suspicioned that his interest in Panthea lay not altogether in her fortune. Had any other woman been involved, Barbara would have shrugged her shoulders and forgotten

Rudolph but that he – her lover and recipient of her favours – should turn from her to someone with whom she had a personal vendetta was unforgivable.

For a moment she contemplated sending for him, then she decided that it would be unwise for him to suspect that she particularly wanted to see him today. He knew enough of her ways to know that, if she questioned him closely about what had occurred last night, she had a reason for it. What Barbara could not understand was that Rudolph should not come to her, naturally and spontaneously, and relate the failure of his mission just for the pleasure of hearing her words of consolation. Two months ago, he had not won or lost a guinea without wishing to tell her of it. She knew now, if she had not known it before, that his interest in her was waning, and mentally she added this to the account she already held against Panthea.

*

Actually, at that very moment Rudolph and Panthea were together, and if Barbara could have overheard their conversation, it would have added one more bit to the puzzle she was assembling bit by bit.

In Lady Darlington's reception room, Panthea sat in the window seat, her face turned towards the open casement, her eyes on the river up which a stately barge was passing, its brown sails full bellowed in the breeze blowing from the sea.

Rudolph was watching her as he sat on a high-backed, velvet-seated chair, his eyes wary as they rested on Panthea's averted face. He was well aware of the tension that lay between them, and one half of him was torn with a desire to plead with Panthea for her forgiveness if he had done anything to hurt or offend her. The other half of him waged a war with anger, frustration and irritation because of what he suspected she was hiding from him.

Lady Darlington had been there when he arrived, and the conversation had been of conventional politeness until at length, to Rudolph's relief, the Dowager had intimated that she must retire and lie down before the evening's festivities. He had opened the door for his aunt and kissed her hand as he bade her adieu, then as he turned to find Panthea, he saw that she had withdrawn from the sofa to the window seat and was sitting looking out with an air of aloof disinterestedness, which somehow discouraged him, despite an inner conviction that underneath her calm composure she was nervous.

He had drawn a chair near to her and seated himself on it. Then there was a long silence as he strove to find some appropriate words with which to begin the conversation, which, now that they were alone, must inevitably refer to the events of the night before.

"You must be tired," he said at length.

"On the contrary, I am rested, for I slept until noon," Panthea replied.

Still she did not turn her face from the scene outside, and at last, with an air of impulsiveness, Rudolph rose, and seating himself beside her on the window-seat, put out his hand to take her fingers in his.

"I want to apologise to you," he said in a low voice.

Her fingers were cold but still within his grasp.

"Thank you."

Panthea's voice was also cold.

"You must hear me," Rudolph said passionately. "What occurred last night was not in the least my fault. I had reason to believe that a gang of highwaymen were using the house. I told Sir Philip of this and from that moment everything was taken out of my hands. I could not withdraw my statement – indeed why should I wish to do so? The destruction and roughness of the soldiers was inexcusable, but I was only the unwilling participator in an abortive attempt to capture a notorious criminal."

Panthea took her hand from his and now at last she turned her face to look at him.

"There is no need for you to tell me all this, cousin Rudolph," she said. "I am well aware of why you went to Staverley."

He flushed at the implication in her voice, but determinedly his eyes met hers.

"It was perhaps unfortunate that we chose a night when you were there," he apologised.

"It was certainly not very pleasant for me," Panthea replied.

"And you were alone, quite alone, until we came?" Rudolph asked.

"For what reason are you questioning me, cousin Rudolph?" Panthea asked.

He was watching her and there was a faint smile at the corner of his lips, as if suddenly he was very sure of himself. Panthea was sitting very straight, her eyes were calm and her lips steady, but there was a little pulse beating at the base of her white throat, and Rudolph saw it. For a moment his glance rested on it, and then slowly he drew from his pocket a small object. He held it tightly in his hand for a second as if it gave him pleasure to crush it, and then he held it out to Panthea.

"Perhaps you would like to explain this?" he asked.

She looked at what he held and felt her heart give a frightened leap. In Rudolph's palm rested a mask – a black silk mask with two open slits in it. She did not move or make any attempt to take it from him, but her fingers were suddenly clenched tightly together in her lap.

"Where did you find it?" she asked, making no pretence not to know what he held.

"At Staverley," Rudolph replied. "It was on the dressing table in one of the bedrooms."

"Which one?" Panthea asked.

"The big room overlooking the porch," Rudolph answered.

Panthea drew in a quick breath. It was her father's room, the room known as the master's room because the head of the family always slept there. There was a great four-poster set in an alcove hung with tapestry. Its curtains were of rich green brocade, and the ostrich feather fronds on the head of its deeply carved pillars touched the ceiling.

When one lay in bed there, one could look out through the low windows over the lake and parkland and on to the far horizon, where the thick dark woods bordered the estate. Panthea remembered asking her father when he was ill if he had been lonely one afternoon, when she had been unable to be with him. He had smiled at her from his pillows and replied.

"I am never lonely here in this room. It is like a watchtower, for I can look out of the windows and see the land I love – and that our forefathers have loved – lying stretched out before me. I can watch the pigeons coming home to roost in the woods, the deer grazing beneath the oak trees, the partridges winging their way towards the cornfields, while the swallows swoop low over the lake and the wild duck rise from it for their swift flight towards other feeding grounds. What man could be lonely when he can watch and enjoy all that he most cares for?"

Panthea heard again her father's words and could see the tenderness in his eyes as he spoke. She had always thought of that room as a watchtower since that day, and now she knew that Lucius too had lain in the historic bed and watched over the lands he loved.

Yes, Lucius had slept in the master's room and there, in the place which was his by right of birth, he had discarded his disguise. Then as she looked at the black mask in Rudolph's hands, she hated it. It stood as a symbol of all that separated her from the man she loved. That little mask, fashioned of a piece of black silk, had first of all hidden Lucius from Cromwell's armies, and then later hid him equally securely from the King's men. But it separated him from her as surely as if it had been a drawn sword laid between them, and it was with the greatest difficulty that she refrained from snatching the mask from Rudolph's grasp and flinging it from her out of the open window. Instead, she spoke in calm even tones which belied the quick beating of her pulses.

"How strange that you should find a mask in my father's room! Perhaps, after all, you are not so much at fault in thinking that the house has been used by a gentleman of the road."

"A polite word for a thief," Rudolph snapped. "But surely, cousin Panthea, we can be frank with each other?"

"About what?" Panthea enquired innocently.

Rudolph hesitated. He could not quite bring himself to come out into the open, to declare that he sought the death of his cousin so that he might inherit the title and estates. He was almost sure that Panthea knew who White Throat was and that she had gone to Staverley for the very purpose of saving him from being captured, and yet he could not bring himself to put his convictions into words.

There was an intrinsic purity in Panthea's face, a shining honesty in her eyes that made him hate his own greed, even while he knew he must persist in it. He was determined that Staverley and all it stood for should be his, whatever the cost – and yet the weakness of his character was such that even in his villainy he could not be strong. While he hesitated, while the words half formed themselves on his lips only to be discarded, Panthea leant forward and took the mask from his fingers.

"I will keep this, cousin Rudolph," she said, "unless of course you find the person to whom it belongs."

She rose then, and almost before he could be aware of what she intended, she had reached the door and made a quick curtsy.

"I too would retire to rest, so pray excuse me."

She was gone before he could stop her, gone from the room with the mask in her hand, and Rudolph was left behind to feel that in some subtle way he had been outwitted and discomfited. But a moment later, in her own bedchamber, Panthea knelt with the black mask to her lips.

"Please, God, guard Lucius and keep him," she prayed. "Protect him and save him, for I love him. Dear God, I love him so much."

9

Rudolph Vyne slammed the door of his lodgings upon the visitor who had just departed, taking with him the last valuable thing Rudolph had possessed – a set of gold buttons that had decorated his best embroidered coat. The coat lay on the floor, and he kicked it disdainfully on one side as he walked across the room to sit beside the hearth in the only armchair that remained to him.

The room was sparsely furnished and in a state of untidiness and dirt of which Rudolph took no notice as he sank down in the chair and buried his face in his hands.

The duns were at him day and night for the bills he owed. He could no longer obtain credit from any reputable tradesman but must seek his food in less frequented streets and by alleys where the shopkeepers were still credulous enough to accept a gentleman at his face value and trust him with their goods.

Rudolph was well aware that the position could not continue. He had got to find money from somewhere and find it speedily. He had borrowed from what friends he had until he could no longer ask for more. He had pledged everything that he possessed of any value and now that even his gold buttons had gone there was, he knew only too well, nothing worth more than a few pence in the whole place.

If only he had been fortunate enough to win at cards last night, the situation would not have been as desperate as it was, but luck was against him and his remaining sovereigns had disappeared into the bank, and while he strove to laugh good-humouredly at his ill fortune, he had felt more like screaming out that this was the last straw and he was utterly ruined. He cursed himself now for the way he had flung his money about when he first came to London, but he had been so sure then that he would obtain funds, one way or another, that he had been improvident with the little he had – with the present disastrous results.

The only hope for him was, as he well knew, the same that had been incessantly in his mind these past few months – to be acknowledged as the owner of Staverley. But although Barbara had promised to help him, and he had pleaded with his aunt until his tongue was dry with the effort, nothing had happened, and his position remained unaltered.

He cursed the King under his breath, then rising to his feet he stared at himself in the cracked and spotted mirror over the mantelpiece. He was looking, he told himself savagely, at the face of a fool or else he was haunted by the most cursed ill luck that had ever dogged anyone. If only he had had the sense when he was in France to attach himself to the exiled King, his position might have been very different at this moment, but down on his own luck, he had no use for another of his countrymen, even if he were a King, in the same position.

He had been amongst those who believed that Charles' supporters were doomed to failure and that a Stuart would never return to the Throne. It had seemed impossible then that the iron rule of Cromwell would ever be broken, or that Charles would come to his own again. He had therefore avoided the exiled King's little band of loyal and threadbare supporters who, desperately in debt and at times even hungry for want of money, appeared of little consequence on the Continent, and were in fact treated by the French Court as impecunious and unwelcome hangers on.

He had been wrong! Rudolph saw it now. But how, he asked himself, could he have guessed that the tables would be reversed so quickly, and that Charles would return to

England in triumph? All his life, Rudolph thought, he had missed success in one way or another.

To begin with he had been a second son, and he had hated his eldest brother for as long almost as he could remember. When Edwin was killed at the Battle of Worcester, Rudolph had, with ill-concealed delight, taken upon himself the mantle of the heir presumptive to his father's position and estates. But he had never got on well with his father, and Lord Arthur Vyne had made it clear that, unless he behaved himself and took his responsibilities more seriously, they could not continue to live under the same roof.

Enraged at such threats, Rudolph had quarrelled bitterly with his father and found to his astonishment that he was cut off with a very small allowance, and that the doors of his own home were closed to him. He had thought it of no consequence until his money ran out, then he had gone abroad, first as companion to a young and rich acquaintance, and later as courier to an old gentleman with peculiar vices.

Neither employment had lasted long, and Rudolph had soon found himself sinking lower and lower in his search for money. There were too many Englishmen of gentle birth in the same position in Europe for his plight to excite any interest or sympathy, and it was only by living a swashbuckling existence of duels, robbery and seduction that Rudolph managed to keep himself in funds.

His only real asset was his good looks. Women fell in love with him, and it was entirely because their hearts beat faster at the sight of his handsome face that he managed to extract himself from several prisons and find a more comfortable bed waiting for him outside than he would otherwise have enjoyed.

The Restoration, however, gave him the chance he was looking for. He borrowed a considerable sum of money from a French family who believed him to be an ardent and loyal supporter of the newly-crowned King, and with his pockets heavy with gold, a state of affairs that he had not enjoyed for a long time, Rudolph came to London. He bribed, cajoled and shoved his way into court circles and then, by a really lucky chance, he managed to attract the attention of Barbara Castlemaine.

Rudolph had, by force of circumstances, been forced to make love to so many women that he thought himself immune from their charms, and that it was impossible for him ever to be swept off his feet by either love or passion. Barbara had proved him wrong, and she aroused his desires as no other woman had been able to do, so that he was even prepared to spend his precious gold on her. He haunted her doorstep and because he was handsome, and had also a buccaneering manner of making love that amused her, Barbara favoured him for longer than the time expended on most of her lovers.

But now Rudolph knew that their passion for each other was dying. Barbara could still arouse him, but the thought of her was no longer the burning flame it had been a few months ago. Instead, he found himself thinking of another face, and of eyes that seemed at times almost purple in their soft depths. So frequently did the image of Panthea come to his mind that he had even asked himself the question whether he would still have thought of her had she been penniless. He had almost laughed at his own question, and then felt frustrated and angry because he knew only too well that he was making no headway in the courting of his cousin.

Staring into his own eyes now, Rudolph suddenly brought his fist down on the mantelpiece with a crash which sent an empty tankard standing there tumbling to the floor. It rolled about for a moment, spilling a few dark drops of ale on to the dirty boards, adding to the general disorder and squalor of the room.

Rudolph's servant had deserted him two weeks ago, taking in lieu of three months' wages his gold ring and his evening cloak lined with fur. Since then. the bed had remained unmade, the hearth unswept. Yet at least the room was somewhere to sleep, though judging by the landlord's threats even that comfort would not be his for much longer.

He had to get either Staverley or Panthea immediately, Rudolph told himself and, if possible, both. He was a desperate man and could no longer brook delay, however plausible the reason for it. He turned from the mirror and going to a cupboard, took out his second-best coat. He put it on. It was by no means as smart as the one from which the buttons had been cut by the importunate wine merchant who had threatened Rudolph with the debtor's prison at Newgate if he did not pay at least a portion of the large sum he owed.

Nevertheless, when Rudolph had changed his shoes and arranged a fresh ruff at his throat, he looked at least passably smart, and his appearance would not be questioned at Whitehall. He had not eaten all day and he was looking forward to the dinner to which his aunt had invited him in her apartments. There would be a number of people there, and although Rudolph knew that the majority of them would be elderly, and to his mind extremely dull, Panthea would be present, and that was enough at least for the moment.

At the thought of her he felt his pulses quicken and decided that astonishingly, though not unpleasantly, he was falling in love. It would have been enough to marry Panthea for her fortune, but that he should also love her was a streak of good fortune he had never anticipated would be his.

As he walked along the narrow streets, avoiding with some difficulty the dirty garbage-choked gutters down the centre of them, Rudolph began to plan his future life at Staverley with Panthea as his wife. There was a swagger in his walk as he approached the Palace, and a smile of elation on his lips which made many a woman stare after him.

Even Lady Gage, so old and withered that it was hard to believe that the springing sap of youth had ever pulsated through her veins, clutched at her husband's arm as the coach swung into the palace and remarked, "See Philip, there is Lady Darlington's nephew – Rudolph Vyne. A finely set up young man, I declare. I cannot imagine why you do not bring him to dine with us one night."

"The man has no brains," Sir Philip answered. "Did I not tell you how he led me on a wild goose chase, telling me tales of highwaymen and the like, and all we discovered was a pretty wench reading a book at the fireside?"

"And that in itself was extraordinary, if you ask me," Lady Gage said snappily. "I cannot believe Lady Darlington knows that her great-niece goes about alone at night. No daughter of mine would behave in such a way, I promise you that."

"Now, Ethel, I have warned you already that you must say nothing of this to Lady Darlington," Sir Philip admonished. "What happens in the pursuit of my duties is no business of yours or of anyone else. I would not have told you of the matter had not it struck me as being most risky for a young girl to ride out at night, when the roads are infested with cutthroats and thieves."

"Then if you think it so dangerous, Philip, surely it is all the more important for me to tell Lady Darlington of her great-niece's escapades?"

"You must say nothing, nothing, Ethel," Sir Philip replied testily.

"Very well, if you insist," Lady Gage agreed grudgingly, "but that girl will come to a bad end, you mark my words."

The coach was drawing up to set them down at the door of the Palace.

"You must find your own way to Lady Darlington's apartments," Sir Philip remarked. "You will remember that I have to make a call on my Lady Castlemaine. I cannot believe that it will take very long."

Lady Gage snorted. "I should hope not indeed. I should like to know what that woman wants with you. I can tell you one thing, Philip, I don't care for your going alone to her apartment. It is, well, it is not safe."

It was a second or two before Sir Philip took in the full meaning of his wife's insinuation, but when he did, he preened himself a little, as if the very thought of what she suspected was by no means unpleasant.

"Duty is duty, my dear," he said pompously. "In my work I must interview many strange people of both high and low degree, but you can, I assure you, trust me to conduct myself with all possible propriety."

"I wish I could be sure of that," Lady Gage answered with asperity. "The woman is shameless, as we all know. You are certain that you must obey her command? Personally, I should pay no heed to it!"

"My dear, if I did that we should doubtless find ourselves on the way back to Bedfordshire. You forget that my Lady Castlemaine, whatever you may think of her, has the ear of the King."

"I have not forgotten it," Lady Gage retorted grimly, "and the only excuse one can make for him is that all men are weak in the hands of a shameless woman who will stick at nothing to gain her own ends. But if the King melts at a trollop's smile, what about you, Philip?"

Sir Philip stroked his fair moustache and tugged at his wig to settle it more firmly on his bald head.

Life should not consist entirely of work, he reflected inwardly, and if work could be combined with pleasure, so much the better. He could not expect Ethel to understand his position. She had been a loyal and true wife to him for over twenty-five years, in fact they had celebrated their Silver Wedding just six months ago. But at the same time. she had never understood him.

It was true, he had married her because her father had been Lord Lieutenant of Bedfordshire and there was no one but Ethelfreda to inherit his very comfortable house and prosperous estate. Ethelfreda had been thin and angular, even as a young girl, and Sir Philip liked his women curved and well covered with flesh. One could not have everything, he thought then, and he thought the same again now as he remembered the lowcut neckline of Lady Castlemaine's gowns which revealed rather than concealed the warm curves of her white bosom.

"Philip, we are here! What are you dreaming about?" Lady Gage remarked, recalling his thoughts to the necessity of alighting from the coach.

They separated just inside the door. Lady Gage turned left towards the Countess of Darlington's apartments over looking the river, while Sir Philip went right in search of Lady Castlemaine's, which overlooked the Privy Garden.

Her Ladyship was housed, Sir Philip noted with a little smirk, not far from His Majesty's own apartments, and he imagined fondly that he was the first to be so sagacious as to notice the fact, whereas the whole court had discussed little else when Barbara Castlemaine first moved to Whitehall.

Lady Gage arrived at Lady Darlington's front door almost at the same time as Rudolph Vyne and, as he swept off his hat in a courtly bow at the sight of her, Lady Gage gave him what she imagined was a beguiling smile, but which in fact was a contortion of the lips that made her appear more than ever like a horse.

"You are dining here tonight, Mr. Vyne?" Lady Gage asked.

"I am, and need I say how delightful it is to know that you too will be a fellow guest," Rudolph said in his most fascinating manner.

He had made it his policy for many years to be exceptionally charming to elderly women. It had paid him a dividend on more than one occasion, and he was particularly anxious now to please the wife of Sir Philip Gage.

As they waited for the door to open, he glanced down at the gown she wore of saffron figured silk and spoke softly.

"May I compliment you on your gown, Lady Gage? It is not often one meets a woman of great intelligence who also knows how to dress."

He could not have chosen a better approach to Lady Gage's heart. She had long considered that she was wasted amongst the dull, quiet-living squires and the wives in Bedfordshire. She believed, quite erroneously, that she was well read and imagined that, had she been given the opportunity, she would have been able to have a salon filled with all the wit and genius that the century had produced. She simpered now, and drawing a little nearer to Rudolph, her eyes fixed almost hypnotically on his, she replied,

"One day you and I must have a little talk together, for I see we have much in common."

"I am yours to command," Rudolph assured her, while he wondered if there was any likelihood of his being able to obtain a loan from the old woman. She was stupid and ugly enough to be flattered into believing he was interested in her, and after that it should not be difficult to obtain some pickings of one sort or another.

His speculations, however, came quickly to an end, for the door was opened by a footman and they passed into the lighted hall. Having left their coats there, they were announced in stentorian tones to their hostess who was waiting for them in her reception room.

A number of people were standing around and, as Rudolph had anticipated, they were elderly and what he termed to himself the pious set at court. He saw Panthea standing on the other side of the room, talking to the Archbishop of Canterbury, and as quickly as he could, Rudolph hurried to her side.

She was looking very lovely tonight, he thought, in a dress of silver brocade embroidered with tiny pearls. She wore a string of pearls round her neck too, and Rudolph guessed them to be valuable, but somehow even he could not continue to think for long in terms of money when he was looking down into Panthea's eyes as she greeted him with a faint smile.

Her fingers were cold as he raised them to his lips, and he remembered for the first time that she might be angry with him for what had passed between them that afternoon. It was then he felt an emotion he had never known before – a mixture of affection, respect, and admiration, which was not far from adoration. It was revolutionary and epoch making that he, Rudolph, should be apprehensive of a woman's anger.

He felt a strange constriction in his throat and a feeling in his heart that he had never known before. He longed to go down on one knee, to raise the hem of Panthea's gown to his lips, then hotly within him rose another emotion, a desire strong and insistent so that he knew, whatever the obstacles in his way, he would override them all, so that Panthea would be his and he could possess her.

She was so small and so fragile that he thought in that moment that he could snatch her up in his arms and force her, by his sheer overwhelming strength, to promise him that which he most desired. And yet, even while he stood fired with these strange feelings, he must utter a conventional greeting and watch her lips move with some banal words in return.

"I have got to see you alone," he contrived to say at last, speaking so low that only she could hear the words.

"Why?" she enquired.

There was a coldness in her voice which should have warned him to go no further.

"I have something to say to you that you alone must hear," Rudolph said. "Meet me tonight when this party is over, in the Privy Gardens or anywhere you wish so long as we can be alone."

He saw a sudden flash of anger in her eyes as she replied.

"I think, cousin Rudolph, that you are forgetting yourself. I am not in the habit of making assignations with young men in the Privy Gardens or anywhere else."

Her words stung him and before he could prevent it, his answer had leapt out.

"No, you prefer to go to Staverley to meet them there."

The blood flamed into Panthea's face at his tone, but her eyes met his steadily, then without a word, she turned her back on him and walked across the room to stand at her great-aunt's side. He knew that she did it deliberately to show him that she was not unprotected, and yet he was not abashed or even repentant at what he had said. He was inflamed now by a desire stronger than anything he had ever known before. Panthea should be his, he was determined on it, and nothing she could say or do would matter, for he intended that she should be his wife.

He made no attempt to pursue her to her great-aunt's side. Instead. he remained where he was and watched her, hoping that she was aware that his eyes were on her and that the fact made her uncomfortable. He felt now as he had felt the first time he ever went stalking. Until the excitement of the chase was on him, he had always imagined it was a dull sport. Then, as he began to manoeuvre his way up the moor, drawing nearer to the princely animal without its being aware of his presence, the lust to kill had come upon him and he had known that the stag could not escape him.

He had the same feeling now as he watched Panthea. She might strive against him, but it would be of no avail. He would conquer her, so that ultimately she must surrender to him. He was so intent on watching Panthea that he did not realise that his aunt had moved to speak to one of her friends and was now at his side.

The Countess of Darlington was looking more than usual like a bird of prey, Rudolph thought. Her eyes were deep set in her head, making her nose as pronounced as the beak of a toucan. Her white hair was dressed with purple ribbons and her gown was of the same colour, so that her skin in contrast was the colour and texture of old parchment. The diamonds she wore round her throat and at her wrists were no brighter than her eyes, which, shrewd and perceptive, seemed to Rudolph to examine him as if he were some strange creature that she had never seen before.

He had no guilty conscience where his aunt was concerned, and yet she made him feel uncomfortable. He seemed to be watching his face, drawing from him some secret that he had hidden there, although what it was he had not the slightest idea.

"Well, what have you to say for yourself, Rudolph?" she asked at length a little sharply, and he felt as gauche and ill at ease as any schoolboy as he replied.

"What should I have to say, Aunt Anne?"

"You know well enough," Lady Darlington replied, and then, as if she saw that his bewilderment was genuine, she added, "Panthea was crying after you left. What had you said to upset her?"

Rudolph made a gesture with his hands as if he disowned all responsibility – then he decided to speak frankly with his aunt and to hide his intentions no longer.

"Why my presence should have upset Panthea I have no idea, Aunt Anne. I but asked her, as I have asked her before, to be my wife. Will you not help her to make a wise decision? I love her and I know that I can make her happy, but apart from that our marriage must obviously be an advantageous one, for together we can unite what is left of the family and restore Staverley to its former glory."

Rudolph spoke eagerly and he was not prepared for the sudden darkening of his aunt's face or the look she gave him of ill-concealed dislike.

"Panthea may wed whom she wishes," she replied, "but as for the marriage being advantageous, that would certainly apply in your case, Rudolph, for Panthea has a rich dowry, as well you know."

"I, in my turn, can offer her Staverley," Rudolph said proudly.

"It is not yet yours," Lady Darlington retorted. "When it is, we will perhaps consider the matter, but until then I do not consider you an eligible suitor for Panthea's hand."

Rudolph bit his lips in an effort to check the hot words that trembled on his tongue, and only with the greatest effort of will could he prevent himself from speaking angrily in reply. He hated his aunt at that moment with a hatred that was almost fanatical, and if she had fallen down dead, he would have shouted his joy aloud for all to hear. Only to look at her was to recall his father, for they were not unlike in face, and he could remember his father speaking in just such a corrective tone of voice, while he had seethed with an inner resentment and longed passionately for revenge.

He loathed all his relatives, he thought at that moment. His aunt Anne with her penetrating eyes, which seemed to bore into him and lay bare the shifty rottenness of his thoughts and feelings, and his cousin Lucius who stood between him and Staverley. He had always hated Lucius even when they were boys. Lucius, elder by several years, had always managed to make him feel small, insignificant and inferior.

He remembered what friends Lucius and his brother Edwin had been. They had all spent part of their holidays together, and for a short period of time before they went to Eton, they had shared a tutor. He was younger than Lucius and Edwin and yet they had tried never to let him feel unwanted or excluded from their games. It was the very effort they made which had infuriated him. He used to lie awake at night loathing them, wishing he could think of some way in which he could prove his own superiority and have them both at his mercy.

All his life he had wanted to be top dog, to be the eldest, the most important, the person to whom everyone looked up, the one who had power and wealth. But life had given him none of these things and he could not even command the affection of those around him. His mother had loved him, and yet even his affection for her had been tainted by the thought that she might perhaps love his brother better.

She had died when he was comparatively young, and he had always known that Edwin was his father's favourite. He had hated every word they spoke together, every look they exchanged. He had wanted to be loved, yet there was nothing he could do to prevent the frustrated yearnings of his pride and emotion from spoiling every affection and tarnishing every friendship. Those who met him casually judged him to be a good-looking, good-humoured young man without much brain and energy. They had no idea of the tempest that seethed within him, and only those who had seen him ruthlessly fighting a duel with someone who had offended him or deliberately pursuing a woman for her money, knew that there was within him a steel-like resolve that could neither be torn aside nor placated.

It was as his aunt turned to leave him, her face wrinkled in a smile for some more favoured guest, that Rudolph knew what he must do. A plan fell into place in his mind. This, he thought, was where his luck turned, where he was no longer the importunate beggar at the gates, but the man in possession, the lord of all he surveyed.

Only once before had he felt so sure of anything and that was when he met Barbara Castlemaine and knew that she was his for the taking. They had met in the Stone Gallery, where all the world could come and go at will to stare at the magnificent pictures, or merely to wander up and down watching the grand personages of the court as they passed to and fro on their errands or met their various friends and exchanged the latest gossip.

Every rumour, every scandal, every intrigue was whispered about in the Stone Gallery almost before it took place. Rudolph, on arrival in London, haunted the Gallery. There he had grown to know who was at court and had made full use of his family's name in obtaining introductions.

"You will forgive my introducing myself, my Lord," he would say to some distinguished nobleman, "but my father spoke of you so often and he would, I know, wish me to pay you my respects."

"May I be permitted to congratulate your Ladyship," he would say humbly to a Lady of Quality.

"On what?" she would enquire, taking in with a swift glance the very presentable appearance of the stranger who had accosted her and noting the fine quality of his clothes and the grace with which he bowed.

"On being the most beautiful woman I have seen since I returned to England from exile in France," Rudolph would say audaciously, managing to convey the impression that he was a Royalist who had crossed the Channel to escape arrest and must therefore, like all those who had been in exile, command a certain amount of sympathy.

Yet all those methods had been unnecessary when he met Barbara. She was passing down the Stone Gallery from a party and he had stepped forward to watch her advance, her dark head held high and surmounted by a hat festooned with ostrich feathers, her white, heavily-ringed hand holding the long, bejewelled stick with which she had set a new fashion among the other ladies of the court. Her skirts were so wide that people must step back to let her pass, and behind her ran a small well-dressed boy, as heavily bejewelled as his mistress.

There was no one in the gallery who did not gasp with admiration at Barbara's flaunting exotic beauty. But where the others stepped back, Rudolph stepped forward. She had come right up to him and still he did not move, then moving her stick as if she would brush him from her path, she spoke haughtily.

"You will permit me, sir, to proceed on my way."

He looked deep into her eyes as he replied.

"Alas, I cannot move, for I am rooted to the spot in admiration and adoration."

His voice had deepened on the last word and it seemed to vibrate between them so that Barbara had hesitated before she spoke, while her eyes were still held by his.

"Who are you?"

She spoke the question softly, and yet he had not bowed as was customary in making an introduction.

Instead, he said, "A man who has seen the heavens open for the first time. I had not known there was such loveliness upon this earth."

She had laughed a little then, a low soft sound within her throat.

"I was in a hurry," she said at length.

"It is not important," Rudolph said. "But there is something else of vital import."

As if he held her spellbound by some magic, she asked, "What is that?"

He told her in a voice too soft, too low for those in the gallery to hear. Speculative eyes watched them move away together and noted that he climbed into Lady Castlemaine's coach which was waiting outside. That was the beginning, and Rudolph knew that fate had directed every move, every word of what had been done and said. Fate was helping him now. He could feel it directing him, seeing as clearly as if he were but a pawn in omnipotent hands, every move he must make.

Beside him, the Archbishop of Canterbury drew a watch from his vest pocket.

"Fifteen minutes after six of the clock," he said a little testily. "I wonder what is delaying the announcement that dinner is served."

As if in answer to his question, the double doors at the end of the long reception room were flung open, but instead of a butler entering, the astonished guests looked round to see that Sir Philip Gage stood there, red-faced and invested with an unexpected dignity, while behind him, quite clearly discernible by the light of the candles in the hall, stood some soldiers.

Lady Darlington, who had been speaking with Lady Gage, did not at first see them. As she saw Sir Philip enter, she moved forward with a conventional smile upon her lips and her hand outstretched.

"So, you have come at last, Sir Philip," she exclaimed. "We were beginning to think you had deserted us."

She had almost reached Sir Philip's side before she saw the soldiers behind him. She looked at them in astonishment and then at Sir Philip, who under her gaze appeared suddenly aggressive.

"It is with considerable regret," he began in a high, autocratic voice, "that I have come here in pursuit of my duty rather than, as I had intended, as a guest of your hospitality."

"What do you mean?" Lady Darlington asked quickly.

"It is my most painful duty," Sir Philip replied, "to arrest your great-niece, Lady Panthea Vyne, and to take her immediately from here for safekeeping pending her trial."

"Arrest Panthea!" Lady Darlington exclaimed. "I have never heard such stuff and nonsense in my life. Why, good heavens, man, what has Panthea done that she should be arrested?"

Sir Philip took a deep breath, and then replied stentoriously, "I charge her in the name of the law with the murder of her husband, Mr. Christian Drysdale."

10

Panthea sat facing her lawyer, her hands in her lap, her eyes serious as she listened to the questions he put to her, the answers to which he jotted down, using a long quill pen which squeaked as it flowed over the paper.

"I want you to give me the most accurate description possible of this highwayman who you say stopped the coach some half an hour or so after you and your husband had left the Church in which you were married."

Mr. Dobson's voice was dry and slightly grating. He was a thin, sallow-faced man of over fifty who looked as if he had never enjoyed a square meal, and whose back was bent until it was almost deformed from poring over papers and manuscripts. But he had the reputation of being the most astute lawyer in London, and Lady Darlington had made most searching enquiries about him before she engaged him to represent her great-niece.

He turned over a page covered with exquisitely formed copperplate writing, and when Panthea did not reply, he looked up at her from under his eyebrows.

"The description, my Lady," he prompted.

Still Panthea did not speak. She was indeed wondering what she could say. She was determined that nothing would force her to give an adequate description of Lucius so that yet another crime could be recorded against him. She was wondering just how much the man who had informed against her had said. Had he, for instance, overheard Christian Drysdale as he stepped from the coach address Lucius by his nickname?

As if her silence irritated him, Mr. Dobson cleared his throat.

"It is, your Ladyship will appreciate, of extreme importance that this crime should be pinned down on the man who actually committed it. You tell me that the highwayman forced your husband from the coach and fought a duel with him. I am, of course, not questioning your Ladyship's word when I say it will be difficult to make such a story sound convincing to a judge and jury."

"But it is the truth," Panthea said.

"They say that truth is stranger than fiction," the lawyer replied, and for a moment a very faint smile twisted his thin, almost bloodless face. "We must, of course, tell the truth yet at the same time we must endeavour to make it sound truthful."

"But that *is* the truth," Panthea protested. "A highwayman – two highwaymen, to be exact, held up the coach and later one of them fought a duel with, with Mr. Drysdale in which he was killed."

She could not bring herself to say the words 'my husband'. They sounded too fantastic, too unreal.

"A duel is, of course, not murder," the lawyer said, "but you know that the charge brought against you is very different. It alleges that these men were not highwaymen at all, but servants or ruffians hired by you for the very purpose of disposing of your husband so that you could obtain his money."

"That is a lie," Panthea answered hotly. "I married Mr. Drysdale secretly at his request, and as I have already told you, I agreed to the marriage only because there was no other way in which I could save my brother's life. He tricked and deceived me, but it was only after I was married to him that I realised what he had done."

"And who conveyed this information to you?" the lawyer said.

Again Panthea was silent, not daring to answer the question. She could see all too clearly how fantastic her story sounded, and she could well sympathise with Mr. Dobson's fear that no one would believe it.

She knew it would be more credible should she reveal that the highwayman in question had been her own cousin. Who else would be so interested in Richard's death? Who else would have risked his own life to give her her freedom? Yet if she told all this even to her own lawyer, Lucius would be implicated and it might spur the authorities on to make even greater efforts to capture him. Whichever way she regarded her story, it seemed to her to be beset by pitfalls. And as if he sensed a little of the tumult going on inside her, Mr. Dobson spoke in a voice suddenly tired and weary.

"If you will not be frank with me, my Lady, then I must tell you there is little I can do to help you. I have a case to build up, a brief to prepare for your Counsel. Unless I know the full facts of what occurred, there is every likelihood of our being confronted in court by something we least anticipate and that might prove us inaccurate at the very commencement of the case, and thus prejudice the jury so that there would be no chance of the verdict being given in your favour."

Panthea knew that he spoke sensibly, but she knew that she dared not reveal the whole truth of what had occurred on that strange night five years ago. How could she explain to the lawyer, for instance, that she had trusted Lucius instinctively from the first moment he looked into the coach and saw her crying on the floor of it, the body of her pet dog cradled in her arms? How could she explain what she had felt when he told her that Richard had been hanged and she had sobbed her heart out against his shoulder? How could she even put into words that a highwayman, a common thief of the road, had never seemed for a moment a stranger to her, so that she had trusted him completely and absolutely as he decided her future and saved her from the horror and degradation of marriage to a brute?

It all sounded so fantastic, Panthea thought, and she felt sure that Mr. Dobson was right and neither judge nor jury would believe a word of her tale.

She felt, with an almost fatalistic calm, that she was doomed. The horror of being taken to Newgate had left its scar upon her, so that now she felt that little worse could happen to her. At first, as she had driven away in the coach from the Palace, she had felt numb so that everything had the quality of a dream, and she could hardly realise that it was actually happening to her personally.

The cries, the consternation, the astonishment of her great-aunt's guests, and Lady Darlington's indignation, had seemed to come to her from a long distance, as if she heard them but faintly and was hardly aware of what they were saying. When Marta brought her cloak and placed it round her shoulders she realised that the woman was crying, and, dry-eyed herself, she reached up to kiss her cheek. But she had found it impossible to say anything. The words of farewell would not come to her lips and in silence she had gone from her great-aunt's apartment, the clatter of the soldiers' boots on the polished boards ringing ominously in her ears as they escorted her down the passages and stairs that led to the palace gate.

Fortunately there were few people about at this hour of the evening, but those there were stared curiously as Panthea was marched past them. She had been half-afraid that she might be taken on foot through the streets, for she had seen other prisoners jeered at by the crowds and even pelted with rotten vegetables, and she felt that, if this should happen to her, she would die at the shame of it.

To her relief a coach was waiting, and when she had climbed inside, Sir Philip followed her with two soldiers who sat opposite them with their backs to the horses.

She had realised when the coach drove off that Sir Philip was uncomfortable. The pompous air of authority with which he had faced her great-aunt and the guests gathered in the reception room was replaced now by an almost apologetic embarrassment. It was as if the crowd of people had given him encouragement, and now, when he was alone with his victim save for their impassive guard on the opposite seat, Sir Philip became a mere man who had insulted a lady, his superior both by birth and social standing.

It must have been hard for him to believe that the fragile, gentle beauty of Panthea's face hid the heart of a murderess. The gravity of her big eyes, the trembling of her soft lips, would have made any man, however hardened, feel that he was behaving like a brute, and Sir Philip, who had a soft spot in his heart for all pretty women, felt a sudden distress sweep over him.

When he had left Lady Castlemaine's apartment he had felt elated, a knight in shining armour going to avenge a foul deed. The way Barbara had spoken to him had appealed to his manhood, the soft flattery of her voice had inspired him with a grandiose conception of his own ability. But now that he had acted, now that he had arrested this girl, of whom he had been told such dreadful things, he felt as if he had inadvertently crushed a songbird between his hands, or tortured a soft Persian kitten which was no more capable of committing a crime than a baby in arms.

His perturbation was not helped by the scene that greeted them when they reached Newgate. Even as the great iron-studded doors were unlocked, the foul stench of the place assailed their nostrils and the shrieks of the unfortunate creatures imprisoned behind the high walls came to their ears.

Panthea said nothing, but her face was drained of all colour as she had her first sight of Newgate's inhabitants. There were women naked to the waist, shrieking abuse at the warders or fighting with each other until the blood poured from the wounds they inflicted with their long nails. There were men fettered to the walls by chains, which had grown into their limbs so that the festered stench of their wounds was almost overpowering.

The disorder and the darkness – for the light came only from a few flickering lanterns – made the place seem like some inferno of hell, and unconsciously Panthea shrank against Sir Philip as if she sought protection from the very man who had condemned her to this. Brusquely, in a voice that was all the more peremptory because he was ashamed of himself, Sir Philip commanded the warders to lead them to the better part of the prison where wealthy prisoners could buy for themselves decent lodgings.

Even the best lodgings, however, did not compare very favourably with the rooms that Panthea had been used to all her life. The wardress, who unlocked the door to show them a sitting room overlooking the street and a bed chamber opening out from it, remarked that it was 'fit for a Queen'. After the horrors they had seen in the other part of the building, Panthea was inclined to agree with her, but even so the small, confined rooms with their low ceilings, tiny windows and dirty, undecorated walls were not particularly prepossessing.

"You can order your food from outside," Sir Philip said gruffly, "and the women prisoners will be glad to wait on you at the price of a few shillings."

"Thank you." Panthea spoke for the first time since they had left the palace.

"You will, of course, be allowed to see your lawyer tomorrow," Sir Philip went on, "and the visits of other people can be arranged, I believe."

"Thank you."

Panthea inclined her head, and when she raised it again she pushed back the hood of her cloak so that the light from the tapers glinted on her fair hair and revealed the frightened pallor of her little face. Almost without meaning to do so, Sir Philip took a step towards her and lifted her hand so that it lay in his.

"I cannot tell you," he said in a low voice, all his pomposity gone, "how much I regret that it was necessary for me to put you under arrest. Perhaps there is some mistake, in fact I am sure there must be, and I beg of you to send for your lawyer the first thing in the morning."

Coldly, and with a pride that surmounted her most tremulous fears, Panthea drew her hand from his.

"You have done your duty, Sir Philip," she said. "I think there is nothing more to be said."

His eyes fell before hers and he turned away towards the door. The wardress was waiting there for him and gruffly, in a voice that was strangely unlike his own, he said, "Have a care of this prisoner and see that she has all that she requires, or it will be the worse for you."

"Her Lidyship will be right enough," the wardress wheezed. "Don't yer trouble yerself, sir. We always does our best for 'em as can pay."

She gave a wheezing laugh as she said the last words, and Sir Philip uttered an oath beneath his breath as he walked quickly away down the long dark corridor. The wardress watched him go and then, turning to Panthea, she said sharply,

"That'll be ten shillings for each of the rooms, my Lidy, and if yer wish to have yer own furniture brought in, that'll be extra. Meals are as yer order 'em and two shillings for the man as fetches 'em from the tavern. If yer want a woman to clean the rooms and wait on yer, that'll be five shillings a day."

Panthea opened the purse that she carried in her hand and gave the woman two guineas. The wardress's eyes noted that the purse was heavy, and her smile was ingratiating as she took the guineas in her dirty fingers and bit each one with her broken teeth to see that they were genuine.

"And what would yer Lidyship like this evening?" she enquired. "A bottle of wine? I will send the boy across the road to buy one for yer if yer but speak the word."

"I want nothing," Panthea replied, "nothing at all."

The wardress looked disappointed. The money clinked as she slipped it into the pocket of her dress.

"I've got to lock yer in," she said as she went towards the door, "so if yer want anythin', shout. Sooner or later, somebody will hear yer, that is if the noise below is not too deafenin'."

She grinned as she spoke. Her two front teeth were missing and the rest, decayed and broken, were not a prepossessing sight. Then she was gone and Panthea heard the key turn in the lock.

She had not slept that night, nor even lain down on the bed, for one look at the dirty stained blankets and torn covers had revolted her so that she sat upright in a chair, almost afraid to lean back against the hard wooden back. She knew that rich prisoners were allowed to take their furniture to prison with them, but she had not realised the absolute necessity for it. The dirty rooms, and what she was certain were vermin-infested walls, appalled her, but even if her bed had been spread with the finest linen and the softest down pillows, it was unlikely that she would have been able to sleep.

She soon realised these rooms were considered some of the best in the prison because they overlooked the street, but even so the howls, screams and shouts from the poorer quarters were very audible and she knew that only the most abject fatigue would have enabled her to rest.

At times it seemed to Panthea as if the noise came not from human beings at all, but from savage animals, and when she remembered the creatures she had seen in the yard of the prison, she thought that perhaps they had lost or forgotten any humanity they might ever have possessed.

Seated in her chair in front of a fireless hearth, she had, as the night grew on, begun to realise all too vividly the predicament she was in. She had no idea how the death of Christian Drysdale had been discovered, but she was quite sure that the person who had been instrumental in discovering it had been Barbara Castlemaine.

Sir Philip had come straight to arrest her after visiting Barbara Castlemaine's apartments, and had he known what he was about to do before he had gone there, Lady Gage would not have come ahead of him as a guest of her great-aunt's hospitality. That much was obvious, though how and by what means Lady Castlemaine had discovered that Christian Drysdale was dead, and that she had once been married to him – Panthea had no idea.

In the morning, her lawyer had brought her fuller details of the charges preferred against her, and a few days later he had even graver news.

"They have discovered Mr. Drysdale's body," he told Panthea on his arrival at the prison. "I knew they had been searching for it these past two days, but last night they discovered it and the remains have been brought to London."

"What difference does that make?" Panthea asked. "They knew he was dead."

"They believed him dead because a man gave evidence of having seen him killed," the lawyer replied. "They had to prove it, and that will not be difficult now that they have the body."

"A man saw him killed?" Panthea asked. "Then it must be one of the coachmen who has given evidence against me."

"That is right," the lawyer agreed. "He is now a Sergeant in the King's Own Regiment and will be, I understand, the chief witness for the prosecution."

Panthea strove to remember what the coachmen had been like, but all she could recall were two shadowy figures lurking in the darkness of the trees then scrambling to pick up the guineas which the highwayman had thrown for them.

"Does the whole prosecution rest on this one man's word?" she asked.

"You were arrested on his evidence alone," the lawyer replied. "It was not sufficient, you understand, but Sir Philip was persuaded to act by a lady whose power at court at times exceeds the bounds of all decency and correct procedure."

The lawyer spoke drily, and Panthea knew that here was someone who was by no means an admirer of Lady Castlemaine.

"I have already lodged a protest," the lawyer went on, "but it can have little effect now that the evidence against you has increased and there appears to be every justification for the action that was taken."

"I can see that," Panthea said quietly.

The lawyer glanced down at his notes.

"They have also interrogated the Priest who married you," he said. "I understand he has made a statement that leaves little doubt that the ceremony did take place at midnight, as is alleged."

"I have not denied it," Panthea said.

"There is now the difficulty of proving that this highwayman did in fact exist," the lawyer went on. "No one is suggesting that you killed your husband with your own hand. That would obviously have been impossible seeing that he was a big man, and you are unusually small. But the prosecution alleges that you hired his assailants, and if they can prove this, then that will indeed be murder."

Gradually as he built up the case, Panthea could see all too clearly the cleverness of Lady Castlemaine's attack upon her. The coachman, Panthea was sure, must have told the truth, for there was no reason for him to hide his facts as regards the highwayman, or to allege that the fight which had taken place had been anything but a fair one, merely two gentlemen equally at home with a sword fighting a duel in the time-honoured manner.

Panthea was sure that it was Lady Castlemaine who had twisted the story just enough to suit her own ends and to make it sound sinister and ominous. But what was going to be so difficult to explain was the fact, as Panthea well knew, that she had taken Christian Drysdale's money and used it for herself.

The question of explaining her fortune had not yet arisen, but Panthea was sure that sooner or later it would come to light that Christian Drysdale carried the taxes that he collected with him in the coach, and then an astute brain would soon put two and two together and Panthea's fortune would be suspect. So few Royalist families had been left with any money by the time of the Restoration and the fact that the Staverley estates had been confiscated was only too well known.

There had been a great number of people who, having known her father or her uncles, had made oblique references to the fact that it was surprising that Panthea was an heiress. They had not actually questioned her, but they had made remarks that invited her to confide in them and which betrayed their curiosity as strongly as if they had said the words out loud.

It was only a question of time before such curiosity was expressed openly, Panthea thought, and then her defence, weak as it was, would be weakened still further by the lameness of her explanations regarding the money. The case for the prosecution was very simple. She could see only too clearly the way their minds would work.

Christian Drysdale, an elderly tax-collector, had become infatuated by the pretty daughter of one of the noblemen he visited regularly. He courted the girl, and because she was afraid to tell her family that she wished to marry him, she had agreed that they should elope at dead of night. But her interest in him lay in the fact that he was rich and that she coveted his wealth. Therefore she hired assassins, who, after dragging the bridegroom from the coach but a short while after the wedding ceremony, stabbed him to death and assisted the bride to make off with the plunder.

It was the sort of story that could be easily believed, Panthea thought, and though she was bound to evoke a certain amount of sympathy as a member of a Royalist family who had continually supported King Charles II, there were also a number of people who would believe her capable of any crime because she was a member of the Court. There were many sober and decent English men and women who were shocked at the loose living and pleasure seeking of those who had their lodgings in Whitehall.

But whatever she said, whatever happened to her, whatever judgment she received, Panthea was determined that not by any word or deed of hers would she implicate the man she loved, the man who had saved her from a life that would have been far worse than death.

"A description of this highwayman," the lawyer insisted again. "Was he tall or short?"

"I cannot remember," Panthea lied.

"What was he wearing?"

Again, Panthea shook her head.

"Surely you can recall the colour of his coat?" Mr. Dobson queried.

"I-I am afraid not," Panthea answered. "I hardly looked at him."

The lawyer put down his pen with a slow deliberation which showed that, if he had acted naturally, he would have flung it on the floor in exasperation.

"The prosecution alleges," he said, and his tone was icy, "that you withdrew into the wood with this highwayman while the grave was being dug for the body of the man who had been your husband. You stayed with him there for some considerable time, and when you came back into the clearing your hand was on his arm."

"I-I cannot recall that," Panthea faltered.

"Did you or did you not go into the wood with this man?" Mr. Dobson asked.

"I-I cannot remember."

"Lady Panthea, you are not telling me the truth," the lawyer shouted. "I cannot pretend to understand why you should wish to shield this man, to refuse to give me a description of him, but it is quite obvious to me that is what you are doing. You saw him, you talked with him, you were in the wood with him, and yet you say you cannot remember anything about him. You must have a reason for this evasion, but whatever that may be, I beg you to tell it to me, for without frankness we are completely lost."

Panthea got to her feet.

"There is something I want to say to you, Mr. Dobson," she said quietly. "You will, I expect, think me ungrateful and perhaps a little mad, but believe me I am neither. I am only doing what I know to be the right thing. Mr. Dobson, I have no further need of your services."

The lawyer stared at her in utter astonishment, then he spoke harshly.

"Do I understand that you would prefer to obtain the services of another attorney?"

"No, no," Panthea said hastily. "You have done everything that it is possible to do for me, and, believe me, I appreciate the trouble you have taken, but I have decided I will not have anyone defend the case. I will answer any questions that may be put to me to the best of my ability, but I prefer not to be represented."

"You are mad!" the lawyer exclaimed.

"That is what I was afraid you would think," Panthea replied, "but my mind is made up. I will stand my trial, and for what it is worth I will defend myself."

"But it is impossible," Mr. Dobson stammered.

"Is it illegal? Am I not allowed to conduct my own case?" Panthea questioned.

"No, it is not illegal, and you may do it if you wish, but no one but a lunatic would attempt such a thing."

"Then you must think me a lunatic," Panthea said with a sweet smile, "but I assure you it is the best way. I cannot answer your questions, I cannot do what you wish me to do and therefore I would not like you to be involved in anything that you know from the start must be a failure from your own point of view."

Mr. Dobson shut up his notebook with a snap.

Then he said, "Lady Panthea, I regret your decision more than I can possibly say, and yet at the same time I cannot but feel that you are perhaps right. If you will not give me the information I require, if you will not let me prepare a brief as it should be prepared, then it is best that you should conduct your own case. You are a very beautiful young woman, if I may say so without impertinence. There is a chance that your beauty may sway the jury as legal arguments might fail to do. As it is, I can only wish you the best of luck and promise that, should you need me or should you change your mind before the case comes to court, then I am at your service."

"Thank you, Mr. Dobson."

Panthea gave him her hand, then as she heard the door close behind him, she heaved a sigh of relief. It had been a difficult decision to make, but she knew she had been right, and now there was a sense of freedom in feeling herself free of his questioning. It had been hard for her to prevaricate, hard too, to look ahead and see the pitfalls that surrounded almost every word she uttered. Now, she would face her trial alone and somehow, for the moment, that seemed infinitely less worrying than having a lawyer to cope with.

She walked restlessly across the floor of her sitting room. What was hard to bear was the waiting. If only her trial could be at once, she would know that the worst was over and that judgment was passed. It was the prison that was so intolerable, as well as the suspense of not knowing what would become of her.

If the prosecution succeeded, she knew what sentence would be hers. For the moment, Panthea covered her face with her hands. She was not brave. She was a coward, she thought. Then she remembered how Richard had died with a smile on his lips and a prayer for the King over the water. She would not be as brave as he had been, and yet she knew that she was not so much afraid of dying as of her own fear.

She wondered if Richard felt as she felt now when he had been imprisoned before his trial. He had not had long to wait, for she had learned later that he had been captured while hiding in a tavern on the outskirts of London, and after but two days in prison had been taken to the scaffold set up in Charing Cross. Sometimes, in the darkness of the night, Panthea would wonder if Richard was near her.

She would whisper his name and strive to send out her spirit in search of him so that she might have the comforting assurance of his survival. What lay beyond the gates of death? she wondered, as so many had wondered before her. Was there utter extinction or was there indeed the life of the spirit, a life fuller and more beautiful than the life on Earth?

She prayed until the very words were meaningless and she became just one aching longing for wisdom, and for the understanding of God. All her life she had said her prayers, gone to church and worshipped her maker in what she thought was an adequate manner, yet now she knew how little she had understood the meaning of the word 'prayer'. Now that her whole being besought the heavens to comfort her, she knew that prayer was no easy repetition of words, but one of the most difficult exercises in the whole world. She prayed and prayed and yet no answer came to her, and at times she felt utterly forsaken, forgotten both by heaven and by the world.

And yet now, as she paced the floor of her room, she felt a sudden glow of satisfaction in that she had been strong enough to dismiss the lawyer. She had questioned her own courage to do it, knowing that neither he nor her great-aunt, not anyone else, would understand her motives, and yet she had done it. She was not such a coward after all – and then in that moment she knew that whatever she was required to face, somehow the courage would be there to enable her to face it.

It was not so much a revelation of the divine which came to her, but merely that a sudden peace descended on her heart, a peace which soothed away the agitated misery of the past weeks and gave her indeed a calm confidence, which was more reassuring than if a thousand angels had visited her in a vision of glory. It was then she found herself becoming aware of the life that was pulsating through her and knew that she was not alone nor forgotten.

There was a new strength shining from her eyes, and when a little later the door was opened and Lady Darlington was shown in by the wardress, Panthea sped across the room into her great-aunt's arms. When they had kissed affectionately, they sat side by side on the sofa, their hands clasped together.

Lady Darlington had sent furniture, carpets, bedlinen, and other things to the prison, but though the room looked very different from when Panthea had first entered it, both to her and to her great-aunt it was still a cell, a place where she was confined forcibly and under lock and key, so that it was the degradation that they both minded rather than the physical discomfort.

"How are you, my dear?" Lady Darlington asked.

"Well enough, Aunt Anne," Panthea replied, "but you have not been taking care of yourself. You look tired, and your gown hangs looser than it did when I last saw you wear it."

It was true that the Countess had suffered deeply from the indignity of Panthea's arrest. Lady Castlemaine had her revenge already in that the Dowager seemed to grow older day by day, to be more withered, more wrinkled and her eyes more deep-shadowed from worry and sleepless nights.

Sometimes, Panthea felt she could cry that her great-aunt should be punished so bitterly for something that was actually nothing to do with her and not her concern in any way at all. Yet because Lady Darlington loved her great-niece, and because in the years they had lived together they had grown close to one another, it was impossible to save her from sufferings or to prevent the vengeance so cleverly planned by Lady Castlemaine from falling upon her and taking its toll of her health and strength.

"Let us not talk about me," Lady Darlington said. "I have news for you. I have come but this moment from an interview with the Lord Chancellor. Your trial is to take place next week unless your lawyers appeal for longer time."

"I have no lawyers," Panthea said quietly, and then before her great-aunt could expostulate, she tried to explain why she preferred to conduct her own case.

The explanation was not easy, for one reason that she could not tell the truth, and for another that the Dowager would not hear her out but argued fiercely with her, commanding her to rescind her decision and to send again for Mr. Dobson. But Panthea was insistent that she should be allowed to have her own way in this matter, and finally Lady Darlington capitulated, but not without the gravest doubts and remonstrances of every sort.

"I shall be glad when it is all over," Panthea said. "It is the waiting that is so hard to bear. Sometimes I feel that I shall go mad here, when we are shut in at night and the prisoners shriek and cry at one another. The warders get drunk and then start fighting outside my window when they come from the taverns."

"I never thought to see the inside of this place," Lady Darlington said sadly, "and now that I have seen it, I am convinced that something should be done for these poor wretches. Men and women must be imprisoned to uphold the laws of the country, but surely the place need not be so nauseous and so ill kept as to endanger life of itself?"

Panthea nodded.

"That is true enough," she said. "The wardress was telling me that no less than sixty-three people are down with prison fever."

"Pray heaven it is nothing worse," Lady Darlington said hastily. "It is in places like this that one gets the plague."

"Do not be afraid for me," Panthea replied. "I see only the two women who come to clean my room. They are healthy enough and are actually not in the part of the prison where the fever has broken out."

"I will bring you some sweet herbs that you may burn them," Lady Darlington said, "and an orange stuck with cloves. Both are a prevention from infection. And now I have news of our friends. Many have enquired after you, and the Queen herself has sent you a most kindly message. She asked me to say that she believes that justice will be done and that you will be free to return to Whitehall."

"Please thank Her Majesty," Panthea said.

It was like the gentle, kindly Queen to believe the best, she thought and Lady Darlington, as if reading her thoughts, said, "The Queen has been most loyal and gracious, Panthea. She was approached by several people of the Court with the suggestion that I should not continue in attendance on her but should be sent away because of the scandal that is now attached to your name, but Her Majesty was adamant. Until the case is heard, she is prepared to believe you innocent."

"Has someone told Her Majesty that Lady Castlemaine is behind all this?" Panthea asked.

"Of course," Lady Darlington replied. "Everyone at court knows how delighted she is to have harmed both you and me. She made no secret of her elation and refers to you openly as 'the murderess'."

"It does not trouble me," Panthea said.

"Indeed, why should it?" Lady Darlington asked. "If anyone can prove that harsh words can inflict no wounds, Lady Castlemaine is the person."

She spoke of several other mutual friends and then with a quick glance at Panthea added, "Rudolph has been to see me every day. He begs that he might be allowed to visit you. He tells me that he has called here repeatedly and that you have refused to see him."

"That is true," Panthea replied.

"There is something else he has asked me," Lady Darlington went on in a troubled voice. "He has begged me to plead with you that you should marry him before the day of your trial. He has spoken very freely of his affection for you, and it is his desire to prove to the world that he will stand by you, whatever the issue, whatever judgment is passed."

Panthea was silent. For one moment she thought perhaps she had misjudged Rudolph and that he genuinely cared for her and was acting in an honourable manner, and then she saw all too clearly what was his motive in pressing his suit at this moment. If she lived, he would be the husband of a rich woman, if she paid the price for her supposed crime, then also he would be rich. It seemed, however, such a grave motive to attribute to anyone that she would not voice her suspicions even to her great-aunt.

Instead, she said quietly, "You must thank Cousin Rudolph for his proposal, but tell him that I do not consider this a moment to think of marriage."

"I felt sure you would say that" Lady Darlington exclaimed and there was a note of relief in her voice, "but Rudolph was most insistent."

They talked for a little longer and then the Dowager rose to leave. She clung to Panthea a little pathetically and Panthea found herself comforting her great-aunt rather than, as it should have been, the other way round. Lady Darlington left a purse of money behind her for Panthea had found that the expenses of the prison were very heavy, and on almost every visit she had to request her great-aunt to bring her more money. Everything was obtainable if one could pay for it, but the bribes were heavy and Panthea found, too, that it was hard not to give money away.

The two women who cleaned her room would talk to her of the other prisoners. She found her heart wrung by the story of one woman, who had given birth to triplets and who had not even a rag in which to wrap the babies. There was another tale of an old woman who had been brought in for stealing an apple. She was almost blind and having kicked against it as it lay on the pavement, had not realised that it had fallen from a barrow outside a shop. She had been dragged to prison and, having not a penny to her name, was forced to share a cell with three women, two of whom were notorious thieves, while the other had long lost her reason and was kept chained to the wall for fear she should in her frenzy injure the other prisoners.

Panthea bought the old woman a room for herself in the better quarters of the prison and had given her money so that she could purchase for herself some better food than the dirty potato swill that was the main diet of the other prisoners.

She took her purse now and concealed it beneath her gown. It was not only the prisoners who were light-fingered – the warders and wardresses also were not to be trusted where money or anything valuable was concerned.

She had taken up a book and had begun to read it when the door opened and the wardress came in holding a note in her hand.

"A gentleman gave me this," she said with her toothless grin. "He paid me well or I should not have come up all these stairs at this hour in the afternoon, I can tell you."

Her breath smelt of gin and she stumbled against one of the chairs. As Panthea took the note from her, she wondered who it could be from, knowing that the wardress was right in saying she had been heavily paid to bring it. After the midday meal, the majority of the prison officials repaired to the taverns and when they had drunk enough, or too much in the usual case, they went to their rooms and slept off the effects. It usually made them querulous and disagreeable, so that the prisoners learned to keep out of their way when they first came on duty again in the later hours of the afternoon.

The warders had complete and absolute powers over the prisoners and the fact that they were not beaten or knocked insensible every day of the week was due more to laziness rather than a sense of decency. Nevertheless, ghastly brutality and acts of violence were very prevalent in Newgate.

The wardress slammed the door behind her, and Panthea heard her heavy, unsteady footsteps going away down the passage. Only then did she glance at the letter she held in her hand. Slowly she raised the wafer with which it was sealed. As she looked at the short sentence written on the paper which she had opened, her heart gave a sudden leap and the blood rushed in a crimson flood into her pale cheeks.

She had seen that same writing twice before. She had never forgotten it. Her fingers that held the paper trembled, not with fear but with happiness, and her face was alive with a sudden light as she read again and again the words that were written by the man she loved.

'Do not be afraid, dear heart. It is always darkest before the dawn.'

11

The court was packed with people. As Panthea was escorted in by two warders, she saw faces swimming before her as if in some terrible nightmare, hundreds of eyes focused on her and seeming to multiply and remultiply themselves. She fought back the inclination to cover her own face with her hands and cower away from the horror of being stared at by the inquisitive, the pleasure-seeking and the curious, all of whom came to the law courts for one reason and one reason only – the gratification of their desire for excitement.

Pride came to her rescue, and she managed to keep her chin high and to walk almost disdainfully to the seat that was allotted to her. She had taken a great deal of trouble over her appearance. She had seen while she was in prison how easily women deteriorated when they were beset by fear. Bedraggled and dirty, they seemed even to gain some satisfaction or comfort from the misery of their own personal neglect.

She had asked her great-aunt to bring her one of her best gowns of pale blue satin, trimmed with rich lace at the bodice and on the sleeves. To her astonishment, it had been brought to her by Marta. It was the first time they had met since Panthea had been in prison, and with the sheer joy of seeing Marta she felt the iron control in which she was holding her emotions slacken a little, so that there were tears in her eyes as she ran towards her maid and embraced her.

"Marta! Marta!" she exclaimed. "How delighted I am to see you! I did not believe that they would let you, for the rule has been that only my relations might visit me."

"It cost her Ladyship several pieces of gold," Marta replied, "but indeed, my Lady, I would have paid it out of my own pocket rather than not see you this day of all days."

Marta's hands trembled as she set down the box containing Panthea's gown, and she made no attempt to disguise the tears that flowed down her cheeks.

"Oh, my Lady," she sobbed, "to think that this should happen to you of all people."

"Pray do not cry, Marta," Panthea said. "I am so overjoyed to see you that I cannot bear that my happiness should be spoilt by your tears."

Marta wiped her eyes with the back of her hand.

"Oh, my Lady I am afraid for you," she said. "They talk of nothing else in the palace but your trial, and those stuck-up servants of my Lady Castlemaine are prophesying that there is no hope for you. They say the evidence against you is overwhelming."

"I am not afraid, Marta," Panthea said quietly.

She hesitated for a moment and then, as if she made a sudden decision, she added, "I have heard from my cousin Lucius. He has bid me not to be afraid and therefore I am free of fear."

"You have heard from his Lordship?"

Marta's tears were checked in astonishment and her mouth gaped open.

"Yes, indeed," Panthea said. "A note was brought to me."

Marta clasped her hands together.

"I told old Harry that his Lordship would find a way of comforting you," she exclaimed. "It was Harry who informed him that you had been taken prisoner."

"I thought it must have been," Panthea said. "But oh, Marta, I hope that he does nothing rash. His own life is in such terrible danger I am half afraid he may risk it to save mine."

"You can trust his Lordship," Marta said. "There has been those who have been about to lay him by the heels these past years, and always they have failed, and he has saved so many from the scaffold, so why not. . ."

Marta stopped suddenly and her hand went to her mouth. She stared at Panthea in a kind of horror, realising what she had been about to say, but Panthea smiled.

"It is all right, Marta. I am well aware what my sentence will be if the case is won by the Crown. As you say, White Throat has saved many a man from the gallows, perhaps now it will be the turn of a woman."

"But, my Lady, what will become of you? If he spirits you away, what sort of life will you have, being pursued, hunted, every man's hand against you?"

"I should not be afraid if he were by my side," Panthea said quietly.

"I often think that with Jack I would mind nothing," Maria said slowly, "but as it is. . ."

She sighed and turned towards the box she had brought with her. Panthea watched her for a moment unpacking the blue satin dress she had asked her great-aunt to send, and then she said quietly, "Tell me a little about his Lordship, Marta, for you must remember I know very little about him, save that he is the most wonderful man I have ever met in the whole of my life."

Marta's face lit up.

"That is the way my Jack talks of him, my Lady, and all those who know him well. He is indeed the most wonderful gentleman, and it is cruel hard that he should have to live as he does."

"Do you know exactly why he took to the road?" Panthea enquired.

"They say he saved the King's life after the Battle of Worcester," Marta replied, "but few know for certain. He never talks about himself, does his Lordship, and yet those who know the kindnesses he does and the thought he has for those in trouble, can never speak too highly of him."

Panthea gave a little smile.

"I can well understand that," she said, "for having met him but twice in my life, I feel that he is quite different from any other man I have ever known."

"That is what Harry says, my Lady," Marta agreed. "He knew his Lordship when he was a small boy. Master Lucius they used to call him then, and everyone on his father's estate loved him. He had always a kindly word for everyone as worked there. There was never a man in trouble or a household in want that he did not find out about it and get their wrongs righted. But if a man was cruel to an animal, he would frighten the offender and make sure that the poor beast was given better treatment in the future. Oh, there's many tales as old Harry tells about him. You should, talk with him, my Lady, and ask him to tell you, what he knows."

Again, Marta's hand went to her mouth, and she realised that perhaps Panthea would never see old Harry again or have the opportunity of speaking to him. Then suddenly she was down on her knees at Panthea's feet crying.

"Oh, my Lady, my Lady, they mustn't do that to you, they mustn't. I would gladly die in your stead."

"Hush, Marta, hush," Panthea said. "We do not know yet if I am to die. Besides, have you forgotten his Lordship? He may yet save me as he has done before."

"'Twas his Lordship who killed Mr. Christian Drysdale, my Lady, wasn't it?" Marta asked in a hushed voice.

Instinctively, Panthea glanced over her shoulder as if someone might be listening.

"Be careful what you say," she replied in a low voice.

"I am careful, your Ladyship," Marta assured her, "but when I heard the lies they were saying about you, I guessed that the person who came to your rescue was his Lordship."

"You may have guessed that," Panthea said severely, "but no one else must know. Promise me that you will keep silent and say nothing."

"I promise you that, my Lady," Marta said, "and it was only because of what you said that night when you rode out to Staverley to warn His Lordship that the soldiers were coming that I had the idea that it must have been him who had held up the coach the night you were married."

"Sometimes it seems a dream," Panthea said. "It was so long ago, and I was so young, and yet I had never forgotten him."

She sighed and glanced towards the window where the pale sunshine was trying to shine through the thick and dirty panes of glass.

"It must be getting late, Marta," Panthea said. "I had best change my dress."

She was ready when the warders came to fetch her. For a moment they seemed surprised by her appearance, so that they stood silent in the doorway. Marta had combed and brushed Panthea's fair hair until it shone like burnished gold. It fell in soft waves on either side of her little face, and her eyes seemed almost exaggeratedly large, for she had grown thinner since she had been in prison.

Panthea was determined not to look crushed and afraid, and therefore she commanded Marta to put a touch of rouge on either cheekbone and redden her lips a little. She was glad that she had done so when she entered the court and felt the blood drain away from her cheeks, and a sudden lightness in her head as if she might faint. Amongst the sea of faces that confronted her, she saw one which she felt would remain permanently in her memory.

It was a beautiful face, and yet Panthea knew the blue, heavy-lidded eyes held hatred in their depths, that the lovely lips, were distorted a little with a smile of triumph and revenge.

Lady Castlemaine had commanded a seat in the front of the court where she could see and hear everything that took place. Her huge hat was decorated with scarlet ostrich plumes, and her dress was laced with crimson velvet ribbons to match. She talked a little excitedly to the crowd of gallants and elegant ladies who surrounded her. She was determined that a number of her friends and acquaintances should be present today, and she had made a point of inviting them to meet her at the court in case, when the time came, they were too lazy to rise early from their beds, or their stomachs were too delicate to endure the stench of the crowds who pushed their way into the back seats and into the gallery.

The floor had been strewn with fresh rushes, the judge carried his bouquet of fresh flowers, but even so the atmosphere was almost overpowering, so that more than one Lady of Quality was forced to sniff vigorously at her vinaigrette for fear of swooning.

Lady Castlemaine, however, had no such qualms, and appeared almost to revel in the excitement that seemed to mount minute by minute.

The case was opened by the prosecution. Sir Balsombe Jones, the Attorney General, rose to his feet and began a long and extremely boring speech in which he took such an inconceivable time in coming to the point that the chatter of Lady Castlemaine and her friends, and the comments of the crowd, at times completely drowned his voice. Panthea felt her attention wandering, even though she realised that what he said was of vital importance to herself. Instead, she found herself thinking of Lucius. The note he had sent her was safe in her corsage and she could feel it pressing against the softness of her breasts.

Ever since it had arrived she had felt calm and, as she had told Marta, completely unafraid. She remembered her instinctive trust of her cousin from the first time she saw him, how she had held out the body of her pet dog to him without for one moment remembering that he was an outlaw from all decent society. She felt now that same trust, that same confidence in his ability to help her, though how he could she had no idea. But the idea that she might be hanged seemed as fantastic now as it might have done six months ago, had she ever imagined such a thing.

She thought she must pinch herself to make herself realise that she, Panthea Vyne, was sitting in this court on trial for her life. She looked round at the face of Sir Balsombe Jones. He was a large, ugly man with a hooked nose and a slightly rotund stomach. His eyes were hard and his lips thin, so that one felt that he had little humanity and certainly no sympathy with those he prosecuted.

His voice droned on so monotonously that Panthea started when at length she heard her name spoken, and heard him refer to her as 'this evil woman'. She suddenly had a wild desire to laugh. It was all so ridiculous! How could anyone ever imagine that she, Panthea Vyne, could have contrived and plotted to kill Christian Drysdale for his money, and then, as the laughter welled up inside her, she saw Lady Castlemaine's eyes fixed upon her and felt herself shiver. There was indeed an evil woman in this court.

She remembered the look that Lady Castlemaine had given her great-aunt that day on the terrace, when the Countess had refused to allow the King's mistress to be introduced to her. Panthea knew that Lady Castlemaine had vowed vengeance at that very moment, and now that she had obtained her revenge, it was very sweet. She was thankful that her great-aunt was not well enough to attend the trial. The strain of the past weeks had been too much for the old lady, and two days after visiting Panthea in the prison, she had collapsed and her physician had ordered her to her bed and forced her to stay there.

It was a mercy, Panthea thought, that she was not here to see the triumph on Lady Castlemaine's face and the avid curiosity on those of her friends. Panthea knew how proud her great-aunt had always been. She knew, too, that the honour of the family and the decent upright life she had led were an intrinsic part of her character. The shame of Panthea's arrest had been almost more difficult to bear than the actual distress of knowing that her great-niece was in prison. However much she trusted and believed in Panthea, it was still almost a deathblow to know that others could sneer and jeer at one of her own blood.

As Panthea sat alone, save for the warders on either side of her, unsupported by relations or friends, she had a sense not of loneliness, but rather of relief that at least she had no one to worry about save herself. She knew that had Lady Darlington been beside her she would have been distressed by every harsh and cruel defamation that was uttered, not because it hurt her, but because of the misery it must inflict upon her great-aunt.

She was glad now that her father was not alive to see this day, or that Richard had not been there to protest eloquently in her defence and to feel outraged and affronted by the lies that were being fabricated, skilfully and cleverly into a noose that would eventually be put round her neck. She was alone, and yet the note between her breasts made her feel as if she were protected and surrounded by a great company of those who loved her.

She had the love of one man and he filled the whole world. She wanted nothing more save that he should continue to love her. At the mere thought of him, her heart began to beat a little quicker and Lady Castlemaine, watching her, felt a sudden fury in that Panthea looked so happy. She turned to make some slighting, offensive remark to the man next to her, and deliberately raised her voice so that Panthea heard what she said. But, like a stone that fails to reach its mark, the words seemed meaningless and unimportant.

Lucius would save her. Panthea was certain of that as she was that she was sitting here, in fact far more certain.

Sir Balsombe Jones was coming to the end of his speech. With eloquent and flowery language, he described the details of Christian Drysdale's death as the prosecution alleged it had taken place. He drew such an exaggerated picture of an evil, scheming woman marrying her infatuated suitor because she craved his wealth, that Panthea felt again that she must laugh. It was too ridiculous to believe that he spoke of her, and she could not believe that the twelve members of the jury, sitting bored and restive in the jury box, would recognise her in the guise of a murderess when they remembered that at the time she was but sixteen years of age.

Looking critically at the jury, though, she had her doubts. They were, she decided, most of them respectable tradesmen. Their faces gave one the impression of being curiously devoid of intelligence and Panthea had the uncomfortable feeling that they would accept the judge's direction, whatever it might be. He would therefore be the deciding factor, and while she appeared to listen attentively to Sir Balsombe Jones, Panthea gave Lord Justice Dalrymple her close attention.

He was a man of some sixty summers, thin to the point of emaciation, his cheekbones prominent on his thin sardonic face. His eyebrows met across the bridge of his sharp, aristocratic nose and the eyes beneath them were shrewd and penetrating. His olive skin was a sharp contrast to the white wool of his wig, and the long pointed fingers of one of his hands cupped his sharp and somewhat protruding chin.

He sat very straight in his highbacked chair and he had an air of almost omnipotent power so that for the first time since she came into court, Panthea felt that here at least was someone with an air of reality, a man who personified all that was meant by both his title and his office, a man in fact who was a judge sitting in judgment.

As Sir Balsombe Jones finished, the judge spoke,

"Thank you, Mr. Attorney General, and who, may I ask, represents the prisoner?"

There was silence, while even those at the back of the Court seemed to wait breathless for the answer. The judge's eyes roved from Panthea's face to the empty bench behind her, then the clerk rose to answer.

"The prisoner has insisted, my Lord, that she conduct her own defence."

"Indeed?"

The judge's monosyllable held both incredulity and disdain – then he addressed Panthea.

"Lady Panthea Vyne, is it your wish that you have no counsel to defend you and that you will reply personally to the charges made against you?"

"That is my wish, my Lord," Panthea said quietly.

"So be it!"

The judge spoke sharply and turned to Sir Balsombe Jones.

"You may continue, Mr. Attorney General."

"I will then, if your Lordship will permit, call my witness," the Attorney General replied. "Call Sergeant Higson."

The Clerk of the Court echoed the name and Sergeant Higson was ushered into the witness box. Panthea knew that this was the coachman who had driven her that memorable night from the gates of Staverley to the church where she was married, and afterwards until the coach was stopped in the wood. She had told Mr. Dobson the truth when she said she had no memory of what he looked like, and she saw now a tall, stalwart man of nearly middle age with a good-humoured countryman's face and a thick head of brown hair the colour of chestnuts.

He stood stiffly at attention and took the oath in an embarrassingly loud voice. He was frightened, Panthea thought, although he was making every possible effort not to show it – and then, as he began to answer the questions Sir Balsombe Jones put to him, he glanced across the court at Lady Castlemaine, as if seeking from her both inspiration and approval in everything he said.

It was then that Panthea understood all too clearly how the story for the prosecution had been built up against her. Sergeant Higson had originally told the truth when questioned about that night in the woods. Panthea had no grounds for assuming this and yet she was sure of it. It would have been no advantage then to the Sergeant to tell a lie, but afterwards it had been made worth his while to say, as he was replying now to the prompting questions of Sir Balsombe Jones, that he had known when he was hired that something unusual was going to happen on the drive.

It was quite clearly thought out, Panthea told herself as she listened. Just a few alterations of the truth and a very different story was presented. Sergeant Higson told the court that he knew very little of what to expect save that his friend, the other coachman, who was now conveniently dead, had told him that there was money in the journey if they did what they were told and kept their mouths shut.

Sergeant Higson said that when he went to the Four Fishermen Inn, where he was told by his friend that Mr. Christian Drysdale would be waiting, he had only the vaguest idea what was to happen or what lay ahead. Mr. Drysdale had asked the landlord to procure him two fresh coachmen. The landlord had spoken both to Higson and his friend, Drover, and they had agreed to drive Mr. Drysdale wherever he wished to go. It was before this happened, Higson said, that Drover had told him there was money in the trip.

The Attorney General had paused then.

"I want the members of the jury," he said, "to make a special note of that point. It was before the unfortunate man who was so foully murdered engaged the coachmen that Drover told his friend there was money in the trip. These men were not yet engaged, and no one save two people in the whole world knew that the wedding trip was to take place. Of these two knowledgeable people one was Mr. Christian Drysdale, who was to be killed a few hours after the wedding ceremony, and the other was his Bride – the woman who sits now before you accused of contriving his murder."

Sir Balsombe Jones spoke dramatically and waited for the theatrical effect to sink home, then continued his examination.

Sergeant Higson then told how he and Drover had picked up Panthea outside the gates of Staverley, how they had driven to the church and how, when the married couple had returned to the coach, their instructions were to travel as quickly as they could to Mr. Christian Drysdale's home in the vicinity of Bishops Stortford.

They had set off and travelled at a quite reasonable speed until they had been brought suddenly to a halt by two highwaymen emerging from the shadows of the trees in the wood, which rose above a part of the countryside known as Drake's Dyke. It was here that Panthea noticed Sergeant Higson glance towards Barbara Castlemaine and lick his lips. He had spoken quite fluently and without hesitation, but now he began to falter as Sir Balsombe Jones pressed him to explain clearly what happened.

The two highwaymen had held up the coach, he said. Mr. Christian Drysdale had been forced to alight, and he and Drover had been told to tie him to a tree. They had done this, but while they were doing it the highwayman and the lady had gone into the woods together carrying something.

"Did you see what they were carrying?" Sir Balsombe Jones asked.

"No, sir."

"Was it large?"

Sergeant Higson hesitated.

"Who carried it?" the Attorney General asked.

"The highwayman, sir."

"Did it look to you like a box or a bag that might contain money?"

"It might have been, sir."

The Attorney General glanced towards the jury.

"Whatever was in this box or bag it was heavy enough to require the highwayman to carry it with two hands."

He turned to Sergeant Higson again.

"It was taken to the wood, and you never saw it again?"

"No, sir."

"When the highwayman and the lady came from the woods, he was not carrying it in his hands?"

"No, sir."

"The highwayman and the lady appeared to you to be on friendly terms?"

Sergeant Higson did not answer.

"Let me put it this way," the Attorney General said. "The lady went with him willingly. She was not screaming or protesting or appeared in any way frightened of this man?"

"No, sir."

"Did you hear her scream on this or on any other occasion?"

"No, sir."

"Did she seem inclined to rush to her husband or to you for protection?"

"No, sir."

"They were talking as they went into the wood, the highwayman and the lady?"

"Yes, sir."

Again, Sir Balsombe Jones paused so that the jury could appreciate the point he had made.

Sergeant Higson then went on to explain how the highwayman had come back from the wood, cut the bonds that bound Christian Drysdale and then, before the freed man could adequately defend himself, had stabbed him to death.

It was all too obvious to Panthea where the story was true and where it was distorted into lies. Sergeant Higson's voice had, when he was not telling the truth, a very obvious apologetic note in it. He also hesitated or stumbled over his words, and yet she felt that no one but herself would notice it, because only she knew the truth of what he told and the untruths with which the story had been supplemented.

"When the highwayman had finished butchering this man and left him lying on the ground for dead, what did he do then?" Sir Balsombe Jones asked.

"He went back into the woods, sir."

"To the lady?"

"Yes, sir."

"Did he say anything to you?"

"Yes, sir."

"What did he say?"

"He told us to dig a grave and bury Mr. Drysdale's body."

"And you did that?"

"Yes, sir."

There were a few questions as to where the shovels were obtained and the attitude of the other highwayman, and then the Attorney General asked, "What happened after that?"

"The highwayman and the lady came back from the woods together."

"Were they walking separately?"

"Her hand was on his arm."

"Did they seem friendly?"

"Yes, sir."

"So when the body of this poor murdered man was disposed of, his wife, or rather his widow, came from the woods on the arm of the man she had employed to murder him, to see that the deed had been truly and properly done. That, in your opinion, was why they came out together, is it not?"

The sergeant looked uncomfortable.

"I only knows that they came out, sir."

"Was the lady smiling?"

"I, I think so, sir."

"She seemed happy, pleased and relieved that her husband of but a few hours ago was dead?"

"I could not rightly say, sir, and yet she was smiling."

"Gentlemen of the jury, you note that. It is a very important point. The lady was smiling. The woman who had watched a man foully and brutally killed, who had taken his money and hidden it in the wood, comes out afterwards smiling, and watches to see that no incriminating evidence is left."

The sergeant then told how the highwayman had paid him and his companion, and told them to make their way back to the village.

"How much did he give you?" Sir Balsombe Jones enquired.

"Four guineas, sir, between us."

"Four guineas! A big sum, was it not, for a coachman?"

"Yes, sir."

"More than you expected?"

"Yes, sir."

"You would, in fact, say it was fantastic wages for driving a coach for a few hours?"

"Yes, sir."

"It was also more money than you expected to obtain from a highwayman?"

There was laughter in court at this and Sir Balsombe Jones continued.

"A highwayman, one always understands, takes money from people, not gives it, yet this highwayman had money to give away, throw away one might say, to two men who were expecting a few shillings for their night's work.'

There was no need to belabour this point now that Sir Balsombe Jones had made it so obvious. He asked one more question.

"This lady, whom you drove from the gates of Staverley to be married, and who appeared on such friendly terms with the highwayman who was waiting so conveniently at a lonely point on the road, could you describe her?"

There was a pause.

"But there is no need, can you recognise her? Is she here in court?"

"Yes, sir."

"Will you point her out to me?"

It was hard for Panthea not to shudder, as the Sergeant's finger went out unswervingly in her direction.

"Thank you, Sergeant Higson," Sir Balsombe Jones said. "You may step down."

The Sergeant stumped somewhat noisily from the witness box to be replaced by a man who had dug up Christian Drysdale's body, a doctor who had examined it, a relative who had identified it by the dead man's ring and personal possessions, and the landlord of the Four Fishermen Inn. When the last of these witnesses had left the box, breathing wheezily with the exertion of giving evidence, the Attorney General bowed to the Judge.

"The prosecution rests, my Lord."

"Thank you, Mr. Attorney General."

The judge glanced towards Panthea.

"Lady Panthea Vyne, as you have no one to represent you, are you prepared to go into the witness box and answer any such questions as the Attorney General may be pleased to put to you?"

Panthea felt her heart sink, but steadily she rose to her feet.

"I am, my Lord."

It was then, as the judge opened his mouth to say something further, as everyone in court bent forward as if to have a closer look at the prisoner, that a loud, clear voice from the doorway resounded.

"I must ask you, my Lord, and all those in court, to keep quite still."

There was an audible gasp, which seemed to echo round the very walls. All turned their heads as it were simultaneously, to see standing in the doorway a black-masked figure with a pistol in either hand. Behind him was another masked figure and two others appeared in the other doorway through which the counsel entered the court. Then, as the heads turned from one to the other in open-mouthed stupefaction, a fifth masked figure entered the court quietly from the door by which the jury retired, and stood with his pistols levelled on the astonished jurors. No less than ten primed and cocked pistols pointed at an unarmed, weaponless crowd. There was a silence in which no one seemed able to draw his breath, and then a voice from the gallery cried, "Lawd save us, if it isn't White Throat!"

A sudden spontaneous cheer went up from at least a dozen throats. White Throat glanced up at them and smiled.

"Yes, I am White Throat," he said, "and I have come as usual to right a wrong. Are you prepared to hear me?"

"We'll hear ye right enough," a man shouted.

"And believe anythin' ye tells us," yelled a woman.

"Thank you, that is what I wanted to know," White Throat said.

He advanced until he was standing in front of the judge and facing the jury. Panthea, watching him with both hands raised to quell the tumult in her breast, thought that he held everyone present magnetised, as if there was a hypnotic quality about him. He stood there weaving a spell over the whole court. Everyone was listening and he did not even have to raise his voice to make himself heard.

"Good people, do you really credit all this nonsense to which you have been listening?" he asked. "Have you looked at the prisoner? Have you seen her? If so, do you imagine her capable for one moment of plotting the death of a man, however bestial, however brutal he might be? You see her now, but I wish you could have seen her as I saw her five years ago when she was but sixteen years of age, only a child, with a child's simplicity and innocence shining forth from her face, and a child's gentle and sweet love of all living things, especially animals.

"You have heard that she was married to Mr. Christian Drysdale, this man for whom the prosecution is ready to weep so many tears because he is no longer on this Earth. Surely, some of you in this court today remember Christian Drysdale, the worst, the cruellest and the most tyrannical tax-collector that ever walked the length and breadth of England? He extorted money from everyone he knew, he levied his own taxes as well as those that had been passed by Parliament, he took bribes from those who had something to hide and then denounced them when they could pay nothing more. He was especially severe with women, the women who were afraid that their sons or husbands might be taken from them or denounced as having Royalist sympathies. He sucked the last farthing from those who were his victims and, when they cursed him, he laughed – laughed and handed them over to the authorities so that they could be hanged or sent to the galleys for crimes, that in many cases they had never committed. That was Mr. Christian Drysdale, a man who with every breath he drew defamed the very name of manhood."

"That be true," someone shouted in the back of the court. "He took every penny my old mother had saved, and then he came for more."

"Yes, it's true enough," White Throat said, "and then while he was extorting his blood money he saw a pretty child, a girl of sixteen, and he, a man of over forty-five, lusted after her. He forced her to marry him, saying that if she did so he would save her brother from being hanged. He had no intention of doing anything of the sort. The Viscount St. Clare had been condemned to death for being one of those who sheltered His Majesty when he visited England. Christian Drysdale was prepared to use any methods to gain his own ends, and by lying to and deceiving this innocent child, he persuaded her to leave her home and her dying father and accompany him at midnight to a chapel where a blind priest was waiting to marry them.

"They were married, and this child, who knew nothing of the devil whom she had married, set off on her wedding journey. She had brought with her the only precious thing she could carry – her little dog. It was the one friend she would have in the strange house to which she was being carried by the man whom she had married. A little dog, so small that she slipped him in her cloak during the wedding ceremony.

"But in his tiny frail body there lived the heart of a lion, a lion who would protect those who attacked what he loved. It is not for me to tell you what happened in the coach as this man of forty-five drove away from the church with his young bride, but whatever he did, the dog, who loved his mistress, resented it. He bit the hand of the man whom, with an animal's unfailing instinct, he distrusted, and for his reward his brains were battered out with a heavy stick, a stick which, doubtless in time, would have been used on his mistress. He was thrown lifeless on to the floor of the coach, and he was taken from there to be buried in the wood by a little stream.

"That, my lord," the highwayman said, looking up at the judge for the first time where he sat, stiff and immobile as if he were turned to stone, "that, my Lord, is the money the Attorney General alleges I carried into the wood to bury. It was something far more valuable than money, something that could never be bought with gold – the affection and trust of a loyal animal who had died to defend his mistress from a man who had been cruel to her.

"When that dog was buried, I went back to where, as the Sergeant has truthfully told you, Mr. Christian Drysdale stood tied to a tree. I cut his bonds, as you have already heard, and I challenged him to a duel. I told him that he fought for his life. It was a fair fight, a fight in which neither of us had the advantage of the other. He was heavier than I, and longer in the arm. He was perhaps of the two the better swordsman, but I was fighting for something which gave me a strength beyond my own. I was fighting for justice and decency. I was fighting to free a child who had been betrayed into giving herself to a lecherous beast who hid his vices beneath a cloak of hypocrisy.

"Her brother had died on the gibbet at Charing Cross the day before she was married. He died with a smile on his lips, a loyal subject of King Charles. He can never return to us, but I ask you, gentlemen of the jury, the men and women of England who love justice and believe in it, to free this woman who has been dragged here to defend herself against the charge of murder. If there was murder done, then I am responsible for it, but I assure you that in a free fight, an honourable one fought in obedience to all the rules of duelling, I killed a man for whose death the world is a cleaner and a better place, for he deserved to die."

As he finished speaking, White Throat glanced round at the court. There was a sudden pause as the echoes of his voice died away, and then, one and all, the crowd rose to acclaim him. They cheered and shouted, the men waving their hats in their hands, women their handkerchiefs. Only Barbara Castlemaine and the ladies and gentlemen attending her sat still, the stiff expressions on their faces an almost ludicrous sight compared with the smiles and excitement of the crowd.

White Throat looked at Panthea for one moment. His eyes held hers almost as if he bade her farewell before he backed slowly to the door, his pistols still held before him, while the crowd cheered and shouted. As he reached the door, he turned to the little crowd of men clustered around it and addressed them. "Hold the door, chaps, for a few minutes."

They gathered his meaning without his saying anymore.

"That we will!" they responded, "And good luck go with you!"

It seemed to Panthea only the passing of a second before at one moment White Throat was standing there, holding them all spellbound as he spoke, and the next minute he had gone and his attendants had vanished with him. In front of the two doors were several burly young men arguing with a number of soldiers who had suddenly become galvanised into action and were striving to force their way through the crowds in the direction in which White Throat had retreated.

A beadle was trying to attract attention by the very stentorian tones of his voice.

"After him, men! *Hold him!* There is a price of a thousand guineas on his head."

The only response he got was a shout of laughter and a lot of suggestions as to what he could do with his own head. For a moment, the pandemonium continued and then the judge's voice restored order.

"After these most irregular proceedings, Mr. Attorney General," he said, "you would perhaps wish to amend the prosecution?"

Sir Balsombe Jones rose to his feet.

"My Lord," he said, "on behalf of His Majesty's Government, I wish to withdraw the charges against the prisoner, Lady Panthea Vyne, and to prefer them at another time against other persons who are not at the moment under arrest."

There were shrieks from the back of the court of, "And he never will be! You won't get him, however hard you try!" before the judge called for order in the court and once more there was silence.

"In that case," the judge said with slow, deliberate tones, "it is my duty and, if I might add, my pleasure to dismiss Lady Panthea Vyne from the case, and to declare null and void all charges that have been brought against her."

This time, the judge could not stop the cheers that rang out. They were deafening and spontaneous, exciting, and almost overwhelming, so that for the first time since she had come from the prison that morning, Panthea found it hard to check the tears that rose in her eyes – tears of joy that the man she loved had once again not failed to save her.

12

Panthea returned to the palace to receive the acclamations and congratulations of her friends, and of a large number of people whom she suspected of having been her enemies until she was vindicated. She was, however, not prepared to quarrel with anyone or to question even the most suspicious flattery of those who fawned upon her.

She was only too thankful to be home, and the very first thing she did on regaining her freedom was to kneel on the crimson hassocks in the Chapel Royal and offer up a prayer of thankfulness which came from the very bottom of her heart. But her gratitude, like her joy at being free from Newgate, was overshadowed by the knowledge that Lucius was now in greater danger than he had ever been before.

It was not likely that the authorities would ignore the fact that he had held both the judge and the jury at pistol point and had made the authority of the law courts a laughingstock. People could talk of nothing else, and there was no doubt at all that Lucius' dramatic appearance, and his championship of Panthea, had made him, at least for the moment, the most popular hero of the City of London.

Small boys put bits of rag over their eyes and played in the street at being White Throat confronting Lord Justice Dalrymple, and it was obvious that the bigger boys took the part of White Throat while the smaller ones, being too weak to protest, were relegated to the unpopular part of His Majesty's Judge.

In the palace those who had not attended the trial begged Panthea, over and over again, to describe to them White Throat's features and declared themselves madly in love with the very accounts they had heard of him. In fact, Lady Darlington's apartments were besieged by women, young and old, anxious to talk to Panthea of her gallant rescuer, all of them uttering sly innuendoes suggesting, if they had but known it, but a half of the romantic truth.

Panthea had not believed it possible to love, yearn and thrill at the thought of a man, and it was hard to conceal her feelings from those whose curiosity kept them incessantly probing for information on that very subject. She was in love so that her whole body ached for Lucius. She was in love so that her mind was beset with anxiety every minute of the day, lest some danger should befall him. She lived, over and over again, that moment of breath-taking excitement when she had seen him entering the court. The slow, unhurried dignity with which he walked, the angle of his proud head and the slightly humorous smile on his lips, which made her heart go out to him so that it was with difficulty she had prevented herself from running straight into his arms. It all seemed engraved on her very soul.

She felt his eyes rest on her and she had known that he sent her a wordless message of love and understanding. She felt then that he knew, as none other, what she must have suffered in the fastness of Newgate, that he appreciated how her pride had been humbled, and all that was decent and most fastidious in her had shrunk from the sordid degradation of the prison.

It was strange, Panthea thought afterwards, how much two people could say to each other with just a glance of an eye because their hearts beat together in unison, and because in spirit, if not in body, they were indivisible. She had known, even in the tumult and excitement of the court, that they belonged to each other. Perhaps they had been one in some previous life, perhaps all through the centuries of times their lives had been intertwined and linked together so that now they had only to meet again for them to take up the thread of their existence where it had been broken off.

She must have known all this instinctively, Panthea thought, on that first night in the wood. Never for one moment had she thought of Lucius as a stranger, but rather she had turned to him as if they had been parted but an hour or so, and behind them lay the past in which they had sought and known so much about themselves. There was indeed no need for words – their spirits recognised one another.

As she knelt in the silence of the Chapel Royal, Panthea closed her eyes and remembered Lucius' lips on hers and his arms around her, when they had clung together in the library at Staverley. She had known then that their love was divine, blessed and given to them by God out of His infinite mercy. She had known then, as she knew now, that there was nothing wrong in their loving each other, and that they were both of them blessed and exceptionally fortunate in knowing such a love – even if for a very short time.

Panthea found she could not think of the future. It was impossible for her to imagine how she and Lucius could ever be together unhunted, unpursued, and taking their rightful place in the world to which they had been born – and yet she dared not face or put into words the alternative.

Lucius was in danger! That idea was ever-present in her mind, and even while she prayed for his safety, she was afraid, as she had never been afraid for herself, that the vengeance and might of the law would overtake him. More than anything, she was at the moment afraid of Barbara Castlemaine.

Panthea had seen Lady Castlemaine's face as she left the court. Frowning, her lovely lips set in a hard line, she had flounced from the courtroom, attended by her friends in an ill-concealed temper that brought some caustic comments from the crowd before she reached her coach outside. It had been galling, too, for her to return to the palace and find that the girl she had thought must be hanged had become the popular heroine of the hour.

Barbara was too used to getting her own way to accept defeat, either gracefully or with a shrug of the shoulders. She was furiously angry, and her household suffered in consequence. She even vented her wrath upon the King, making him so uncomfortable by her tantrums that to sweeten her he parted with yet further treasures from the palace, and more money from the Privy Purse, all of which, however, did little to appease Barbara's anger.

As she listened to the flattery of the gallants who courted her, she suspicioned that there was a hint of amusement at the back of their fulsome compliments, and the thought that she was being laughed at was an irritation beyond all else. She had not forgotten that when she first came to London she had been poor and had appeared in very plain country clothes. Her beauty had been enough to command attention, but she had never forgotten the sniggers and laughter, and the patronising amusement on the faces of those in court circles who had thought her a figure of fun.

She had soon altered her clothes and, once recognised, her beauty had, so many people told her, added a new lustre to the gaiety and elegance of the social world. But she had not forgotten those first weeks of misery, and throughout her triumphant progress there still existed deep down in her heart the feeling that, after all, she was the same girl who had amused rather than dazzled the very people who now acclaimed her.

It was perhaps these memories, allied with her mother's incessant complaints of poverty, that made her rapacious, greedy and grasping to the point of avarice. If her father had lived, things might have been very different, but the

Viscount Grandison had died of wounds received at the Siege of Bristol. All who knew him spoke of his personal valour and courage, of his love of justice and integrity, and his example to all those who served under him. Had Lord Grandison lived, he might have moulded the passionate nature of his young daughter into finer channels so that her beauty could have been used to advantage, rather than to seduce and allure all those who saw her.

Barbara without a father had been brought up by a weak, complaining mother and a stepfather who was not particularly interested in her. She had felt unwanted and unimportant, in a household to which she seemed to belong only on sufferance. She had craved then for the things she could not have and when at length she obtained all for which her ardent young nature had pined, she found herself unable to be satisfied but wanting more, and always more with a greed that seemed completely insatiable.

Yet, life at Whitehall had left Barbara with the belief that anything she required must be given her and now, having received a check in that Panthea was free, and the vengeance she had planned had not been executed, she turned over in her mind how best she could stir up more trouble. Her mind was shrewd and, being observant, Barbara Castlemaine had not missed the look that had passed between White Throat and Panthea in the court.

She had guessed immediately that Panthea was in love with the highwayman and had stored the knowledge carefully in her mind for future use. Then, as she had studied the masked man's face and heard him speaking eloquently to the listening and the hushed court, she had found that his voice had a strange, mesmeric influence upon her. She had liked the full, deep tones of it and while the words he was saying angered her because they were freeing Panthea from the net that had been so carefully prepared for her, Barbara found herself not only listening with a strange attention, but remembering both White Throat's voice and the movement of his lips long after he had finished speaking and the drama had ended.

His voice had haunted Barbara and she found herself thinking of it when she was back at the palace. She woke in the night to remember the carriage of his head and the flash of his eyes behind the velvet mask. There was little subtlety about Barbara's desires, and when they were aroused, she was concerned only with the gratification of them, and it was perhaps a point in her favour that she never pretended or prevaricated to herself.

The night after Panthea's trial had ended, Barbara had lain awake thinking of White Throat and she knew that she wished to see him again. The very difficulties that this presented merely made her the more anxious and the more determined to obtain what she desired. Almost before she formulated the wish, her brain was contriving, scheming, plotting how she could achieve her ends.

The following night, and the night after that, found her wakeful, her brain as agile as a monkey swinging from bough to bough. Eventually, she discarded a thousand schemes and ideas for one, and her maid, entering the room at nine o'clock, found that her mistress had already risen from her bed.

"You are early, my Lady," she ventured, surprised to find the curtains drawn and the bed unoccupied.

But Barbara merely snapped at her to mind her own business and sent her in search of her Major Domo. Waiting was always the most difficult thing Barbara must endure because she had no patience, and self-control was almost impossible for one of her passionate temperament.

By far the most tiresome part of the many intrigues she had instigated at the palace was to wait for the information she required once she had sent someone out to obtain it. More often than not, when one of her hirelings returned successful from the chase, he would find himself not warmly congratulated but cursed for having been so long in bringing back the news.

Barbara had not long sent her Major Domo off in search of information before she despatched a footman for Rudolph, to his lodging off Charing Cross. Rudolph, on receipt of the message, came immediately, for he was well aware that it would not be wise at this moment to antagonise Barbara in any way. He, like the King, had borne the brunt of her anger when the case was over, and he had no intention of annoying her further, so that although it was inconvenient to come hurrying to the palace, he wasted no time and entered Barbara's apartment to find her pacing up and down the room, her eyes hard and chill as the North Sea on a December morning.

There was something about Barbara's beauty that always reminded Rudolph of the ocean. Her moods changed as swiftly as the colour comes and goes from the moving waves. One moment she would be warm and sunny as the sea beneath a Mediterranean sky, her eyes as blue, a smile on her lips as gentle as the sunshine playing upon the untroubled water. Then the next minute she would be shaken as if with a tempest, her eyes flashing with the fury of her feelings, her voice as thunder, and her whole being tumultuous as the waves that dash and crash against the sharp pointed rocks.

No one, Rudolph thought, could fail to be afraid of Barbara when she was in one of her tempestuous moods, and he was thankful now to see that, while she was sulky, she was not as yet in one of those rages when the whole air around her would vibrate with the violence of her emotions.

He kissed her hand, but when he would have drawn her in to his arms and kissed her lips, she shook herself free of him.

"Do not touch me," she said sharply. "I brought you here because I wished to learn the truth. Who is that man?"

Rudolph was well aware of whom she was speaking, but he played for time, asking innocently enough, "Of whom are you speaking?"

'You know full well of whom I speak," Barbara replied. "I wish to know the real name of this highwayman they call White Throat."

Rudolph made an expressive gesture with his hands.

"But why ask me?" he enquired. "Sir Philip Gage should have the information you require, if anyone has it."

Barbara scowled at him so ferociously that instinctively he took a step backwards.

"Do not lie to me," she snarled. "You are well aware who White Throat is, indeed I know myself for that matter."

"Then you must tell me what I do not know," Rudolph replied.

She looked at him then, her eyes meeting his, and after a long second, when he forced himself to meet her gaze, he felt the sweat break out on his forehead.

"Pah," she said at length, almost spitting the exclamation at him as she turned on her heel. "You are as chicken-hearted as the rest of those who have not the courage of their own convictions. Why do you not tell the truth instead of shrinking behind your own incompetence? White Throat is the true Marquess of Staverley, and you have not the guts either to denounce him or to murder him and make sure of your succession to the title."

Rudolph made no effort to argue with her.

"How do you know this?" he asked lamely.

"For two reasons," Barbara replied. "One, that you were so anxious to capture this highwayman. Since when have you been interested in law and order save when you benefit from it? Secondly, because there is a likeness between you that is quite remarkable. I could see but half of his face, but there was a distinct resemblance to yours. You are about the same height, and there is a similitude too in the way you walk, although why I cannot explain. His voice is deeper than yours and it has a more manly note in it. When I see him unmasked, I am certain that his face will be more masculine, and his looks have something that yours have always lacked."

"When you see him unmasked?" Rudolph questioned.

He bent forward eagerly and there was no mistaking the glint of hope in his eyes. Barbara looked at him slyly.

"If you think White Throat is captured, you are mistaken, but I wish to see him unmasked. That is why I asked you here to tell me where I can find him."

Rudolph looked at her in astonishment, which was quite obviously not assumed.

"But . . . why should . . . I know?" he stammered.

"Why not?" Barbara enquired. "He is your cousin."

Rudolph swore suddenly.

"What in the name of the devil are you trying to do?" he enquired. "To blacken me with the same brush, or force me into declaring that my claim on the estates is null and void because the rightful heir is alive? You promised to help me, Barbara. Is this your idea of assistance?"

"You conceited idiot," Barbara retorted. "I am not in the slightest interested in you or your efforts to seize a title to which you know full well you are not entitled. I wish to get in touch with this relative of yours who calls himself White Throat. I want to speak with him."

"But that is impossible!" Rudolph said. "No one knows where he is."

Barbara leant back in the chair and regarded Rudolph with narrowed eyes.

"I did not believe that you could be so dense," she said, wearily. "The other night you went off on some wild goose chase in search of this very man. You, failed, I understand, to find him, but where did you look for him and why?"

"We went to Staverley," Rudolph answered. "I heard rumours that White Throat and those who robbed with him had made Staverley their headquarters. I was not, as it happened, misinformed, but my cousin Panthea got there before me, and warned Lucius so that he escaped by the back entrance to the house while we were busy breaking down the front."

"That does not appear to me to be a very intelligent approach," Barbara sneered. "When one goes hunting, it is wise to stop the fox's earth at both ends, otherwise he is liable to find a bolthole, however hard one pursues him."

"It is easy to be wise after the event," Rudolph said sulkily.

"Who gave you this information?" Barbara enquired.

"That Lucius was making Staverley his headquarters?" Rudolph asked. "Oh, nobody of any consequence."

"Tell me," Barbara insisted.

"It was a woman as it happens," Rudolph replied, looking uncomfortable.

"Who is she?"

"No one you would know."

"I asked who she was."

"Her name is Moll Pettit."

"Where does she live?"

"At the Green Dragon at the end of Fleet Street."

"Why did she tell you this?"

Rudolph looked embarrassed and Barbara said impatiently, "Oh, for Heaven's sake answer the question, and don't sit there looking like a dumb dolt. It is obvious you pleasured the girl, and if you think I am jealous of every little strumpet that walks the streets of London, you are very much mistaken."

"I was in wine," Rudolph said apologetically, "and you were with the King."

"Never mind about that," Barbara snapped. "What did she say?"

"It was almost what you said just now," Rudolph answered, "that I was extremely like my cousin. She did not know he was my cousin, of course, but from what she said I guessed whom she was talking about and led her on. It appeared finally that one of Lucius' gang had come to the Green Dragon for supplies of some sort. He had been taken with Moll, which was not surprising for she is an attractive woman of her sort, and to save him the trouble of taking the things back with him, she had offered to drive them out of London the next day with a horse and cart. He had agreed, and I gather they had spent the rest of the night comfortably enough. He had left her as the dawn broke and she had the feeling that he did not want to be seen in the streets once it was light.

"She had taken the stores out to the meeting place agreed on, which I knew from her description was at the edge of the park that borders Staverley. The man had met her there and with him had been another, one who strangely resembled me. It was this second man whom she knew to be a gentleman. He paid for the goods and then bade her say nothing of whom she had met or seen, or to whom she had sold her wares.

"She had kept her promise, it appeared, until the resemblance to me of the stranger she had met in the country was too much for her, and she began to pump me as to who he might be and whether he was my brother."

"So you knew then that he was living at Staverley?"

"If you come to think of it, there could not be a better place," Rudolph replied. "A big house empty and forgotten, full of secret passages, underground cellars, and priests' holes for those who know them. I for one never would expect to find a gang of highwaymen living in an empty house. It is the first time I ever heard of such a thing."

"Do you think he will go back there now you have disturbed them?" Barbara asked reflectively.

"I believe so," Rudolph replied, "and Sir Philip thinks as I do. He is therefore biding his time."

"And you? Are you also prepared to wait?" Barbara asked cruelly, knowing the answer.

Rudolph's face flushed.

"Curse you, but you know the position I am in. You lent me that money a fortnight ago. It has kept the wolf from the door, but it won't last for ever."

"Now that your cousin is free, I should ask her to help you," Barbara said with a bitter smile.

"She shall help me," Rudolph retorted. "You can be certain of that."

His voice was suddenly harsh and Barbara looked at him, then seeing the resolution on his face, she bent forward.

"What are you going to do?" she asked.

He told her, and there was a faint smile on her lips as he finished speaking. Then she reached out her hand and took the embroidered purse from the table where it was always kept waiting so that she could pay her spies. She took from it ten florins and tossed them to Rudolph with a disdainful gesture. They fell on the floor at his feet, and for a moment he stared at them stupidly as if he could hardly believe the coins were real.

"Take them," Barbara said. "You will need them, for such things cost money you will find."

There was something nasty in the way she spoke which incensed Rudolph beyond endurance. The money Barbara had thrown him was insulting, as they both knew. It was not nearly enough for his requirements, in fact it would do little but buy him a meal of which he was greatly in need. Barbara had gold in plenty for those she favoured. Silver was a coinage she used but seldom, and Rudolph suspected that she had it ready now for the very purpose of mocking at him. He knew that he should walk from the room, or better still throw the money in Barbara's face. But he was hungry. Rudolph bent down, slowly picked the florins from off the floor and put them in his pocket. Then he straightened himself and looked at the woman he had once loved more deeply than he had ever loved anyone else in the whole of his shallow dissolute life.

She was lolling back in the chair, one foot supported on an embroidered footstool. Her dress had slipped from one shoulder, giving her an abandoned look which was almost irresistibly fascinating. Her eyes were half closed, her lips parted provocatively, and yet he knew she was laughing at him.

Suddenly in that moment Rudolph hated Barbara – hated her for the depths of passion into which she had drawn him, for the emotions she had stirred in him, for the love he had expended so wantonly upon her. He looked at her and knew that she waited for him to fall at her feet, that she was deliberately enticing him to desire her, even though she had just made him scramble like a servant for the bounty she had thrown him as she might throw a bone to a dog. It was then as she waited, her skin dazzlingly white against the velvet on the royal chair she had purloined from the King's own apartment, that Rudolph knew himself free of her. Without a word, but gauchely because he was ashamed, he turned and went from the apartment, slamming the door behind him.

Alone, Barbara Castlemaine stretched her arms high above her head and yawned. It had been amusing to bait the fool, it was perhaps annoying that he had finally taken the bit between his teeth and run out on her when she had least expected it, but it was of little consequence. She had other and more important things to consider, and a plan to make that would require a cool unheated brain.

She went to her desk and after some deliberation wrote a few lines on a piece of white paper. She would have sealed it with a piece of gold sealing wax that she had cajoled from the King, and which he had obtained from his sister in France as there was none to be obtained in England.

But even as she lifted it in her hand, Barbara realised her mistake and set it down again. A plain red sealing wax would be less distinctive. She applied it, then taking up the gold bell that stood on her writing desk, she rang it vigorously. When her footman answered it, she berated him for being so long in coming and sent him hotfoot for one of the grooms.

The man was brought to her after some delay. He was an undersized creature with pale eyelashes over shifty eyes, and a habit of speaking without opening his mouth, which made him almost incoherent. He was wearing an old pair of breeches and a tattered shirt, and on reaching Barbara's presence he immediately broke into a muttered apology for not having been given time to put on his uniform.

"You will not need it where I am sending you," Barbara said. "Go exactly as you are. It is important, you understand, to go exactly as you are."

The man nodded. Barbara walked across the room and picked up her purse. She jangled it so that his eyes glinted at the sound and she saw the sudden expression of greed flash across his face. Still fingering the purse but not opening it, she sat down again at her writing chair and began to speak.

*

It was some ten hours later that Barbara peered through the open window of her coach as it travelled slowly along the narrow dusty road. They had been moving at a good speed when they first left London, in fact she had commanded the coachman to make the horses go as quickly as they could, but now the animals were tired, for the coach was large and heavy and the night was sultry with never a breath of wind to blow away the stale heat that lingered from the hours of daylight.

It seemed to Barbara that she had been travelling for hours and every so often she had put her head from the window and cursed the coachman for not going quicker. Now she was intent on wondering if they were on the correct road, and putting her head once again from the window, she shouted.

"Are you certain we are not at fault?"

"No, my Lady, the wood is but half a mile ahead," the coachman replied.

Barbara gave a sigh of relief and sank back again against the soft padded cushions. They were, in reality, but fifteen miles from London and had taken only just over an hour to do the journey, which was surprisingly quick going.

Barbara was still wearing the magnificent gown in which she had supped with the King in his private apartments. He would have escorted her home, for when she had pleaded a headache and said that she was too unwell to continue the evening's amusement but must retire to bed at once, he had been full of concern. She had, however, persuaded him that she could find her way alone, knowing that, if once he came back to her apartment, it would be difficult to persuade him to leave.

She had her way as always, and Charles had sat down again at the gambling table although he was not particularly interested in cards, while Barbara had slipped away, hurrying not towards her apartments but to the palace yard where her coach was waiting.

She had it all carefully planned. Like the groom who had been sent off earlier in the day, none of her coachmen wore the famous Castlemaine livery. It was in fact, a very shabby retinue that swung out of the gates of London into the countryside. Few people accorded it a second glance and Barbara, sitting well back from the windows of the coach, made certain she was not seen.

Her dress of dull gold brocade embroidered with diamonds, and her necklace and earrings of the same gems, would not only have rendered her the center of all eyes had she been seen but would also have made her the natural prey of robbers and highwaymen.

Barbara was well aware that her coachmen were trembling with apprehension and fright at having to drive into the countryside without outriders, but they were far too frightened of her to protest and they obeyed her unquestionably, for they had learned from long experience of the strange vagaries of their mistress and knew that they must be obeyed at all costs. Barbara was not afraid, but there was an excitement within her so intense that she felt as nervous as her coachmen, but for a very different reason.

The adventure and danger appealed to her, making her appear more beautiful than ever. Her eyes shone like stars, and her whole body seemed to vibrate with the mounting emotions within her breast. The coach travelled on and finally came to a stop at the place Barbara had commanded them to find. It was the ruins of what had once been a lovely chapel of Norman architecture. It was a favourite beauty spot of those who wished to ride out from the City to some specified rendezvous. Barbara had been there on several occasions, when the ladies of the court chose to go rustic and picnic amongst the rural beauties of the unspoilt countryside.

The chapel, surrounded by high fir trees, stood a little away from the road. Its broken and ruined walls cast strange shadows in the moonlight, but the centre of the roofless building appeared to be bathed in silver, an oasis of loveliness protected from prying eyes, a secret place for those who would be alone and private. The large arched doorway remained and Barbara, stepping from her coach, went swiftly through it to stand looking around her as if in expectation that someone would be awaiting her arrival She looked breathtakingly lovely, a creature from another world, the wide billowing skirts of her evening gown rustling as she moved, her diamonds twinkling and sparkling around her neck, her dark hair framing the exquisite beauty of her face. She stood there pulsating, it seemed, as if driven by some extraordinary urgency that would not let her rest but propelled her as powerfully as if she were but a puppet in its hands. She stood there waiting and then, as nothing happened, the elation died from her face, and she seemed irresolute.

At that moment, from the shadows at the far end of the broken walls, a figure detached itself. He advanced so softly that he had come several paces before Barbara saw him, but as her lips formed themselves into a soft sound and her hands were clasped together as if in an excess of joy, White Throat stepped into the moonlight.

Barbara did not move from where she stood, and he walked across the clearing towards her, neither hurrying nor lagging, but moving almost determinedly so that one sensed there was something important in his coming. He drew near to Barbara and she saw the glitter of his eyes behind the mask, the sudden tightening of his lips before he spoke to her.

He swept his hat from his head, and although the bow was polite, it was neither flattering nor cordial.

"You are Lady Castlemaine?" he said.

'You recognise me!"

"Your face, like your name, is well known."

She did not know whether he spoke sarcastically or whether he stated a fact. There was a little pause and then White Throat asked, "Why are you here?"

She looked up at him, and her eyes widened as if in surprise before she replied.

"Why not? Is there any reason why I should not come to this place?"

Again, she saw his lips tighten and after a moment's pause, he said, "I think your Ladyship is playing with me. I came here to meet someone very different, and I imagine that you have a knowledge of this."

"Why should I have a knowledge of any such thing?" Barbara Castlemaine asked. "I came here to look at the moonlight. I had a sudden desire to escape from the affectations and the pretensions of the Court. I came here alone in search of something new."

She was watching him as she spoke, expecting him to appear uneasy, a little bewildered and nonplussed as to whether she spoke the truth or not. To her surprise, for few had ever questioned Barbara's acting, the highwayman appeared completely at his ease even though his face was severe, and she had the uncomfortable feeling that he sat in judgment on her, although why or how she should feel this she could not explain.

"Now that you are here," he said, "have you found what you sought?"

It was then that Barbara threw back her head and the moonlight was full on her face as she replied softly, "Yes, for I have found you."

13

For a long moment there was a silence which seemed to vibrate between them and then, with an impulsive gesture, Barbara Castlemaine laid her hand on White Throat's arm.

"I want to talk to you," she said very softly. "Is there not some place we can sit down, for what I have to say may take a long time?"

His face was turned towards her, but the mask hid his expression and from the firm line of his lips she learned nothing. There was, however, no perceptible hesitation before he replied,

"There is a tombstone over there on which your Ladyship could sit, that is if you are not afraid of ghosts."

"I am not afraid of ghosts or of anything else," Barbara Castlemaine replied. "What other woman of your acquaintance would have come here at night without outriders?"

"My acquaintance with ladies who have such accessories is somewhat limited," White Throat said drily.

He moved beside Barbara in the direction of the tombstone, and when they reached it she sank down on the flat marble surface, spreading out her skirts as if she seated herself on one of her own satin and cushioned sofas.

White Throat stood looking down at her and after a moment she patted the stone beside her and said invitingly, "Will you not be seated, for we cannot talk while you tower over me? I find very tall men curiously fatiguing."

He did as she asked, and now the moonlight was on his face as it was on hers. The broken stone wall made a background for them and protected them both from prying eyes and the night wind. The delicate stone tracery of a broken pillar beside the tomb gave their seat a curiously classic look so that Barbara, in her brocade and diamonds, seemed to mingle the ancient with the modern until the mind became a little confused and one wondered where the past ended and the future began.

She was lovely enough to make any man's heart beat faster as she said pleadingly, her hands clasped together, "I want you to do me a favour before we talk together."

"What is it?" White Throat asked.

"Will you please remove your mask?" Barbara said. "I have a very urgent desire to see your face."

"Why should that be of interest to you?" the highwayman enquired. "Are you hoping that you will be able to identify me on another and perhaps less happy occasion, or are you merely curious, as so many women are, as to what sort of brutal monster a mask may hide?"

Barbara laughed, a little tinkling laugh of genuine amusement.

"Are you really so stupid as to believe that I am not already aware of your identity, my Lord of Staverley?"

"I wonder who gave you that information," Lucius said. "Could it have been my cousin Rudolph?"

Barbara laughed again.

"Rudolph wishes you were dead," she said, "so that he might claim your title and estates. It is a pity from his point of view that you are so persistently alive."

"The odds on my inconveniencing him for long are in his favour," Lucius said drily.

As he spoke, he reached up and untied the bow which held the mask and drew it from his face. There was a faint smile on his lips as he faced Barbara.

"Now are you satisfied?" he asked.

Her eyes searched his face and she gave a little exclamation of pleasure.

"You are like Rudolph," she said, "but there is just that difference, something that I have always felt was missing from his features. I cannot explain it save to say that it is of the utmost import to a man – and to a woman."

Lucius put the mask into the deep pocket of his velvet coat, then turning sideways on the tombstone so that he faced Barbara almost squarely.

He said, "And now, if Your Ladyship will be so kind as to inform me why you are here and why you sent me a note purporting to be from my cousin Panthea."

"How do you know I sent you the note?" Barbara Castlemaine enquired.

"I am not entirely devoid of brains," Lucius replied. "I came here tonight expecting to see my cousin, but at the same time suspicious that it might be a trap into which someone wished to lure me. I saw your coach when it was at least a mile from here and took care to see that it was not followed, nor contained either armed soldiers or eager justices of the peace out for my blood. When I saw that the coach contained a woman, I naturally thought at first that it was, in truth, my cousin Panthea coming in search of me at this very spot, as had been written in the note that I had received earlier in the day."

"So, you *did* receive it," Barbara Castlemaine said. "You must give me credit for being extremely astute."

"The groom you sent to Staverley found the house locked and barred," Lucius said quietly. "He knocked on the doors and rattled on the windows without receiving any response. He would have failed to contact me had he not been more frightened of failing you than of endangering his own neck."

"What do you mean?" Barbara Castlemaine asked.

"Terrified, I imagine, of returning to you to say that he could find no one at home, the poor wretch tried to climb up the outside of the house to a half-open window on the first floor. He had almost reached the window ledge when a piece of rotten guttering gave way and he crashed to the ground, falling some twenty feet on to the flagstones of the terrace. He was dying when two of my men found him and he was dead before I could reach his side and give him any attention."

"Yet you found the note?"

Barbara's face expressed neither sympathy nor horror at the story she had heard. Her interest was concentrated all too obviously on the matters that concerned herself.

"I took the note," White Throat said quietly, "from the man who had died in his efforts to bring it to me."

"And so you came here," Barbara said.

"And so I came here, to meet my cousin Panthea," Lucius amended.

"And instead, you found me."

The words were spoken almost coquettishly and for a moment Barbara's long dark eyelashes swept her cheeks, then she raised her eyes again and said,"I have already told you, I wanted to see you."

"And now that you have done so, are you content?" Lucius enquired.

There was a sarcastic note in his voice, which one would have been deaf not to hear, but it appeared to leave Barbara unmoved, for she bent a little nearer, the heavy exotic fragrance of her perfume scenting the air about her as she moved.

"There is much that I have to say to you," she said, "but first tell me about yourself. Are you happy, living the wild, hard life of an outlaw, or do you crave for the things you have lost, the comfort of home and hearth, well cooked food, soft music and of course women – women like me to talk with and to make love to whenever you wish?"

Barbara's voice was as soft and seductive as a violin playing a love song, and Lucius' reply was quick.

"What are you attempting to do, my Lady?" he enquired. "Entice me back into civilisation so that I put my head in the waiting noose?"

The look Barbara gave him was almost sorrowful.

"Can you not trust me?" she said. "If you imagine I have come here as a decoy for the law or from His Majesty, you are much mistaken. I have come here entirely on my own and no one, save the two coachmen who have driven me here, have any idea where I may be found."

"And why have you come?" Lucius asked.

"I have answered that question already," Barbara replied. "To see you!"

His eyes searched her face as if to find the truth there, and when he did not speak, Barbara continued.

"I saw you for the first time in the law courts, but I had heard of you for many years and I think your exploits and adventures have always stirred my heart and aroused with in me an interest that grew greater and greater, until finally I looked up to see you standing in the doorway of that hot crowded courtroom. It was then I knew that I wished to speak with you and to learn what sort of a man you might be. I know your cousin well, but Rudolph is a poor fellow. He tries to swashbuckle his way through life and succeeds only in being a failure."

"How would you have him then?" Lucius asked.

"I would have him as brave as you are," Barbara replied. "Why, he has not even the courage to come here and murder you himself but must fetch a lot of bungling soldiers to try and do the job for him."

"So, you would have me murdered by my cousin Rudolph," Lucius said. "A pretty scheme, and what part do you play in it?"

"I have not said I would have you murdered," Barbara Castlemaine said. "On the contrary, I much prefer you alive, Lord Staverley."

"That name is not mine to use," Lucius answered. "I renounced my family years ago. I am White Throat, the highwayman, the robber and the thief, the man who takes gold and jewels from those who travel to London in their coaches."

"And would you take mine?" Barbara asked.

She put up her hands as she spoke to the diamonds round her neck.

"If I took them from you," Lucius said, "you would only replace them from the Privy Purse, and as it is the country can ill afford your extravagances. I would not add to them."

"How severe you sound," Barbara pouted. "Would you deny a woman the pleasure of looking beautiful?"

"It depends for what reason she uses her beauty," Lucius said. "Some women create only misery."

"Am I one?" Barbara enquired.

"That is a question for you to answer," Lucius said.

Barbara shrugged and putting out her right hand she laid it softly on his.

"Why do you fight against me?" she asked. "Your eyes are hard, your voice when you speak to me is harsh. I have come here to see you and I have taken risks that I might do so. Are you not glad? Is there not some warm soft spot within your heart for a woman who has dared so much?"

"What do you want of me?" Lucius enquired.

"Are you not man enough to know the answer to that?" Barbara asked. "I have told you that when you came to the courtroom my heart beat quicker and I knew then I could never rest until we had met, until I knew if your heartbeat in unison with mine."

Slowly, Lucius removed his hand from beneath Barbara's, then rising to his feet he said, "Lady Castlemaine, I think we speak at cross purposes. I am not foolish enough to imagine that your interest in me is what you pretend. I cannot guess why you came here tonight, but I am not vain enough to accept at its face value that which you tell me. If you will not be frank, and if you have nothing further to say, then I must ask you to excuse me for I have work to do elsewhere."

He spoke softly but Barbara's response was not what one might have expected. Instead, she leant back on the tombstone, her throat and neck very white in the moon light, her lips very red as she smiled a slow, seductive smile.

"How stupid you are," she said, "or are you one of the few men left without vanity? You would, I promise you, be unique at Whitehall."

"May I go?"

Lucius' tone was patient, almost to the point of long suffering.

"No!"

The monosyllable came sharply from Barbara's lips.

"No, you will not go, for there is much I would say to you. Sit down again, Lord Staverley, or White Throat if you prefer the name." Barbara straightened herself and held out her hand invitingly. "Come," she said. "There is no reason to be afraid of me."

It was then Lucius laughed, a laugh of sheer untrammelled amusement.

"I am not afraid of you," he replied, "and I have the strangest suspicion that you are trying to seduce me. Tell me if I am at fault."

"Would it surprise you so very much if you were right?" Barbara asked.

"Then the stories about you are true after all," he remarked.

"What stories have you heard?" Barbara enquired.

"That you are as promiscuous as you are beautiful, that you are utterly without modesty, and that when you desire a man, you do not always wait for him to pursue you."

"So that is what they say of me," Barbara said, by no means displeased. "Well, what if it is true, Mr, Highwayman? Shall I add to it that, as yet, no man has refused me?"

"And what would you do to him if he did?" Lucius enquired.

"I think I would kill him with my own hands," Barbara replied. "They say there is no fury like that of a woman scorned. No man shall scorn me and live."

Lucius laughed again, but the sound was low and had a modicum of pity in it, then his face was surprisingly gentle as he sat down on the tombstone and took Barbara's hand in his.

"Listen, Lady Castlemaine," he said. "You are beautiful and life has heaped so many favours upon you. Take my advice and do not flout the laws of nature unnecessarily. You are very lovely, you are also in many ways intelligent. Use that intelligence to rule your heart and your body so that they become the servants of your brain not the masters of it. You will not thank me for this advice now, but when you are old, if you do as I say, you will be grateful. Leave men to do their own wooing, Lady Castlemaine. You will learn then a great deal about love which at present you do not know."

"I know all there is to know about it," Barbara retorted, and for the moment Lucius, watching her, saw the expression of a spoilt child in her face rather than that of a pampered beauty.

"Love is a subject that is inexhaustible," Lucius said. "There are many kinds of love, Lady Castlemaine, but only the highest and best is worth pursuing."

"How can you be sure of that?" Barbara asked. "Only by seeking love, by sampling it not once but a thousand times can you be certain that it is not what you want, until ultimately you find perfection."

"How wrong you are if you think that is the way to find perfection!" Lucius said quietly. "Have you never been in love – really in love?"

Barbara turned her face, away from him and for a moment the expression in her eyes altered.

"Yes, once," she replied in a low voice, "and it tore me to pieces so that I prayed never to feel like that again. The love I seek now is the joy and excitement of a heart beating in harmony with mine, the rapture of feeling warm lips against my mouth, of knowing that strong arms hold me close, and feeling that a flame mounting within my body is leaping hot and passionate within the man who holds me."

Barbara had gradually turned her face back towards Lucius as she spoke, and now, as if the very words she had spoken conjured up an excitement within herself, her eyes were glowing, her breath came quickly from between her parted lips, and the white curves of her breasts seemed to move tumultuously among the jewels that bordered the lowcut bodice of her dress.

But as Lucius watched her, the gentleness of his expression seemed to alter so that his eyes were hard and almost like granite as he said, "That is not love. There is indeed an ugly name for it."

But Barbara was past hearing him. Even as he spoke, her hands came out to lie caressingly against the soft velvet of his coat, and her voice hungrily and endearingly whispered, "I want you! Kiss me and then you will know how much I want you."

Lucius was still for a long moment before he replied.

"You have made a mistake! You have forgotten to whom you are speaking! You, Lady Barbara Castlemaine, the most famous woman at Whitehall, should not talk of such matters to an outlaw and a man who lives only by his wits. You dwell among courtiers and Kings. There are men at Whitehall who live only to hear such things as you are saying now. But they are not for me, and so I beg of you to forget that you have said them."

Lucius rose to his feet.

"Your carriage is waiting, Lady Castlemaine," he added. "London will seem a drab place unless you return to it."

He had hardly finished speaking before Barbara too had sprung to her feet.

"Why are you saying this?" she asked. "Why are you striving to be rid of me? Can it be that you are afraid to take what you are offered?"

"Let us say that is the reason," Lucius replied soothingly. "The hour is late, and it is dangerous for you to stay here any longer,"

"Dangerous? From whom does the danger come?" Barbara asked a little wildly. "From you?"

She stood there palpitating, her eyes fixed upon him as if she would wrench some secret from behind the impassive severity of his face, then suddenly she exclaimed, "You do not want me, that is the truth, is it not? You do not want me?"

"I have not said so," Lucius replied.

"But it is obvious," Barbara Castlemaine shouted. "I have come here, I have told you what I feel about you, and all you can do is to send me back to London."

"I am thinking of your Ladyship's safety," Lucius said.

Barbara gave a cry of rage.

"You are thinking of nothing of the sort," she exclaimed. "You have refused me, you – a thief, a robber, an outcast, a man with whom no decent woman would associate."

"That is what I have already told you," Lucius said, apparently unmoved by the tempest of Barbara's rage.

"But it is not true," she cried, her mood veering like a weathercock in the wind. "You are not some lowborn robber, but the Marquess of Staverley, the bearer of a noble name and. A great title. We speak as equals, you and I, and yet you have refused me. You are sending me away because you do not want me. I am as safe here as if I were in a nunnery surrounded by women, safe with you, my Lord Staverley! Is the appearance of your manhood but pretence?"

Barbara's tone was insulting, but still Lucius remained unmoved.

"You are tired," he said. "In a little while you will forget – in fact let us both forget this night and our meeting."

"But I wish not to forget it," Barbara said. "I wanted to meet you and I came here for that very purpose. You are all the things that I looked for in Rudolph but could not find. You are a man as handsome and appealing as the one to whom I once lost my heart. I could love again, and love this time would be very different for I know so much more. I am much wiser and have had so much experience."

"But why should you love me?" Lucius asked. "You are talking wildly! Let me persuade you to go home, for I promise you it is the right thing to do."

"And have I ever done the right thing in my life?" Barbara asked. "You cannot be rid of me as easily as that. You cannot really want to refuse me. It is but your chivalry, your desire to remain obscure in the dangerous life you have chosen."

"Think what you please," Lucius said, "but I promise you that it is best for you to leave without our speaking of such things anymore."

"But suppose I refuse?" Barbara cried.

She came nearer to him then, suddenly, before he could move or prevent it, her arms were round his neck and her lips, hot and burning, were pressed against his. Just for a moment he held her, then with a gentle strength that could not be withstood, he took her arms from his neck and set her aside from him.

"You force me to be frank," he said very quietly. "I am in love with someone else, someone whom, if circumstances were very different, I would ask to be my wife."

The fury in Barbara's eyes and the contorted anger of her mouth made her like a creature from hell. She seemed to quiver all over as her passion and desire changed in a split second into a fiery virulent rage. Her fingers were clenched until the knuckles showed white, and she stamped on the ground while her dark curls danced round her face.

"Curse you," she stormed, "that you should do this to me, you of all people. I will make you pay for this. I will have you strung up on the nearest gibbet and I shall stand below it and laugh. Do you hear me? I shall laugh. And afterwards you shall be drawn and quartered and your head, green with mould, shall be stuck on the spikes of Tower Hill. I shall drive by and jeer at you. I hate you now as I have never hated any man in my life before, and I swear by everything that I hold holy that I will punish you for this by death."

But Lucius, as he heard and watched Barbara's temper, seemed completely unmoved, and there was indeed a sadness in his eyes which lightened their severity.

Only when Barbara paused for breath, her voice hoarse in her throat, did he say quietly, "All these things will doubtless come to pass but, in the meantime, if you will not go from here, I must leave you. All the same, you will be wise to take my advice and leave immediately while I am present. I am not the only highwayman abroad in these woods and there are those who would respect neither your Ladyship's person nor your possessions."

The full fury of Barbara's anger was passing from her and suddenly she shivered a little, although whether from the reaction of her own anger or the warning in Lucius' words he did not know. It was, however, enough to make her move across the grass towards the doorway of the broken chapel through which they had entered. Below her on the road, Barbara's horses and servants waited patiently, too used to her Ladyship's peculiarities even to question her keeping them on duty at an hour when the moon was sinking down the heavens and dawn would soon break in the east.

As Barbara appeared in the doorway of the chapel, one of the men sprang down from the box and opened the door of the coach. Barbara hesitated for the first time since she had walked away from Lucius and, turning, found him close behind her. For the moment there was an almost pathetic expression of defeat in her face and then, as she looked at him, at his clear-cut handsome features, at the square, intelligent forehead, and deep-set eyes, she set her lips as if with an effort she restrained herself from further abuse, and with a flounce of her skirts she ran down the short incline towards her coach and stepped into it.

The footman looked up to see if Lucius was following and then closed the door and sprang up on the box. Neither he nor the coachman thought it strange at seeing a well-dressed man emerge from the ruins which her ladyship had just left. They were used to clandestine meetings and to assignations in strange places. They were thankful that the encounter, or whatever it had been, was over and they could return to the City.

Lucius stood bareheaded in the moonlight as Barbara bent forward to take a last look at him. Then, as if the unruffled serenity of his appearance was too much for her, she suddenly leant forward and shouted.

"You will be sorry for this when you hear what has happened to your cousin Panthea. She is not for you!"

The last words were lost as the coachman whipped up the horses and the coach started forward, but Barbara was rewarded by the sight of Lucius roused as she had not been able to rouse him the whole evening. He took two or three quick steps forward, his face suddenly distraught with anxiety, his hand raised as if to stop the coach, but it was too late. Barbara was carried away from him and now, because she had managed to disturb him, she threw herself back against the padded seat and tried to laugh.

But the sound that came from her lips was not one of merriment, indeed it broke almost harshly on something that was suspiciously like a sob. Then, drawing her handkerchief from where it had been tucked in her waist, Barbara applied it first to her eyes and then tore the delicate embroidered linen and deep valuable lace into small shreds.

"That hurt him," she said aloud. "That will teach him to prefer that pale-faced doll to me!"

Yet somehow it was no consolation to know that Lucius was perturbed about another woman. It did nothing to relieve the aching pain within Barbara's breast, or the feeling she had of being crushed and humbled until every bone in her body ached as if she had been physically instead of mentally insulted.

She could not quite believe it to be true that she, the most acclaimed beauty in the land, had offered herself to a highwayman and been repudiated. She could hardly credit her own memory of what had been said, of the invitation that had been given to him so boldly, so unmistakably, and that had been refused. It must be a mistake! Yet she knew there was no mistake. She could still feel the unyielding coldness of his lips beneath hers. She had known then, if she had not guessed before, that she did not attract him. It was unbelievable, almost incredible, and yet it was true, she did not attract him. Here was one man who could remain immune to her charms, to the blandishments and allure that had made every other man on whom she had ever looked her abject and adoring slave.

It was then, for the first time in her life, that Barbara began to be afraid of her old age. It was still a long way ahead of her, and yet she knew that she would feel as she felt now when the time came when men passed her by, when she could no longer pick and choose her lovers but must sink lower and lower until the presents she would give them would be worth more than the favours that had once been prized higher than all the wealth in the Kingdom.

She thought of the King and of the power she had over him, of the men who had preceded him and those who haunted her apartments, pleading and praying for just the touch of her hands, a glance from her brilliant blue eyes.

How often she had laughed at them and threatened that her servants should turn them away for daring to be so importunate. How would she feel when the day came when there would be no one waiting there, when younger and more eager beauties would take her place with the King? She had been afraid of the Queen but that was before she had seen her but, though Charles had returned to her after his marriage, there was nothing to say that he would remain her protector for ever.

She could hold him now by her beauty, by the passion that she aroused in him and by the fact that she had borne him two children and would doubtless bear him more, but men were not faithful out of gratitude, they were faithful because a woman was lovely and more desirable than her fellows. For a moment, Barbara felt a presentiment that made her shiver as if a cold hand had touched her and she knew it for the hand of time.

Clairvoyantly, she thought she could see the faces of those who would rival her. She could see them as if they sat beside her in the coach as it rumbled over the stony road – women whom Charles would love, women who would take the presents, the money and the power that had been hers. There would not be one but many, but she knew she would fight every inch of the way to retain all she had gained, to acquire more to hold the vacillating affections of the King.

But ultimately, she would fail. Time would take the last vestige of her beauty from her and with it the last particle of her power. This was the beginning tonight, when a man had refused her because he loved another woman. He had spoken to her of love and told her that she did not know what was finest and best in love. He had given her, too, some advice which, while she knew it to be both true and right, she knew she would never follow. She would pursue what she wanted, whether it be a man, a jewel, or merely some delicate dish, with the greed and hunger that could not be denied because always her body, beautiful though it was, would master her brain.

Barbara had it in her heart to be sorry for herself, and yet even while she strove to be honest, she could not prevent her anger burning furiously within her against Lucius. She hated him with a fierce searing hatred that seemed to burn her up like a fever, to parch her lips so that she felt as if they cracked for want of water, and she knew that she had desired him as she had never desired a man before, not even Philip Chesterfield, whom she had loved beyond anyone else until this moment.

It was not love that she felt for Lucius. It was an aching want that made the whole world seem empty and meaningless because she could not know him close and feel herself possessed by him. It was like being isolated in a desert of stagnation and unhappiness, it was a loneliness that she knew was only physical and yet was no less intense because of it. It was the first time in her life that Barbara had ever felt the pangs of unrequited passion, and they were to scar and torment her and never cease to rack her memory as long as she was to live.

Lucius was the first man who eluded her. There were, in the long years to come, to be many more, and yet never was anything quite so soul-destroying as the pain she endured in those first moments as she drove from the ruined chapel, and as the heat of her desire died away within her. But the aching want of it remained long after she was cold and still, her fingers still clutching the torn, tattered pieces of her handkerchief.

*

The coach must have driven for nearly five miles, and they were travelling at a good speed for the horses were fresh after their rest and were also impatient to be home in the comfort of their stables when, with a jerk that flung Barbara on to the floor, the horses were pulled up on their haunches and the coach came to a sudden standstill. At a sharp command, the coachmen held their hands above their heads and Barbara looked out to see a highwayman astride a black horse, a primed pistol pointing directly at her heart.

She rose from the floor, and it took a moment or two before her scattered senses realised that the highwayman confronting her was Lucius. He wore his mask, but there was no mistaking his black embroidered coat or the bunch of lace at his neck that was so characteristic of him. She knew, too, the square outline of his chin, the firm strength of his lips that she had touched with her own but a short time ago.

"What do you want?"

It was typical of her to say the words defiantly, but unexpectedly they seemed to be strangled in her throat.

"Get out! I wish to speak to you."

He still sat astride his horse, but as he saw that she intended to obey him, he swung himself to the ground, still with his pistol pointing at her. He waited while she stepped from the coach and the door swung shut behind her.

"What do you want?" she asked again.

"Tell these men here to wait until you have finished speaking with me?"

"Why should I?"

"Because I tell you so, and hurry. There is no time to be lost."

Wonderingly, but with her confidence slowly returning to her, Barbara gave the order and then glanced a little mockingly at Lucius.

"What now?" she enquired. "I am, of course, only too ready to obey you."

He took no notice of her sarcasm. Instead, he said curtly,

"Move a few steps away from the coach. I do not wish your servants to overhear our conversation."

She did as he suggested then, when they were out of earshot, she turned to face him with a twirl of her silken skirts.

"Well?" she enquired. "Have you regretted sending me away?"

"I followed you for a very different reason," Lucius said. "As you left, you spoke of my cousin Panthea. Where is she, and what did you mean by the last words, you shouted at me?"

"So, you *are* curious," Barbara jeered. "But you will hear no more from me. The news will doubtless reach you in good time."

"Tell me what you mean and at once," Lucius insisted.

"And if I refuse?" Barbara enquired.

"Then I shall shoot you," he said, and he raised his pistol threateningly.

"If I am dead that will do you but little good," Barbara smiled. "You will still know nothing of what is happening to your cousin."

"I shall not shoot to kill, Lady Castlemaine," Lucius answered. "It is not my habit to kill anyone unless they are so foul and depraved that the world is well rid of them. It is not for me to sit in judgment on you, but I fight for my cousin Panthea. She is dearer to me than life itself, dearer to me than the chivalry that I was brought up to accord to ladies like yourself. As I have already told you, I am a desperate man. You will tell me what has happened to my cousin or else I shall shoot and wound you. You have already told me your men are not armed, so there is nothing you can do to prevent it. You will not die, Lady Castlemaine, but you will be scarred, and scars are not becoming to a beautiful woman. A long scar across the whiteness of your shoulder for instance. . ."

"You would not dare!" Barbara cried out, but Lucius seemed hardly to have heard them.

"A woman with a finger missing is an object of pity. You would be pitied, Lady Castlemaine, and I do not think you would like it."

"I shall not tell you, and I do not believe your threats."

Barbara spat the words at him, and in answer Lucius raised his pistol and pointed it at the point of her white shoulder where it rose seductively from the bodice of her dress. He took careful aim, and then quietly began to count.

"One . . . two. . ."

His fingers appeared to tighten on the trigger and Barbara gave a little cry.

"Damn you," she cried, "but if you want to know, and I hope the news pleases you, she is being married at this very moment to Rudolph. He has need of her money, and she will marry him so that he can live at Staverley and restore

the estates to what they were. I hope the information pleases you, my Lord Staverley, and you will soon find yourself hanged as you so rightly deserve."

"Where is Rudolph marrying her?"

The words cut across Barbara's vindictive threats. For a moment she thought to refuse, and then she saw that she had already hurt him, and with a sudden elation she cast all caution, and Rudolph's plan of secrecy, to the wind.

"They are being married in the church at Staverley. Does that please you? The church that should be yours – the church where, if you were not a hunted man with a price on your head, you could have married her yourself and made her your wife."

Barbara's last word ended in a sudden shriek as she shouted it so that Lucius might hear, for he was no longer by her side. As she told him the place at which Panthea was to be married, he swung himself into the saddle and, gathering up the reins, dug his spurs into his stallion's side. He did not glance at Barbara as he rode past her, nor did he look back.

She watched him as he galloped hotfoot down the road until he and his horse vanished into the shadows of the trees and were no more to be seen.

Then a slow bitter smile curled her lips. Already the moon was fading from the sky and the first pale fingers of the dawn were lightening the sky in the east. It was a long journey to Staverley. Lucius would be too late!

14

The Queen finished the last stitch of her embroidery and held it out for Panthea's approval.

"It is pretty, is it not, Lady Panthea?" she asked.

"It is lovely, ma'am," Panthea exclaimed, "and Your Majesty's work is exquisite. I doubt if there is anyone in England who can do such tiny stitches."

"I was taught by the nuns in Portugal," the Queen said with a smile.

She folded her embroidery and then, as if the thought of the good women who had been her instructors drew her thoughts to more spiritual things, she raised her eyes to the holy pictures that decorated the walls of her room and her lips moved so that Panthea knew she was murmuring a prayer.

It always struck Panthea as strange that the Queen's apartments in the palace were so plainly and simply furnished, whereas people talked continuously of the magnificence of Lady Castlemaine's apartments. But the Queen, as everyone knew, never bothered the King with requests for presents, nor did she covet the valuable and ornate furnishings of many of the other state rooms which could so easily have been transferred to hers. She was content with her holy pictures on the walls, her books of devotion by her bedside and her stoup of holy water over her head, and Panthea often had the feeling that, although she never said so, Her Majesty felt gentle pride in being so different from the other ladies who sought her husband's affection.

Like most people who rely on their expression and charm for their good looks, the Queen sometimes looked remarkably attractive and at others dull and uninteresting.

Panthea noted with pleasure that today the little Queen looked almost pretty as, putting aside her embroidery, she began to change her gown for supper with His Majesty.

Her maids brought several different dresses for her approval and the Queen hesitated over which to choose, considering as she did so the jewels she could wear with each *ensemble*. There was a gown of stiff, white-figured satin over a petticoat of crimson lace, with which she could wear her necklace of rubies which had been one of the wedding presents given to her by her relatives in far-off Portugal. This dress was Panthea's favourite, for the touch of crimson was exceedingly becoming to Her Majesty's dark eyes and hair, and Panthea was anxious that Her Majesty should look her best tonight, for the King had notified her that they would dine quietly and with only the minimum of ladies and gentlemen in attendance on them.

These were the occasions, Panthea knew, when the Queen had a chance to win her husband's affection and to prove to him that she was in many ways far more desirable than Barbara Castlemaine, with whom he spent so much time. In looks there was, of course, no comparison, for Barbara's beauty was unrivalled not only at court, but also over the length and breadth of the land.

She had a smile that could charm the very heart of a man from beneath his ribs, and even the rough crowd who had threatened to mob her coach because they were incensed by the stories of her extravagance and greed, turned their curses to blessings when she opened her coach window and smiled at them with the magic of Circe, turning in her case not men into pigs, but pigs into men.

No, the Queen could not challenge Barbara when it came to looks, but she had other and more subtle qualities that the King both liked and respected. The Queen was witty, and he adored wit – Barbara's sense of humour was almost negligible. The Queen was good-tempered and easy-going, while Barbara was turbulent and her outbursts of temper seemed to increase in number month by month. The Queen had a dignity and self-control that well became her position, while Barbara was swayed and guided only by the desires and hungers of her body, behaving when she wished as badly as any fishwife from the market, or a harlot from the taverns round Fleet Street.

"Choose the white and crimson, ma'am," Panthea said now, as the Queen seemed about to decide on a brown and orange brocade that made her skin look sallow and took the sparkle from her eyes.

She spoke impulsively, forgetting for a moment the court etiquette which decreed that she should not have given her opinion until invited to do so. But the Queen smiled at her and said gently, "Your taste is always good, Lady Panthea. I will do as you say."

The maids carried the gowns from the room and when they were alone again, the Queen remarked a little wistfully, "I dare say it matters little what I wear for I am no beauty, as I know full well."

There was something so wistful and woebegone in her tone that Panthea felt the tears rise in her eyes.

"Oh, ma'am, you must not say that," she exclaimed, "for there are many degrees of beauty and I often think that the goodness of Your Majesty's heart, and the sweetness of your mind, shines from your face with a loveliness that is not of this Earth but has something spiritual about it."

The Queen was plainly touched even while she shook her head as if she could not credit the truth of what Panthea said.

"You are always loyal and true to me, Lady Panthea," she said. "I owe both you and your great-aunt a gratitude for the kindness and loyalty you have always shown me since I came to England."

"It has been a great honour to serve you, ma'am," Panthea replied, and she meant it.

"We like having you at Whitehall," the Queen went on. "I can say now in all sincerity that I am deeply relieved that the wicked and dreadful charges that were lodged against you were proved wrong."

"I thank you, ma'am," Panthea answered.

"All the same, it has taken its toll on you," the Queen said gently, "You are looking pale, Lady Panthea, and under your eyes there are dark lines which I do not recall when I first came to Whitehall."

It was then that Panthea felt the opportunity had come for her to tell the Queen what lay within her heart. She had thought of it for some time before the trial, and after she had warned Lucius that Rudolph was determined on his capture. It would, in many ways, be easier to approach the King, but she felt that Charles might not listen to her, especially after his sharp rebuke the day they had been riding in the park and Sir Philip had galloped up with his request for a company of soldiers.

She had been afraid since then of bringing up the matter, but she had been sure that the Queen would listen attentively and with sympathy. Katherine might be young, but she had an understanding far beyond her years, and no plea for help or comfort, Panthea knew, would be refused if it were humanly possible for her to attend to it.

There would never be a better chance than this, Panthea thought, for it was seldom that she was alone with the Queen, and the fact that they were together this afternoon was only because a Lady in Waiting had been taken faint and another had escorted her back to her apartment.

A quick glance at the clock by the Queen's bedside, where the lamp that was one of her most precious possessions burned at night, told Panthea that she had perhaps five minutes' grace to spare, and without further hesitation she spoke hurriedly.

"I have something of the greatest import to tell you, ma'am. Is it too much to ask that Your Majesty will at least hear me?"

"But of course I will hear you," the Queen replied. "Come and let us sit down by the window."

She moved across the room to the two highbacked, velvet-cushioned chairs overlooking the garden below. As she followed, Panthea felt the urgency of her plea within her, and at the same time a sense of her own incompetence to make the story sound as appealing as she believed it to be. Lucius' life depended on the efficacy of her tale. Suddenly she felt bereft of words and eloquence, and was conscious only of the aching yearning of her own heart that he might be pardoned and restored to the position in society to which he was entitled by birth.

Her anxiety must have shown very clearly on her face for the Queen, having seated herself, put out her hand and said kindly, "Tell me in your own words, my dear. I know myself how hard one tries to be fluent when one would petition for something about which one cares very deeply. But words are only a vehicle for our feelings. Speak simply and I shall understand – and indeed it is best that you should speak simply, for at times the English language is still hard for me to follow."

It was then that the words came to Panthea. Dropping on her knee beside the Queen's chair, she poured out her heart, telling Her Majesty all she knew of Lucius, what he had done for her personally, and how he had saved from the scaffold and from transportation others unjustly accused of crimes that they had never committed. If the Queen sometimes found it hard to follow Panthea's words, her white face and pleading eyes were eloquent enough to convince a far harder judge that she pleaded a just cause.

When Panthea had finished speaking, the tears were running down her cheeks and her eyes were still wide, fixed on the Queen's face, and her fingers laced together suppliantly.

"I have told you all this, ma'am," Panthea finished, "believing that you might find it in your heart to speak with the King. I have told you the truth, the whole truth as I know it – and I know that, whatever wrongs my cousin Lucius may have committed, he has remained true and honourable and that there is not a more loyal servant to His Majesty in the whole length and breadth of the land."

The Queen gave a little sigh and bent forward to lay her hand on Panthea's shining head.

"I can see how much it means to you, my dear," she said. "You love him, do you not?"

"With all my heart and soul," Panthea said simply.

"And if you could marry him, you would do so?" the Queen enquired.

"I would follow him barefoot across the world," Panthea said, "if he would but raise his finger to beckon me. I love him, ma'am, and he me with a love that is so perfect that it can only come from God himself."

The Queen sighed again. For a moment there was a shadow on her face, and Panthea knew she was thinking of her own love for the King and how it was unrequited. Then with an effort which was obvious to see, she forced herself to concentrate on Panthea's problems rather than on her own.

"I will see what I can do," she said at length. "It is not easy, as you well know, but when the right opportunity presents itself and His Majesty is willing to listen to me, I will tell him all that you have told me at this moment."

Panthea kissed the Queen's hand.

"How can I ever thank you, ma'am?" she murmured.

"Thank me when something has been achieved," the Queen said. "I think, if in nothing else, His Majesty will admire your loyalty to Lord Stav . . . how do you pronounce it? To Lord Staverley."

"That is right, ma'am, Lord Staverley," Panthea approved.

She would have said more, but at that moment there came a knock on the door and one of the Queen's maids entered with a jug of perfumed water in which Her Majesty would wash while she was changing her gown.

It was time for Panthea to withdraw and, pressing the Queen's hand once more to her lips, she curtsied low to the ground and then stood on one side while two other Ladies in Waiting made their obeisance to the Queen before taking up their duties.

As Panthea walked towards the door, the Queen said quietly, "I will not forget what you have told me, Lady Panthea, and we must both remember it in our prayers."

It was a direct effort, as Panthea knew, to comfort her and to give her hope. As she went down the long corridor that led from the Queen's apartments, she felt both warmth and gratitude mingle with her affection for the little Queen. It was no easy task to be the wife of the vibrant and most popular King who ever sat on the Throne of England. The crown indeed lay heavy, not on her head but on her heart, for she loved the man who had set a wedding ring on her hand, and unlike so many other women at court, she would have been happier had he been a plain gentleman rather than a King with so much more than love to offer those who were both greedy and ambitious.

Panthea reached her great-aunt's apartments and found, as she expected, Lady Darlington resting on the sofa, a book open on her lap and her eyes closed in sleep. The book, Panthea well knew, was only a gesture. Lady

Darlington invariably opened it with the determined air of one who is about to occupy the next few hours in reading some instructive treatise, but long before she had reached the end of her first page, her eyes would drop and she would fall peacefully asleep, the book open on her knees at exactly the same place as it had been on the day before and the day before that.

Panthea's entry into the room, however, disturbed Lady Darlington and after a second her eyes flickered and opened slowly to find Panthea smiling down at her.

"Have you had a nice rest, Aunt Anne?" she enquired.

The Dowager gave what was almost a snort of annoyance.

"I have been reading," she said frigidly. "I only closed my eyes for the passing of a second."

With an effort, Panthea tried to look contrite but her eyes twinkled despite herself.

"I am sorry to interrupt you, Aunt Anne, but it is time we dressed for dinner. Have you forgotten that we dine tonight with Lady Hyde?"

"Of course I had not forgotten," Lady Darlington replied, though she had done that very thing. "Why, Lady Hyde is giving the dinner especially for us."

"I hope there will not be many guests there," Panthea said. "Everyone will ask me about Newgate, and I swear I have no desire to think of prisons again, let alone to talk of them."

"You are the fashion at the moment," Lady Darlington replied drily. "There have been no less than fifteen callers today already. I cannot help being amused when I remember that all the time you were away, but half a dozen people came to pay their respects and those almost surreptitiously for fear other people should see them."

"It makes one realise how much friendship means in the Palace, and how little account one should pay to the protestations people make, both of fidelity and affection," Panthea smiled.

"Rudolph will be there tonight," her great-aunt said. "He has at least been faithful, for he called here almost every day while you were in prison."

"His reasons were obvious enough," Panthea answered sharply. "I had no idea he was to be there this evening, or I would have asked you to refuse the invitation."

"Why should you do that?" Lady Darlington asked. "There is no need for you to run away from Rudolph or to be shy of meeting him. If you have no wish to marry him, you can say so firmly once and for all."

"But he will not take no for an answer," Panthea sighed. "It is my money he wants, Aunt Anne, I am very sure of that, and he has no real love for me, however much he avows to the contrary. I have seen him look at Lady Castlemaine and I know full well that there is where his affections lie."

"A man can love one woman and desire another," Lady Darlington retorted. "At the same time, I have no particular wish to see you married to Rudolph. There is something about him that I do not trust, though what it may be I cannot state with any certainty."

Panthea could have told her, but she checked the words on her lips. Her great-aunt was old and it would only upset and disturb her to realise that Lucius was living, but in danger. For the moment, it was best to keep things to herself and to let the Dowager remain in ignorance of the very complicated truth.

Alone in her bedchamber, Panthea wished that she could be frank with her great-aunt and with everyone else. If only she could declare her love and loyalty to Lucius, she felt it would make things so much easier for her. It was the lying and subterfuge she hated, and the pretence that she did not know who White Throat was, and why he should have rescued her. She felt a traitor every time she denied his identity, and yet she knew it was for the best. It would do neither him nor herself any good if the authorities realised they were linked together in any way, even by a blood relationship.

With a sigh that seemed to echo through her room, Panthea looked around her to decide, as the Queen had done, what gown she would wear that night. There was no particular reason for her to dress elaborately or for her to look her best, and yet when she had finished dressing she was forced to admit, both to Marta and to herself, that she did look her best.

It was Marta, in the end, who had chosen her gown, bringing her one she had completed that very afternoon and insisting that Panthea should wear it that evening, despite the insistence that it was far too grand for Lady Hyde's party.

"I have worked on this, my Lady," Marta said, "all the time you have been in prison. Wear it to please me, for I have wished so much to see you in it."

Panthea complied with her request and knew as she looked in the mirror that the gown was the prettiest she had ever owned. It was white, as the Queen's gown had been, but of a very different material and design.

The Queen's gown had been of heavy figured satin, stiff and unyielding, which seemed to flow from her waist in almost regal lines. Panthea's was of satin too, but a satin as soft as silk, so subtle, so pliant that it appeared to cling to her figure, revealing every exquisite line of breast and waist and falling in shimmering folds to the ground over a petticoat of lace so delicate, so exquisite, that it seemed as if it must have been fashioned by fairy fingers rather than by human ones.

There was lace at the sleeves and at the edge of the low bodice, and lace too on the linen handkerchief that Marta had made for her to carry in her hand, and which reminded her of another handkerchief she had once owned and which lay now, as she well knew, against the heart of the man she loved.

Panthea had no elaborate jewels to wear with her gown and instead she had set two white roses in her hair, and another deep in the laces at her bosom. Their fragrance made her think of the roses at Staverley and she had a sudden yearning for her home.

She knew then that the life in the palace had no real appeal for her. It could be fun, exciting and thrilling for a short while, but she would rather be home in the country with the song of the birds to replace the King's minstrels and the scent of the flowers to perfume the house and garden, rather than the exotic aromas of the perfumes that Charles had sent from France and which had become fashionable amongst all the lords and ladies of the Courts. It was Staverley where she wished to live, but not alone. She felt the truth of that seep through her with a sudden pain, not even at Staverley could she find happiness and contentment unless Lucius was with her. She knew then that without him life held no savour, no interest. She belonged to him, and nothing was of interest unless he was beside her and could share it.

Panthea felt the tears well up in her eyes at the thought of how unsupportable the future would be unless she and Lucius could be together. But she knew there was no time now for her to linger or to let herself become sorrowful. She looked at herself in the mirror, but instead of being elated at her own loveliness and the delicate fragile beauty of her new dress, she thought only that she wished to show it to Lucius.

Her great-aunt's voice calling out from the hall made her catch up her fur-lined cloak in sudden haste, drop a kiss on Marta's cheek and run from the room. They had only a short distance to walk to Lady Hyde's apartments, yet it took quite a considerable time because they met such a number of guests and friends moving along the corridors, all of whom must stop and congratulate Panthea on her new-found freedom.

Panthea found herself answering them mechanically, while her thoughts were elsewhere, and this mood continued until long after dinner was over and the more elderly members of the party had seated themselves round the card table, while Panthea, Lady Hyde's daughters and several young gentlemen played games in the next room.

It was then, at last, that Panthea felt her detachment leave her. She was young enough to be entranced by 'I Love My Love with an A . . .' which was one of the court's favourite games, and the fun waxed fast and furious as, sitting in a circle, they played 'Hunt the Slipper' beneath the billowing skirts of their pretty gowns.

It was long after midnight before Lady Darlington made an effort to leave and then, as she rose from the card table and took up her winnings with an air of satisfaction, she heard Panthea's laugh ring out and remarked to Lady Hyde how glad she was that the child seemed happier.

"It is a hard ordeal through which she has passed."

"That is true," Lady Hyde nodded. "You will have to be very careful with her for a long while. Such experiences leave deep scars which are not easily cured and erased."

The two ladies sat talking on the sofa, and it was after two o'clock before Panthea realised the time and hurried with a guilty air to her great-aunt's side.

"Aunt Anne, why did you not tell me you were waiting to go home? You must be exhausted, and I am deeply ashamed that I have kept you up so late."

"I was glad to see you enjoying yourself, my dear," Lady Darlington replied.

"We have been laughing a great deal," Panthea said, her cheeks flushed and her eyes bright. "It was childish fun, but so joyful."

"May I escort you to your apartments, Aunt Anne, if you are really determined to go?" Rudolph asked.

His voice was politely solicitous, and Panthea glanced at him from under her eyelashes.

She had been a little surprised by Rudolph's behaviour this evening. He had made no effort to seek her out, but had been just friendly and unobtrusive, taking part in the games wholeheartedly and doing nothing that she could condemn as being tiresome or in any way unpleasant. She wondered now, for a fleeting second, if she had misjudged him and if he was no longer interested in her personally. Then she remembered his attitude towards Lucius and her heart hardened against him.

"We can find our own way, thank you, cousin Rudolph," she said before her great-aunt could speak, and he fell back apparently abashed.

They were back in their own apartments half an hour later and Panthea, having kissed the Dowager good night, retired to her own bedchamber. For a moment, she did not begin to undress but sat at the window looking at the moonlight on the smooth water of the Thames. She was thinking of another moonlight night, five years ago, when she had waited in the shadows of the trees for Lucius to return to her, after he had freed her from the bondage of her marriage.

She wondered where Lucius was tonight, if the moon was shining down on him, if he slept in the shelter of some wood, or if he had returned to Staverley, flaunting the authorities who had dared to disturb him in his hiding place.

She was so lost in her own thoughts that for the moment she did not hear the soft knock on her bedroom door. It was repeated, and only then did Panthea become aware of the sound and bid whoever it was to enter.

To her surprise, one of the footmen came to the door. It was a man who had recently come into her great-aunt's employment, and she supposed that he did not know that, if he had anything to say to her, it would have been correct for him to have awakened Marta and sent her with the message.

"What is it, Thomas?" she asked coldly.

"A note, my Lady," he said. "I was told to give it to you personally."

Panthea checked the words of reproof on her lips. For one quick moment of joy, she thought that the note might be from Lucius and that Thomas had therefore been right in bringing it to her.

With fingers that trembled, she tore the note open and then the light died from her face and was replaced instead by an expression of disappointment. The writing was not Lucius' – she could see that at first glance – and then she saw that the note was signed by a very different name.

'I must see you immediately. It is of the utmost import and it concerns Lucius, Rudolph.'

Panthea read the message through twice. Then, rising to her feet, she said to Thomas, who waited in the doorway, "Where is the gentleman who gave you this note?"

"He is outside the apartment, my Lady."

"Ask him to come in," Panthea said.

"I suggested that, my Lady, but he replied it would not be wise to do so at this hour, and that it was imperative that he should have a word with you alone."

Panthea hesitated. It seemed a strange request and yet so many things had been strange lately. She thought that Rudolph might wish to tell her something about which it was best for her great-aunt not to know. She picked up her cape and placed it over her shoulders again. She could talk with Rudolph outside in the corridor if that pleased him, but she hoped they would not be seen, for she was well aware how quickly and easily gossip arose in the palace, and that at the moment any action of hers that was unusual would incite comment and speculation.

Panthea hurried across the hall and outside into the corridor. Rudolph was waiting a little distance from her great-aunt's front door. When he saw her appear, he came towards her. The light was dim, and it was difficult for her to see the expression on his face.

"What do you want?" she asked.

"You must come with me at once," Rudolph said. "Lucius is in grave danger and I have arranged for him to cross to France tonight. He wants to say goodbye to you."

"You have arranged for him to go to France?" Panthea enquired incredulously.

"Yes, he came to me and asked my help," Rudolph replied. "I have friends who can convey him across the Channel, but he wishes to tell you about it himself."

"But I do not understand," Panthea said. "Why has he taken this decision?"

"He asked me to tell you nothing," Rudolph answered, "but just to bring you to him. He is here in London. He is waiting outside the walls where he will take a boat down the Thames. There is one sailing at dawn and he must not be long delayed. Are you coming?"

Panthea stood palpitating. She did not trust Rudolph and yet he sounded so convincing. This was something she had least expected. For the moment, she could not think clearly save that Lucius had sent for her and she must go to him at once. Before she could answer, before she could make up her mind, Rudolph had set his hand under her arm and was guiding her down the passage.

"We must not be seen," he said and, as Panthea had done on the night she had gone to Staverley, they slipped from shadow to shadow, avoiding the night watchman and the parties of ladies and gentlemen returning to their own apartments. The effort at concealment took Panthea's mind from anything else save Rudolph's desire not to be seen, and the sense of urgency that seemed to be transmitted from him to her so that she found herself as impatient as he was to reach the palace gate, where he whispered to her that a coach would be waiting.

It was a shabby vehicle, badly built and none too well upholstered, but as Panthea sank back against the seat, she felt the horses start forward with a bound and knew that they would travel swiftly, if in discomfort.

"Now tell me what this is all about," she said to Rudolph, as they rattled down the empty streets with only the moon light to guide their way.

"There is no need for me to explain anything," he replied. "You will learn all about it very shortly."

A sudden jolt of the coach threw her against his shoulder and instinctively she recoiled and settled herself more firmly in the corner of the coach. He was right, she thought. There was nothing to be gained by talking to him. She had best keep silent and wait until she saw Lucius.

It was then that the full purport of Rudolph's words became real to her for the first time since she had heard them. Lucius was going to France. She knew then an agony she had hardly believed possible within herself. She was losing him – he was going away from her and she would not be able to see him. In that moment, Panthea determined that he should not go alone. She would go with him. If he were to be exiled, then she would be exiled too. At least they would be together. She had not thought at that moment as to how it could be achieved, whether she could take any money with her, or any possessions save the clothes in which she stood up. Everything seemed supremely unimportant except that she should be with Lucius.

She loved him! She loved him so much that, if he went away, she could not live.

The coach had reached the open countryside by now, and the horses seemed to be galloping at almost a furious pace down a long road. Panthea glanced through the window. The moonlight was on the meadows and there was not a house in sight. She turned towards the silent man beside her.

"You said Lucius was just outside the walls," she said. "Where is he? How much further have we got to go?"

"A little while yet," Rudolph said, and Panthea sank back again in her corner.

What could have happened? Why should Lucius, who had evaded capture for so long, be suddenly in greater danger than he had been for these past five years or more?

There was a sudden doubt within her, so that she turned again to Rudolph and said, "Where are we going to? I insist that you tell me."

There was a moment's silence as if he hesitated as to what to tell her, and then he replied, "We are going to Staverley."

"To Staverley?" Panthea questioned. "But you told me Lucius was outside the walls. What does this mean?"

"We are not going to the house," Rudolph replied, "but to the church. You remember it, I think. The church outside the park gates. You must have gone there often as a child."

"Of course I have been there," Panthea said impatiently. "But why are we going there? Is Lucius hiding in the church? And why did you tell me he had come to London?"

"If you want to know the truth," Rudolph said, and she noticed a change in his voice, "I have no idea where Lucius may be. He may be in London, in Staverley, or in prison where he ought to be. I am not his keeper, neither have I any knowledge of his whereabouts at this particular moment."

"You have no idea?" Panthea repeated breathlessly. "Then why am I here? Where are we going to? I demand an answer."

The questions poured from her lips, and as she finished speaking, there was a silence – a silence so sinister that she must scream with the horror of it. At length, Rudolph answered her and in his voice was a note of amusement, and some other emotion that frightened her more than anything else.

"We are going to Staverley Church, Panthea," he said, "so that you may marry me and we can put an end once and for all to these doubts and maidenly frustrations that have been keeping us apart."

"So this is a trap," Panthea cried, trying to calm the panic that was rising within her so that she had only a wild desire to scream and strike out at the man lounging back beside her.

"Yes, a trap," Rudolph repeated, "but quite an ingenious one, you must admit. You walked into it very confidently, my dear. I had not expected it would be quite so easy."

"Then Lucius is not in danger!"

Panthea could not help the note of elation in her words. At least it was a relief beyond words that she need not be afraid for him.

"Lucius is in the same danger as he has always been," Rudolph answered testily. "His good fortune cannot continue for ever – sooner or later he will be captured. But that will not concern you or me. We are to be married, Panthea, and with your money I intend to restore Staverley to its former magnificence. When we are living there as man and wife, the King will, I think, hardly fail to grant me the title."

"And why do you imagine you can claim the estates when they belong to Lucius?" Panthea asked.

"I have been given to understand," Rudolph answered, "that should any member of the family wish to live at Staverley and spend money on doing the place up, there will be no legal objection to his doing so, provided the rightful heir does not lodge a complaint."

"If you imagine I will agree to any of this, you must be mad," Panthea said. "You have connived at Lucius' death – you are doing all you can to have him hanged so that you can take what is his by right of birth. I hate you, cousin Rudolph. I *hate* and despise you – and now, having told me your mad scheme, you will please turn this coach back and take me to London."

"Do you believe it possible that I should do anything of the sort?" Rudolph enquired. "For one thing, I have not even the money with which to pay the coachmen. I am looking to you to provide that little necessity, my wealthy cousin."

"I will pay as many coachmen as you please," Panthea said, "if you will take me back to Whitehall."

"Do you really imagine I should give up my plans so easily?" Rudolph enquired. "I have arranged things very carefully, Panthea. You do not realise what it is like to be a pauper, to be down to one's last penny and to owe thousands of pounds to creditors who will wait no longer for their money. That is my position today, and that is the reason why we must be married at Staverley. There was only one Parson who would give me credit when I tried to arrange our marriage. I told the old fool there who I was, the fourth Marquess of Staverley, and so he was content to wait for his fees until after the ceremony had taken place.

The pious shylocks in London will not even put on their surplices until one has greased their palms."

The roughness and bitterness in Rudolph's voice made him seem a complete stranger. Panthea had never heard him speak to her before save with courtesy and an ingratiating pleasantness that was now completely absent. It was this that made her more fearful than anything else, for it told her all too clearly that Rudolph was supremely confident of getting his own way and need no longer plead with her but could show himself in his natural colours, a man bent on a dastardly course and quite certain that he could achieve it.

"Cousin Rudolph, you must listen to me," Panthea said quietly. "I do not believe that you intend to do all you say, nevertheless you have put me in a most compromising position by bringing me out here alone with you at night. You know what people would say if they knew, and I can only beg of you to behave like a gentleman and take me back to my great-aunt's protection as quickly as possible. I, in my turn, will promise you on my honour that tomorrow a sum of money will be deposited with your lawyer, or in your name with a goldsmith. I have no idea exactly what your debts amount to, but I am sure it would not be impossible for me to arrange to pay them and to leave you with something in hand."

"How very generous!" Rudolph sneered. "But I have no wish for your charity, cousin Panthea. I have asked you repeatedly to become my wife, and even apart from the money and the fact that you are in love with Lucius, the idea is pleasing to me. I will not say that I love you, for that is a word that has been much misused, especially in the circles in which you and I move, but I want you, Panthea. You attract me and I desire you. That is surely enough, and as many women have found me an attractive lover, I cannot believe that you will be an exception."

"How dare you speak to me like this?" Panthea cried. "I have told you before and I tell you again that I would not marry you if you were the last man in the world."

Rudolph laughed.

"At least you have spirit," he said. "It is a Vyne characteristic, and I expect our children will have it too. My dear, you have no choice in the matter. You will marry me and like it – and when we return to London, you will accompany me as my wife."

"I will not marry you," Panthea replied, "and I think it doubtful that the Parson of Staverley, who has known me since I was a child, will allow me to be dragged forcibly to the altar."

"I shall not have to drag you," Rudolph said. "You will come willingly enough."

There was a menace in his voice, which was all the more obvious because he spoke quietly. Despite every effort Panthea's voice trembled as she asked, "And why?"

It was too dark in the coach for her to see Rudolph's face, but she felt instinctively that he smiled.

"Because, my dear," he answered, "if you do not promise to marry me when we reach the church at Staverley, I shall stop the coach here and take you away into the woods. The men who are driving us have been well paid. They will not listen to your cries, and I do not think that even the most optimistic person would back your strength against mine. I have told you that I desire you, Panthea, and I shall make you mine whether it be with your consent or not. I think, after that, you would not be so ready to say that you would not marry me."

"You would not dare to touch me."

"Dare!"

The word broke on a laugh, and Rudolph's arms reached out in the darkness and drew Panthea to him.

She struggled desperately against him without avail. She heard the lace of her dress tear as she struggled, then suddenly she found herself utterly helpless in his grasp. His one arm imprisoned her as completely as if it had been a band of steel, and then, putting his free hand under her chin, he tipped her head back against his shoulder and she felt his lips on hers.

His mouth was hard and hot against her lips for a long moment, and she felt she must faint at the misery of her own powerlessness. And then, as suddenly as he had caught her to him, Rudolph released her.

Gasping for breath, Panthea moved away from him, back into the corner from which he had taken her. She could still feel the strength of his arms bruising the tenderness of her skin, she could still feel nauseated by the touch of his lips on hers, but she knew that he had mastered her, that his strength rendered her helpless and impotent. There was no appeal and she knew it, and then, as she covered her face with her hands, she heard Rudolph laugh.

"Shall I stop the coach, or will you marry me?" he said. "I would show you again that it is hopeless to struggle against me, only the fact is that I have a distaste for kissing in coaches, 'tis so cursed uncomfortable."

Panthea felt then that she was humbled to the very dust. This was a degradation such as she had never known or never imagined. She could not answer Rudolph, could not force any sound between her lips, which were dry with a constriction of her throat, and which seemed completely closed with fear and misery.

"Silence, I believe, means consent," Rudolph said with an almost intolerable cheerfulness, "and so, since you have consented to marry me, we will waste no more time, but hurry on to Staverley."

15

They journeyed for a long way in silence. Panthea's first feeling of abasement was so intense that it was impossible for her to think of anything, save through a fog of darkness that seemed to sap her brain and leave her lost and desolate. Then panic rose within her breast, and it was only by the greatest effort of will that she could prevent herself from striving to escape and battling fruitlessly against Rudolph's strength. Common sense told her, however, that such a course would gain her nothing and would merely pander to his sense of power and conquest.

She knew by the tone of his voice, and by the very way in which he had kissed her and flung her from him, that he was enjoying to the full this moment in which he held her completely in his power. Frightened as she was, Panthea could still understand that this, for Rudolph, was a triumph in which he could avenge himself on her for all the slights and insults he had endured in the past in being a poor relation and an unpopular one.

Rudolph had never been particularly subtle, and it was not hard to perceive the workings of his mind. He had been driven to desperate methods to achieve his ends, and now that he believed himself the victor, all the pettiness of his shallow nature was revealed in that he not only would demand her obedience to his commands but would inflict as much humiliation on her as possible.

Even while he desired Panthea as a woman, he hated her because she was all those things that he should have been himself. It was not only her wealth that he resented, but the honour and the integrity that he sensed were as much a part of her character as the reverse of those qualities were a part of his. And because he knew now that, even though he could subdue and violate her body, her mind would always remain superior to his and her spirit beyond his reach, he must, as all boasters will do, bully someone physically weaker than himself.

He sprawled beside Panthea in the coach in a deliberate effort to prove himself at ease, and began to talk, the rough coarseness of his voice revealing all too clearly his real nature which before had been hidden under a plausible veneer of social graces. He boasted of his conquests, revolting Panthea with the tales of women who had loved him and who had enjoyed his mastery of them.

"You are no different from the rest of your sex, my dear," he said at length, "and though you shrink from me now, you will be pleading for my caresses in a very short time. Girls invariably have fanciful ideas about men, and you will soon forget Lucius when my arms are round you and I have taught you some of the tricks that make life worth living. You are pretty now, but you will be a damned sight prettier when I've finished with you. There is always something lacking in a virgin and you will bloom after marriage into a woman who will make men's eyes goggle when they look at you.

"I shan't be too strict with you, I promise you that. You will have to learn to shut your eyes where I am concerned, but I am all for a little give and take. We will go back to Court after we have got Staverley in order, and who knows, the King himself may take a fancy to you, and that may lead to anything. I promise you one thing, though, I am not likely to be such a damned fool as Roger Castlemaine and go hopping off to France to leave you with the spoils. I shall be there, you can wager on that, and anything that comes your way comes mine."

He gave a little chuckle to himself and, stretching out his hand, patted Panthea familiarly on the knee.

"Cheer up," he said. "You're going to have a damned good husband in me, even though I say it myself."

"I refuse to marry you."

Panthea spoke through clenched teeth, but even as she said the words, she knew they were empty and meaningless not only to herself but to Rudolph.

"You've got no alternative, my dear," he said drily, "and you know that as well as I do. Let's make the best of what will eventually prove to be a very good business, and by midday I'll have you safely back in London, though we must not forget to call at your goldsmith's and collect some money to pay for the coach."

He laughed heartily as if at a great joke, and added with what was almost a disarming honesty, "I'm a rogue, but one who enjoys his own roguery, and from all accounts I will make you a more pleasant husband than the one you chose first."

Panthea felt there was no answer to this, for it was in many ways true. If she were forced to choose between Christian Drysdale and Rudolph, she would prefer Rudolph even while she loathed and despised him for the way he was behaving to her. Both men had forced her into marriage, she thought, and it was a coincidence that both marriages had taken place at night and in the environs of Staverley.

Even as she thought of it, she prayed for yet another coincidence. Lucius had saved her from her first marriage – would he appear now to hold up the coach and rescue her as he had rescued her before? Even while she prayed for such deliverance, she knew it was most unlikely. Coincidences happened more often in storybooks than in real life. It was too much to hope that Lucius would be riding this very road on this very night, that he would discover her by chance and thus prevent Rudolph from putting his nefarious scheme into action.

It was too much to hope for, Panthea knew, and yet she went on hoping. At the same time, her brain gradually began to seek another avenue of escape, trying almost frantically to think of some plan, some plea by which she could circumvent Rudolph.

She wondered if it was worthwhile defying him openly, telling him to do what he wished to her, rather than placidly agree to marry him. Perhaps he was only bluffing, perhaps he would not do what he said and rape her into acquiescence, but she was afraid to put it to the test. Rudolph was a desperate man, and desperate men do desperate deeds. Besides, what he contemplated would mean very little to him from all accounts. He had already boasted to her of the women he had seduced on the continent, both willingly and unwillingly, and she could readily believe that his conceit made him genuinely credit that women protested more from convention than because they disliked being conquered.

The strength of Rudolph's arms, the greedy possessiveness of his lips, were still too vivid in Panthea's mind for her to risk inciting him again to a show of strength. It was no idle boast that he could possess her if he wished, and she was afraid to challenge him.

There must be some other way, Panthea thought, something she could say or do to gain her freedom. Then, with a sense of dismay, she realised they were nearing Staverley. They had not been travelling so quickly for the past few miles, for the horses were tiring and she guessed that they were not thoroughbred beasts who could endure a long journey, as Socrates could, without showing physical signs of fatigue, but were the flashy hacks that could be obtained from hostelries that catered for ladies and gentlemen who wished to hire good-looking horses, often pretending the horses were their own.

Panthea had no way of knowing the time, but she guessed that they had taken immeasurably longer to reach Staverley now than the last time she and Harry had come this way. Already the moon had faded from the sky and the first pale fingers of the sun were showing in the east.

Quickly and impulsively, because she knew that very shortly they would arrive at the church, Panthea turned to Rudolph and spoke.

"Cousin Rudolph, we are nearing Staverley, the house that has meant so much to our family. Do you really mean to do what you have set out to do, to marry me against my will, to force me to take the most solemn vows of matrimony with hatred in my heart and a deep loathing for you in my soul? We are of the same blood, you and I, and many of our ancestors have died rather than do a dishonourable deed. So many of them have lived lives that have enhanced the glory and the splendour, not only of the family but of the country they have served. What you are about to do now is not worthy of those who bear the name of Vyne. You know it and I know it, and the knowledge of it will lie between us always so that we can never find happiness together, however hard we try. Let me go, cousin Rudolph. Prove yourself worthy of the name that my father and my brother bore, and I promise you that you will never regret it. All that I have shall be yours, every penny that I own shall be given to you freely and willingly and without reservation, but for your own sake as well as mine do not do this thing."

Panthea's voice broke a little as she finished speaking, and she waited, quivering in the darkness of the coach, for Rudolph's answer. It came swiftly and without hesitation.

"You make a good advocate for your own case, Panthea," he said jokingly. "As I have already told you, I want both your money and you. Are you so modest as to believe yourself completely unattractive to me?"

"Are you so utterly steeped in your own evil that you cannot see that what you do is wrong and wicked?" Panthea asked.

"Words! *Words!*" Rudolph retorted. "What is wicked and what is good in this world are things I have never been able to distinguish to my own, or to anyone else's, satisfaction. Is it wrong to bed with a woman when it gives both you and her pleasure and satisfaction? If that is wrong, then what a sinner is our King and the majority of those who wait upon him at Court! Is it evil to wish for money? Then indeed the whole of this country is inhabited by miserable sinners. Is it wrong to wish to be wed, to settle down in domestic bliss and breed children that will carry on the family name? No, no, cousin Panthea, you cannot denounce me in such a manner. I am as good and as bad as most men, if it comes to that, a mixture of both, and one who is not without his virtues, as you will find out when we live together as man and wife."

"But I love Lucius," Panthea said, the words bursting from her as if she could no longer contain them.

"And what of it?" Rudolph asked coldly. "You cannot wed him, and to remain single for love of a nefarious highwayman who will sooner or later be hanged for his crimes would be as ridiculous as if I refused to wed you for love of some other woman who would have none of me."

"You love my Lady Castlemaine," Panthea said accusingly.

"She has attracted and beguiled me as no other woman has ever done, and I suspect as no other woman ever will," Rudolph said coolly, "but that does not mean that I am prepared to renounce the pleasure of marrying you, my dear cousin. Come, what is the use of arguing? 'Tis all arranged, and all you have to do is to say, 'I will'."

Panthea gave a little shudder. There was nothing she could reply, nothing she could say. She thought how often recently she had dreamt of saying those very words, but not with Rudolph beside her.

They were nearing Staverley Church now where it stood on the roadside on the extreme boundary of the Staverley estates. It had been built by Panthea's great great-grandfather, who had put it as far as possible from the house because he hated the sound of bells. If only it had been nearer, Panthea thought now, perhaps Lucius might have seen them arrive, if he was still in hiding in Staverley. But there was no hope of that. The church, while it was surrounded by the big oak trees of the park, could only be seen from the top windows of the house, and a coach driving to the door was therefore unlikely to attract the attention of anyone save those who lived in the adjacent vicarage.

And now they had arrived, and Lucius had not intercepted them, Panthea felt her heart sink into the depths of despair as the horses drew to a standstill and one of the men on the box climbed down to open the door.

The windows of the coach were fogged and dirty, but the sunshine made a gallant effort to pierce the gloom, and Panthea could see Rudolph's face as she turned to him with a last appealing gesture, her own face white and desperate as she said, "Please, cousin Rudolph, please do not make me do this!"

There was no smile on his lips now, nor any jovial good humour in his eyes as he looked down at her, and taking her wrist in a cruel grip, he said, "You will marry me if I have to kill you to make you do it."

Panthea gave a little cry of pain. The hurt of his fingers made the blood seem to drain away from her body, and she knew that her last hope was gone and there was nothing that she could do. She alighted from the coach and glanced around her, as if some hope of rescue might be lurking amongst the trees or coming down the winding narrow road that they themselves had just traversed.

But there was no one in sight. There was only the fresh, sweet smell of the country, the weakening of the morning breeze, the song of the birds and the fragrance of the honeysuckle that grew profusely over the porch of the church.

The very sight of the building itself brought back to Panthea so many memories. She could remember holding her father's hand as she toddled rather than walked the narrow path between the tombstones. She had been but three or four when she had first been taken to church to sit in the great family pew, her legs dangling over the velvet cushions which made her high enough so that she could just peep over the carved front of the pew.

Her mother had been buried in the family vault and her father too, and although Richard had been drawn and quartered and what remained of his poor mangled body had been scattered to the winds, they had laid his sword amongst his ancestors, so that he too rested in spirit if not in body under the shadow of the square Norman tower.

It was before the altar of this church that Panthea had always imagined herself being married. When she had first taken to dreaming the dreams that every girl in adolescence hugs in the secrecy of her heart, she had thought of herself passing up the aisle on the arm of her father, a lace veil shielding her downcast eyes, a sheaf of lilies from the gardens of Staverley held in her arms. She had dreamed dreams of the man who would be waiting for her at the chancel steps. At first his face had been shadowy, later it had been real and vivid, haunting her dreams, the face of the man she knew had been meant for her since the beginning of time.

She could have cried out now at the pity of it. For all she knew Lucius might be sleeping at Staverley, or lying concealed in the woods that stretched far away to the north as far as the eye could see. He might be thinking of her as she was of him, and yet he would have no idea what was happening, or that she was crying out in an almost intolerable agony for him to come and save her.

Panthea's thoughts were roused by Rudolph's hand on her arm and his voice saying curtly, "Come!"

Mechanically she walked through the gate into the churchyard, and then to her joy she saw that a woman was approaching them. She came hurrying, a fat, smiling, good-humoured woman with a red face, her hair untidy beneath her cap, her gown but half-laced together as if she had robed herself in great haste.

"My Lady, my Lady," she cried as she approached, and Panthea gave a little exclamation of joy.

"Mistress Bonnet," she exclaimed. "How glad I am to see you!"

The Vicar's wife curtsied to the ground.

"Oh, my Lady," she exclaimed again. "When my husband told me who was coming here this morning, I could hardly believe my ears. You are earlier than we expected, but he will be here in a few minutes. Will you not come into the house and have a sup of wine? You must be sadly weary after your journey from London."

"Thank you," Panthea replied, and glanced at Rudolph as if afraid he might refuse on her behalf the offer of hospitality.

"I can do with a glass of wine myself," he said roughly, and followed Panthea and Mistress Bonnet down the path that led to the vicarage.

The blinds were drawn in the house, which had an untidy homeliness about it. Mistress Bonnet fussed about the room into which she led Panthea, patting up cushions and exclaiming at the untidiness of the ash-strewn grate.

"If only I had known you were coming, Lady Panthea," she said, over and over again. "But my husband never mentioned it to me until long after we were in bed. I doubt if he would have told me then, for I believe that Mr. Rudolph had sworn him to silence, but he was doubtful if he would wake up in time, for he was always a heavy sleeper, and I vow that if I did not call him on a Sunday morning, the congregation would wait for him until late in the afternoon. And then, as it happens, he need not have imparted his secret, for over two hours ago little Tommy Hodge comes a-beating on the door to say his granddad is breathing his last. You remember old Jacob Hodge, my Lady? Blacksmith he was for nigh on fifty years, until his nephew took the forge over from him."

"Yes, of course I remember him," Panthea answered.

"A God-fearing man for all that he could be too, free with the ale at harvest time," Mistress Bonnet went on. "Well, I'm sure the Vicar will not be long, but old Jacob won't pass on without a struggle. A fighter he's always been in his lifetime, and he'll not let death take him easily."

Still talking, she brought a bottle of wine to the table, and when Panthea refused it, fetched a glass of milk from the kitchen.

It was over an hour before the Vicar appeared, despite Rudolph's ill-concealed impatience, and Panthea had time to tidy herself and wash her hands. As she cleaned the dust of the journey from her face, Mistress Bonnet chattered all the while, making it easy for Panthea to conceal her sense of utter desolation, which seemed to intensify itself minute by minute.

She half thought of appealing to the Bonnets to save her, but she knew they could do nothing to help her, and some stiff-necked pride within her revolted at the idea of revealing to these simple trusting people, Rudolph's infamy. He was, after all, her cousin, and the Bonnets had respected the Vynes since they had first been granted the incumbency of which her father had been the patron.

They were obviously impressed by Rudolph, believing implicitly his story that he was the heir to the Marquessate and that he would soon be arriving to take up his residence at Staverley. They could not save her – one whitehaired old man and his kindly, chattering wife. Indeed, there was nothing they could do nor anyone else. If she flouted Rudolph now, Panthea knew that she would not be able to escape him, for he kept a watchful eye on her and even when she went into another room with Mistress Bonnet, she guessed that he was listening through the half-open door, ready to prevent her escape or even to interrupt any confidence she might make.

For one moment, Panthea played with the idea of locking herself in one of the rooms and sending Mistress Bonnet in search of the villagers who would protect her, at least from Rudolph's violence. But the vicarage was some way from the cottages in the village and she knew that long before the stout old woman could find assistance, Rudolph and the two coachmen could force open any locked door and she would once more be in his power. Besides, there was something degrading in involving in this sordid scheme of Rudolph's people whom she had known all through her life.

No, there was nothing she could do, she thought, as she walked from the vicarage into the churchyard, the Vicar leading the way into the church. It was very quiet and still beneath the ancient arched roof and the sunshine was shining through the stained-glass window over the altar. Panthea had the feeling that her father was watching her as she moved slowly up the aisle at Rudolph's side, and they stood waiting while the Vicar went into the vestry to fetch his surplice and book.

She cried out with all her heart for help and then turned her face to Rudolph, believing that now, at the very last minute, he might relent and some long-forgotten decency within him give her the reprieve she supplicated. But there was a faint mocking smile on his lips as he looked down at her, and his eyes held an expression that made her put her hands instinctively to her breast as if she would cover the nakedness of her white skin from his gaze.

"You are damned pretty," he said in a thick voice.

She felt the blood rush suddenly into her cheeks. She had no idea how lovely she looked as she stood there in her white satin ballgown, with its shadowy lace fluttering with the movement of her hands and her fair head silhouetted against the old grey stone walls. She was concerned only with the lust she could see in Rudolph's face, and the sacrilege of his oath which besmirched the sacredness of the ground on which they stood. She would have spoken, would have said something to rebuke and silence him, had not the Vicar at that moment come from the vestry and walked towards them ready to begin the ceremony.

His presence put all other thoughts from Panthea's mind, save the fact that she was now to be married. It was then that the panic that had been rising in her took possession for one second and she would have turned and rushed from the church had not Rudolph, with a quickness that came from many years of living on his wits, realised her intention and put out his hand to prevent her going.

He gripped her arm above the elbow and sank his fingers menacingly into the soft flesh, and holding her with a grip of steel, he drew her to his side and held her there so that, like him, she faced the Vicar who, seeing nothing amiss, opened his book and started the service.

His words seemed to come from very far away. Panthea could hear his voice droning monotonously as a bluebottle against a windowpane. She could not understand his words because she was conscious only of her own weakness and the hurt of Rudolph's fingers.

But when she believed that at any moment a merciful darkness must overtake her, she heard all too clearly the Vicar's voice saying as he looked directly at her,

"I, Panthea Charmaine. . ."

He paused, and as Panthea did not speak, he said, "You must repeat this after me. 'I, Panthea Charmaine. . .'"

Rudolph's fingers were like bands of fire. Panthea winced, and repeated in a voice that seemed very unlike her own, "I, Panthea Charmaine . . ."

". . . take thee, Rudolph Henry Alexander."

". . . take thee, Rudolph Henry Alexander."

". . . to my wedded husband."

Panthea tried to say the words, but somehow they would not come.

As she tried to speak, as the Vicar and Rudolph both looked at her, waiting for her words, she heard a sudden clatter of horse's hooves outside and, immediately after, the sound of someone running up the path to the church door. She knew who it was long before she heard his footsteps on the stone floor or heard his voice. She knew by the sudden wild exciting leap of her heart, by the sudden quickening of her pulses, by her joy, which seemed almost like pain in its very intensity.

"Stop!"

Lucius' voice rang out, echoing loudly round the walls of the church, and as Panthea turned towards him, he came striding down the aisle, his eyes ablaze with anger, his spurs jingling on his high-polished boots so that the whole Church seemed to ring with the sound of them.

"Lucius, my beloved, you have come in time!"

Panthea's words were whispered almost beneath her breath, but Lucius heard them. With a swift movement, she wrenched herself free from Rudolph's slackened grip and ran towards him. She was swept into his arms, to hide her face for a moment against his shoulder, in the utter relief of knowing that he was there, and she need no longer be afraid.

"What does this mean?"

It was the Vicar who asked the question with a quivering note of authority in his astonished voice.

"It means," Rudolph said furiously, "that we have a witness for our marriage, Vicar. This man will attempt to stop the ceremony, but he is too late."

"You are not married!" Lucius asked, making it a statement rather than a question.

It was then Panthea spoke from the protection of his arms.

"No, we are not married," she said. "I prayed that you would come in time and my prayer has been answered,"

"He has not arrived in time," Rudolph raged. "He is powerless to stop this marriage, and I know that you, Vicar, will not listen to a thief and a robber who has no right to cross the threshold of a church."

But the Vicar was peering at Lucius with short-sighted eyes.

"But surely it is Mr. Lucius Vyne?" he said. "I have not seen you for a long time, sir, but I cannot believe myself mistaken."

"You are not mistaken, Vicar," Lucius said. "I am indeed Lucius Vyne, whom you last saw some twelve years ago."

"But they told me you were dead," the Vicar said. "Indeed, Mr. Rudolph was telling me but yesterday that you died on the scaffold."

"Unfortunately for my cousin, in this case that wish was not fulfilled," Lucius said.

"Enough of this nonsense," Rudolph said sharply. "I insist, Vicar, that you continue the ceremony where we were interrupted."

"It is you who are talking nonsense," Lucius said. "You know full well now I am here you can no longer bully or threaten Panthea into becoming your wife."

"You shall not stop me," Rudolph said threateningly and put his hand to his sword.

As he drew it, Panthea gave a little cry of horror, but Lucius stood his ground and made a sudden sign with his hand. There was the sound of running feet and almost before he realised what was happening, Rudolph found himself gripped on either side by the strong hands of two highwaymen. They had been waiting in the doorway for just such a signal and they had swept their hats from their heads in reverence for the sacredness of the building, but they had not removed their masks, and Rudolph's anger at being made a prisoner was only equalled by the astonishment on the Vicar's face as he stared at them.

"I will not fight you, cousin Rudolph," Lucius said quietly. "Unlike you, I have no desire to shed the blood of one of my own family, but these men of mine will keep you prisoner until I have decided what to do with you."

Lucius glanced at the highwaymen as he spoke and said briefly, "Take him away."

They obeyed him, and although Rudolph struggled as they escorted him down the aisle, he was powerless to escape. They heard him cursing as the highwaymen took him outside into the churchyard and then, as the sound of their footsteps and Rudolph's voice died away, Panthea looked up into Lucius' eyes and saw there an expression of love and tenderness such as she had not believed it possible to find on a human face.

"Oh, Lucius, thank God you came in time," she whispered. "I was so afraid."

"He has not hurt you, my darling?" Lucius asked.

She shook her head, so happy now to be able to remember the insults that she had endured. Her heart was beating so quickly that she could hardly draw her breath, and she knew that even beneath his strength Lucius, too, trembled a little at the wonder of knowing that she was close to him. The voice of the Vicar aroused them to a consciousness that he was beside them.

"My children," he said very gently, "would you not have me bless the happiness that I see in both your faces?"

Lucius looked up at him quickly and then at Panthea, and in a voice broken with emotion she said, "Please, Lucius . . . please say yes."

She felt him stiffen and then, looking at the Vicar, he said, "Vicar, I am an outcast, a man who has nothing to offer the woman he loves save a heart overflowing with adoration and a body that will be vowed to her service so long as life shall last. Would this be enough for any woman, a life without security, a life without even a future?"

The Vicar did not answer. Instead he turned his kind old face towards Panthea, and she knew that he waited for her reply.

"What does anything matter," she said softly, "save that God has sent us into the world to love each other and that we are together, whether it be for a long time or a short, whether it be in security or in fear of every man, I care not. It is our love that matters and already we are united by the divinity of that love and our souls are one, however separate our bodies."

She felt Lucius' arm tighten on hers and he raised her hand to his lips. For a moment, she felt the warm ardency of his mouth against her fingers and then, still holding her hand, he turned towards the Vicar.

"Will you wed us, sir?" he asked simply.

The Vicar opened his prayerbook and started the service again, but this time Panthea heard every word, for they seemed to ring out clearly so that she responded to every one, her whole being concentrated in an act of worship so wonderful and so glorious that she felt herself in the company of angels. Lucius' calm grave voice made the responses, and when at length the moment came for him to put the ring upon her finger, he drew from his right hand a gold signet ring that he wore upon his little finger. He slipped it on and it fitted her perfectly, then they knelt together for the Vicar's blessing.

It seemed to Panthea then as if a golden light encircled them both, and that the blessing they received came not in the feeble tones of an old man, but with the strength and majesty of a power beyond the Earth and one echoing far into the spheres themselves. It was in an enchantment beyond words, and with Lucius' hand on hers, that she prayed that she might have the chance of giving him a little of the happiness he deserved.

They were still kneeling side by side as the Vicar went from the altar to the vestry and it was then, while they were still on their knees, that Lucius drew Panthea to him and kissed her lips. It was a kiss holy and tender, a kiss as if they both stood on the threshold of another world, and with their faces radiant as the morning light, they rose to their feet and, hand in hand, followed the Vicar into the vestry.

Having signed the register and with the Vicar's blessing still echoing in their ears, they were moving slowly down the aisle, hardly conscious of where they were going or what they were doing save that they were together, when, as they neared the door of the porch, Panthea gave a sudden start. Her eyes widened as she saw that, standing in the doorway, there was someone watching them.

For a moment, she could only stand and stare at the man waiting there with a faint smile on his lips and a cynical look in his tired eyes, and then she swept to the ground in a deep curtsy.

"Your Majesty," she whispered, and she felt fear rise with in her like some poisonous snake.

"So, you have been married, Lady Panthea," Charles said. "Not a very fashionable service even though it was honoured by your King's presence."

He was teasing her, Panthea felt in a sudden agony, and her eyes went from the King's face to that of Lucius' standing beside her. He stood as straight and proud as if he were a soldier on parade, but she knew that his face had paled as he waited for the King to acknowledge his presence.

With his long tall figure barring the door, blocking the only way of escape from the church, the King, holding his plumed hat in his hand and his riding whip in the other, faced the man whom his military and the magistrates had long been striving to bring to justice. They were of the same height and their eyes met each other levelly. For a moment they were not King and subject, but two men of equal rank appraising each other and taking stock of each other's manhood.

"You are Lucius Vyne," the King said after a moment. "It is a long time since we met."

"It is nigh on fifteen years, Sire," Lucius replied.

The King nodded.

"I have not forgotten. I have indeed often laughed to myself at the spectacle you made as you galloped away with my hat on your head and the Roundheads spurring after you, believing you to be me. It was not, however, particularly humorous at the time, for I believed, until you rescued me, that my last hour had come."

"I was fortunate in being able to serve Your Majesty," Lucius answered quietly.

"And now you have married the Queen's favourite Lady in Waiting," the King said.

Panthea felt as if she must cry out at the suspense. Did not the King realise who Lucius was? Was he unaware that he was not only speaking to Lucius Vyne who had saved his life, but also to White Throat, the notorious highway man whom he had given instructions must be arrested and brought to justice?

She felt as if the strain was too intolerable to be borne, and while she waited, wondering if Lucius would petition the King for pardon or make a dash for safety, the King turned in the doorway, saying, "You must meet the gentlemen who escorted me here this morning. After all I had heard of Staverley from the Queen and other people, I had a desire to see it for myself, so I took my ride in this direction instead of towards Hampton Court as is my wont. But before we entered the park, we saw some strange happenings."

He came out into the sunlight as he spoke and then Panthea knew that it was too late to do anything, and this was indeed the end, for standing around the churchyard gate, yawning as was usual with the gentlemen who had to escort His Majesty on his very early morning rides, were several courtiers whom she recognised by sight, and among them Sir Philip Gage. She thought then that this must be a trap, and the King had brought Sir Philip here so that he could arrest Lucius. She put her hand quickly on his arm and even as she did so, remembered that she was now his wife and with a little stifled sob of relief knew that whatever punishment he must endure, she could demand to share it with him.

As if he sensed what she was feeling, Lucius' hand sought hers and she felt the comfort of his fingers, but he said nothing. With an added sense of horror, she saw coming towards them from the right of the churchyard, where the leaves grew thick and concealing, a little company of men with Rudolph in the centre of them. There were four highwaymen with him now, and they still wore their masks, but driving them forward were two gentlemen of His Majesty's entourage, drawn swords in their hands.

She saw Lucius look now towards his followers and his jaw tightened in a sharp outline. They were all prisoners now, she thought, and realised that the King was waiting until the masked band was brought to him. They came nearer and nearer, in a silence in which Panthea felt that everyone must hear the frightening throbbing of her heart. But, like Lucius, she stood still and immobile, feeling thankful that the despair and utter misery that she was experiencing did not show either in her face or in her bearing.

The band of highwaymen drew level with the crowd of courtiers, and then through the eye-slits of their masks, the four men saw who was waiting for them. With one accord, they swept their hats from their heads and one of them, whom Panthea recognised as Jack, remarked in a loud voice, "Long live Your Majesty."

Rudolph's hands were tied behind his back, and his face was crimson with fury, but there was no mistaking the relief in his face as he saw the King, and that behind him stood Sir Philip Gage. There was an unpleasant smile on his lips as he said, in a loud voice with a note of triumph in it, "May I crave an audience with Your Majesty?"

The King raised his hand.

"One minute, Mr. Vyne. We have other matters to deal with first."

He turned to a crowd of waiting courtiers.

"I have the very great pleasure, gentlemen," he said, "to introduce to you someone whom I have long wished to meet and whose prolonged absence from our court is much to be deprecated. I refer to Mr. Lucius Vyne, who saved my life at the Battle of Worcester and who has now fortunately returned to our midst. He has, I think, been away so long that he will not have learned that he is, in fact, the Marquess of Staverley, and entitled to the estates that were confiscated by our enemies and which must now be restored to him. Gentlemen, and especially to you, Sir Philip Gage, let me introduce the Marquess and Marchioness of Staverley."

Sir Philip's eyes almost protruded from their sockets, but he bowed with the rest of the courtiers and mechanically, hardly knowing what she did, Panthea curtsied in response.

She saw the amusement in the King's face as he watched them, and as Lucius appeared about to speak, he forestalled him with a raised hand for silence and moved towards the band of highwaymen. Going up to them, he pointed at their masks and said, "Remove those things from your faces."

They did as they were told, and four pairs of eyes, apprehensive and beseeching mercy, were turned on the King, to whom they had always remained loyal and true whatever crimes they had committed. Charles considered them for a moment and then, still with a little smile at the corners of his lips, he spoke.

"Sir Philip Gage has need of men such as you to keep law and order in the City of London and in its environs. I also have need of new recruits in the King's Own Regiment. Are you prepared to serve me?"

There was an audible gasp, then the four men went down on their knees, and it was Jack who spoke for all of them in a voice which was suddenly tremulous with emotion.

"We are all ready to die for Your Majesty," he said.

"I would rather you lived to serve me," the King replied. "You will all report to the Captain of the Guard at Whitehall."

"Your Majesty, I protest."

It was Rudolph who spoke, and his voice seemed like a sudden discord as it rang out harshly and with ill-concealed anger. The King's hand went to his chin.

"Ah, Mr. Rudolph Vyne," he said reflectively. "I had not forgotten you. In fact, I have heard a great many things about you recently."

The King paused a moment and then with a sudden indifference, as if he were already impatient and anxious to be gone, he said, "I think England is hardly the place for you, Mr. Vyne. You spent many years on the continent, I understand. I must advise you to return there, where your very peculiar talents may be put to better use than they are here."

Rudolph was exiled and he knew it. He would have spoken, but the King did not wait for his reply. Without a glance, either at the kneeling highwaymen or at Panthea and Lucius, he walked through the churchyard gate and mounted his horse, which was waiting for him outside. There was a sudden scurry amongst the courtiers to mount and follow him, and almost before Panthea could realise what was happening, the sparkling and colourful cavalcade had ridden away down the road, the dust rising behind them, obscuring them as surely as if they had vanished over a misty horizon.

Panthea stood staring after them for a long moment and then was conscious that Lucius was watching her, his eyes on her face. He may have made some gesture with his hand, or they may have known instinctively what he wished, for the four highwaymen had turned to walk away to where their horses were waiting in the shadows of the wood and despite his shouted commands to release him, they took Rudolph with them. In a few seconds they were out of earshot, and at last Panthea turned towards her husband.

The expression on his face told her all that she wished to know. It was true! This had not been a dream but had happened in all reality. Lucius was free – free to love her, and they could live together at Staverley and bring up their children under the protection of the great house that had stood steadfast and true through so many vicissitudes. *Lucius was free!*

It seemed to Panthea as if the whole world was singing with happiness, and the sunshine was so golden that she was dazzled by the brilliance of it. She moved towards him with a little incoherent murmur, which was lost against the soft velvet of his coat as she hid her face.

He held her for a moment without speaking, and then very gently he raised her face to his so that he could look down into the glowing loveliness of her face and into her eyes, which shone with a love so great that she must tremble with the very ecstasy of it.

"My darling, my lovely wife, this is the beginning," he said, and held her closer still until their lips met and she knew once again the thrill and wonder of his kiss.